FILTHY GAY STORIES 2

C.D. TRUNCHEON

MAYONNAISE PRESS

Copyright © 2024 by C.D. Truncheon

All rights reserved.

No part of this publication may be reproduced, distributed, or transmitted in any form or by any means, including photocopying, recording, or other electronic or mechanical methods, without the prior written permission of the publisher, except as permitted by U.S. copyright law. For permission requests, contact Mayonnaise Press: editor@mayonnaisepress.com.

The story, all names, characters, and incidents portrayed in this production are fictitious. No identification with actual persons (living or deceased), places, buildings, and products is intended or should be inferred.

Book Cover by Mark Watkins

Illustration by Desiree Poole

1st edition, 2024

Contents

1. Scout's Secret   1
2. Trained by Coach   37
3. Capturing the Finish   77
4. The Nutcracker Prince   108
5. Friarhaven   146
6. Wildwood Heat   187

Scout's Secret

I stood alone at the side of the two-lane highway outside my Connecticut hometown, the predawn darkness cloaking the world around me in mystery. A shiver ran through me, not from the chill of the early morning, but from the expectation sitting heavy on my shoulders. I had done it—I had graduated high school and ascended to the rank of Guardian Trailblazer, scouting's highest honor. My parents, my friends, my aunties and uncles—everyone swelled with pride except the one person whose pride mattered most. Me.

"Mason Marcotte," they'd say, "what an achievement!" The words were hollow and echoed against the empty chambers of my self-doubt. I differed from the other boys. I didn't want to be, but had always known.

My achievements were badges sewn onto a sash of solitude. While they boasted muscles and braggadocio, I navigated the wilderness with a cautious mind and a silent step, my slim build more a whisper in the wind.

There was a kindness in the eyes of my Scoutmaster, Scoutmaster Thomas, when he spoke to me—a softness that told me he saw beyond the badges and handshakes. "Camp Hardwood," he said one evening, "in the wilds of Maine. It's led by Scoutmaster Clark, one of my former Trailblazers. It's for Guardian Trailblazers—the last chance you'll have to go camping as a scout now that you're out of school. The place has answers, Mason, to questions you haven't even asked."

The prospect of finding those answers both terrified and excited me. What did Thomas see in me that made him think this camp and Scoutmaster Clark could sieve through the mire of my internal struggles?

A distant rumble broke the silence, and I tensed as the familiar silhouette of a rusted-out school bus emerged. Its gears groaned with age and disuse. The same bus that had ferried me to countless scouting adventures now felt like a vessel destined for purgatory, its yellow paint flaking away like old scabs.

The headlights washed over me, a harsh glare against blackness, and the bus shuddered to a stop. With a hiss of brakes and a screech of metal, the door swung open, revealing a dim interior and the stink of aged vinyl. A sight frozen in time greeted me; the cracked seats where eager children once sat were now occupied by slumbering figures, their bodies draped in sleep.

I chose a seat near the front, distancing myself from the others and their quiet snores. I didn't recognize anybody.

As the bus rumbled down the road, I leaned my head against the cool window, watching as the world outside illuminated with the first hints of dawn. My thoughts spiraled around Scoutmaster Clark, the man Thomas spoke of with such subtle reverence. Was he truly the epitome of a Guardian Trailblazer who could mold me into something more? Could he instill in me something I lacked?

"Find out who you are, Mason," Thomas had said, his voice in my head over the engine's droning hum. "Not just as a scout, but as a man."

The darkness retreated, giving way to the unforgiving clarity of daylight. I felt the pull of anticipation knotting within me. Maine loomed ahead. I closed my eyes, inhaling deeply, trying to calm the restless energy that coursed through me. Guardian Camp wasn't just a destination; it was a crucible, and I was steel about to be tested. The question wasn't whether I would change, but how—and whether I would recognize myself when I emerged on the other side.

Light seeped through the windows, tinting the world in hues of amber and gold. The bus jolted to a halt once more. A cacophony followed as another scout boarded with the subtlety of a storm. He was just under 6 feet tall with wide shoulders and dark brown skin—more like a quarterback than a scout. The air charged with his reckless energy; his immediate and all-consuming presence.

"Room for one more?" he bellowed, his voice interrupting the muted, waking wilderness.

He didn't wait for an answer, his movements brash as he tossed his duffel bag onto the aisle, indifferent to the sleeping passengers it narrowly missed. He carried the audacity of someone who had never been told *no*, who moved through life with the certainty of a runaway train, untamed and unapologetic.

The seat behind me gave a sudden jolt as he threw himself into it. His presence engulfed the surrounding space; his exaggerated laugh vibrating through the metal frame of the old school bus.

"Name's Quamir," he announced, slinging an arm over the back of my seat, his fingers inches from my shoulder. "Quamir Madison." I could almost feel the heat radiating off his skin, the scent of him—a mix of sweat and cologne—wrestling with the stale air inside the bus.

"Mason," I replied, without turning around. The pressure to keep my voice steady was immense, like holding back floodwaters with nothing but sandbags.

"Mason," he repeated, tasting my name on his tongue, giving it a weight I wasn't sure it deserved.

I couldn't help but notice the strength in Quamir's arms, the way his chest filled out the fabric of his tank top, the powerful stretch of his legs clad in basketball shorts. In the front, outlined against the thin material, hung a bold declaration of his masculinity that drew my eyes despite my best efforts to avoid it.

"You don't got no leg hair," Quamir observed, his tone playful yet commanding. "You're a Trailblazer? How old are you?"

"Eighteen."

"You look fourteen."

His words were like a hook, snagging my self-esteem. I was all too aware of my physique. Not just a late bloomer, I wondered if I would ever bloom at all. I was only five-six with a mop of black hair on my head. I hope he never had to see me in the showers.

"We'll put hair on your chest at camp," Quamir said with a booming confidence that felt both magnetic and dangerous. He was like some mythic figure, a guardian at the gates of manhood, challenging me to rise and meet him.

I smiled, but inside, doubt gnawed at me. I wondered if this summer would mark my transformation or merely deepen the chasm between who I was and who I hoped to become. I would head to college in the fall—a threshold I felt unprepared to cross.

"You have one last summer to sprout," Quamir continued.

"Maybe," I said, latching onto the hope in his words.

The relentless rumble of the bus engine sputtered into silence as we stopped. Dust floated in the air like a fine mist. The camp loomed before us—a circle of tents perched around a crackling fire that looked far too feeble to fend off the encroaching wilderness. The outhouse stood sentry at the edge of the clearing, its door swaying slightly as if beckoning us into despair.

"Out, everyone!" the bus driver barked, his voice slicing through the uncertainty that settled over us like morning fog.

One by one, we disembarked into the crisp Maine air, each exhale materializing as a ghostly vapor before being swallowed by the forest. The other scouts shuffled their feet, casting wary glances at the primitive setup. I could feel their forlorn gazes, the silent question in their eyes: how would we survive this?

"Man, this is some real Survivor shit," Quamir boomed from behind me, his voice echoing off the trunks of towering pines. He hopped down from the bus with a thud, muscles rippling under his skin. Even here, in the raw embrace of nature, he seemed impossibly large, impossibly sure. "Think you'll grow a beard out here?" Quamir teased.

His comments were getting old. Maybe I'll grow claws and fangs instead, I thought.

The other scouts dragged their gear from the back of the bus, faces drawn and shoulders slumped beneath the weight of their packs—and their doubts. They introduced themselves in the minutes that followed, but I didn't catch most of their names. Only Barrett—the ugly one who seemed unusually competent and no-nonsense—stuck.

"Alright, boys," I said, more to myself than to them. "Let's set up camp."

And with that, we moved toward the tents, our steps hesitant yet determined, propelled by an unspoken resolve. For two nights, this would be home.

***

The moment Scoutmaster Clark strode into the clearing, an electric charge crackled through the camp. He was 21 or 22—finishing college, from what I heard. His boots thudded against the earth with the confidence of a man who knew every inch of the wild as if it were the lines on his palm. My gaze swept over him and marveled at the way his presence commanded instant respect and attention. He was a living statue, with chiseled features that looked hewn from mountain stone, then sculpted with an artist's precision. The short-cropped hair atop his head gleamed like polished ebony under the dying sun, a stark contrast to the deep forest greens and browns of his uniform that clung to his perfect muscular body.

"We're in for a blustery night," he announced, his voice resonating through the trees. "Let's make sure we've secured our tents properly. We won't have any getting carried away on my watch."

His words didn't simply fill the air; they commanded the very wind that was picking up, sounding through the leaves with a sense of urgency. Scouts scrambled to heed his command, their movements suddenly more precise, more deliberate, attempting to mirror the strength and certainty he exuded.

I stood there amongst them, strangely adrift. I was invisible to him—a mere shadow amidst a sea of faces—and I hated it. A burning desire ignited, a yearning that clawed at my chest with sharp, insistent fingers. I needed his approval, needed to be seen by those piercing eyes, to be acknowledged. I wasn't the only one. Quamir was already cracking wise in a stage whisper loud enough for Scoutmaster to hear.

"Mason!" I heard my name as if from afar, realizing too late that one of the other scouts was addressing me. "Are you with us?"

"Y-yes," I stammered, snapping to action. My hands grasped some tent pegs nearby and drove them into the soft earth, each strike of the mallet an echo of my determination. Sweat soon beaded on my brow and soaked into my shirt.

Clark's indifference was like a physical weight. It stifled me, suffocating the small embers of confidence I had nurtured. I thought he might never see me. Then, suddenly, he was there.

"Need a hand, Mason?" Scoutmaster Clark's voice cut through

the thickening air, surprisingly close.

"Uh, no, Scoutmaster. I've got it." My words sounded weak even to my own ears.

"Good," he replied with a nod that might have been approval or simple acknowledgment. "Discipline is key out here. Can't let the elements catch us off guard."

"Understood, sir," I managed, though the pounding of my heart drowned out the assurance I tried to imbue in my response.

My knees weakened. Somewhere within the tangled thicket of my insecurities, something dark and dangerous unwound—a forbidden curiosity.

The wind howled like a beast in the distance, tearing at the edges of our hastily erected sanctuary. It was a sound that set my nerves on edge. I had just finished securing my tent, knots double-checked with meticulous care, when chaos erupted.

"Damn it, Quamir!" The shout resounded through the campsite as one tent—one I knew Quamir had claimed responsibility for—crumbled like a house of cards. The fabric whipped violently in the gusts, snapping ropes and flailing poles creating a spectacle of confusion.

"Hold down that corner!" I yelled, rushing over to help salvage the disaster.

"Quamir, what the hell did you do?" Barrett screamed.

Scoutmaster Clark was there in an instant, his silhouette a tower of calm amidst the frenzy. "Explain," he commanded.

"I—I thought if I tied it this way it'd hold better," Quamir's voice was defensive, his broad frame blocking most of the collapsed tent from view, his hand holding a failed knot.

"Thought or assumed?" Scoutmaster Clark's tone was icy. "Your shortcut has compromised the integrity of this tent. It would have collapsed in the night, if not now."

"It should have worked!" Quamir shot back, jaw clenched, refusing to meet Clark's gaze.

"Thinking isn't enough. You need to know, to be certain, especially when the safety of others is at stake." Scoutmaster Clark's rebuke was absolute, his disappointment palpable even to me.

"Whatever, man," Quamir spat out before storming off into the gathering darkness, his departure leaving a wake of unease.

"Always gotta be the smart guy, huh, Quamir?" Barrett muttered, loud enough for a few of us to hear.

"Quiet down," I cautioned, but my heart wasn't in it. Barrett's frustration was justified.

"Seriously, Mason," he continued, shaking his head and assisting with the tent repair. "I've been on three trips with that guy. He's all sizzle and no steak. Loud, obnoxious... Why do they even let him stay?"

"Let's focus on getting this tent up," I said, though inside I wondered the same thing. Why did Quamir act like such a dick?

"Clark's got his hands full with that one," Barrett added under his breath. "If that was me, I'd be out on my ass, no second chances." We finally secured the tent back in place.

"Clark's fair. He sees potential in everyone," I offered, though my confidence in my words wavered.

"Potential for trouble, maybe," Brad retorted.

***

Hours passed. Quamir returned for dinner and had some private words with Scoutmaster Clark out of earshot. The night wrapped the camp in a shroud of darkness; the wind murmuring through the trees. The other scouts' breathing had settled into the steady rhythm of sleep, but rest eluded me. I lay on my back, eyes fixed on the canvas ceiling that fluttered with every gust, casting ominous shadows.

A soft rustling broke the cadence of slumber, followed by muffled noises that seemed out of place in the stillness. The sounds weren't just the wind's handiwork. They were coming from Quamir's tent.

The sounds grew more frequent. Curiosity clawed at me. I slipped from my sleeping bag, threw on my shirt and shorts, and pulled my socks up. The cold, dry ground crushed beneath my feet as I crept across the campsite, drawn inexorably toward the source of the noise.

Near Quamir's tent, I positioned myself behind an old pine tree, its bark rough against my palm. The flap was open, and I glimpsed the interior bathed in the silvery glow of moonlight.

Scoutmaster Clark knelt beside Quamir's cot, his face etched with stern concern. "This behavior," he began, low yet commanding, "it's not acceptable, Quamir. Is there a reason you're behaving like this?"

Quamir lay motionless, staring upward, and didn't answer.

"Is there?" repeated Clark.

At last Quamir muttered, "sometimes I got so much energy I feel like I'm gonna explode. Happens all the time. Just who I am."

"What do you do to manage it?" Clark probed, leaning in closer.

"Nothing," said Quamir. "It helps me play better at sports."

"But you aren't always playing sports," said Scoutmaster Clark. "You're a Guardian Trailblazer. A high school graduate. You've found *some* way to control your attitude."

Finally, Quamir snorted. "One thing helps," he said, "when I get too full and heavy."

"You're joking," said Clark.

Quamir snorted a laugh.

"Fine," said Clark. "I'll go. You can handle your needs." He moved to stand.

"I'll just be bad again tomorrow," said Quamir. In his voice was a plea for attention. A plea for Scoutmaster to stay. "I'll fuck up. That's how it is. What can you do to help *that*?"

"Would you like me to help?" Clark's question hung in the air, filled with unsaid implications.

My pulse hammered in my ears. I could hardly breathe, waiting for what was next. Quamir's gaze never left the tent's peak. He nodded, his response a silent surrender. "Try anything," he said. "I dare you."

The moment teetered on the edge of something forbidden, the lines of power, control, and discipline blurring before my eyes.

Scoutmaster Clark's hands, firm and sure, disappeared beneath the sheets covering Quamir's prone form. I watched, my back pressed to the rough bark of the pine tree, as those hands began a rhythmic dance, up and down under the thin layer of fabric.

The soft gasp that escaped Quamir was nearly lost in the sound of the rustling leaves outside.

"You've got quite the manhood, Quamir," Clark murmured, the sound blending with the quiet night. "Not a kid anymore."

I couldn't see their faces, but the words painted images more vivid than daylight ever could. Clark's hands stilled for a moment, and even from my hidden vantage point, I sensed a shift. Quamir gasped again, accepting a gentle squeeze between his legs.

"Nice, tight balls. Full enough to make a baby," said Clark. I imagined the weight of his touch, the silent communication between skin and skin, Scoutmaster Clark's hand up the baggy leg of Quamir's shorts.

"Help me, Scoutmaster?" The plea was barely audible, but it rattled the cage of my own desires.

The pumping resumed beneath the veil of fabric, and my hand drifted to my own shorts, the pressure there painful evidence of my arousal. I fumbled, trying to ease the constriction, my movements jerky and desperate.

Quamir closed his eyes tight and breathed through his mouth. "Hey Scoutmaster?" asked Quamir. "How'd you get so strong? You work out or..." he gasped, "...or something?"

"Rock climbing... boating... you know," said Clark. "You don't need a gym when your job is outside." His rhythm increased.

Quamir giggled. His resistance crumbled under the steady push and pull of Clark's ministrations.

"You're getting sticky," said Clark.

"You do it how I like," said Quamir. His giggles turned into squirms, and Clark pressed his forearm down, holding Quamir in place.

"Can't keep still, can you?" Clark's tone was teasing, but his grip was unyielding.

"It's getting so tight. Take off your shirt, Scoutmaster?" asked Quamir. "Can I see your chest?"

Clark unbuttoned his shirt and drew it back over his shoulders. "Wanna feel?"

Quamir placed a hand between Clark's sinewy, hairy pecs. "Nice," he moaned."

"Let's lower these sheets," said Clark. He whisked the sheets to Quamir's feet, then tugged at Quamir's shorts. Quamir thrust his hips up, and Clark drew them off.

"Never... you know..." mumbled Quamir. "...with a dude."

"But you've wanted to," said Clark.

Quamir nodded rapidly. His body was a landscape of shadows and peaks, every muscle taut with anticipation, his masculinity as rigid as a tire thumper.

Clark's mouth descended. Gentle slurping joined the quiet night.

I bit back a groan, my hand moving in a shadow of Clark's actions.

My fingers gripped my heated bulge through my shorts, squeezing to anchor myself to reality. I was adrift in this sea of darkness and desire, lost to the sight of Quamir's arching back, the bobbing head of Scoutmaster between his thighs.

"Scoutmaster," Quamir choked out, his voice strained with a pleasure I could only guess. "It feels so good, you suckin' me off. It feels so good! No girl ever did it like that" His head whipped back and forth. "Oh, shit!"

Quamir's control slipped away, replaced by a raw need that throbbed in time with my own quickened pulse. Unable to contain myself any longer, my hand fumbled at my fly, releasing the pressure of my hard length. My heartbeat pulsated through my girth, and my fingers wrapped around it. I began a slow, deliberate motion—up and down, twisting slightly, mimicking the tempo of Scoutmaster Clark's motions within the canvas walls.

"Scoutmaster," Quamir groaned, his low voice strained with pleasure. Each kick and thrash of his legs sent jolts of electric need coursing through me. I watched, rapturous, as Quamir's fingers tangled in Clark's hair, holding him firm, demanding more.

"I can't hold it no more," said Quamir, spiked with the edge of release. "I'm gonna nut! I'm gonna... I'm gonna... Oh shit!" Quamir cramped, crunching forward, an almost pained expression on his face as his body shook and twisted and finally succumbed to the rhythmic beating of climax.

Clark didn't miss a beat, swallowing and humming an approval that resonated through the tent fabric—a sound so commanding it made me shudder. When Quamir settled back, Clark cleaned him meticulously with his tongue, each stroke a promise of discipline and care.

"Nice and sweet," said Clark. "You were really full. You needed that."

Then, he rose, standing tall like a deity of the night. His shorts hit the ground, revealing a backside carved from stone and a virility that seemed to pulse with power. "Your turn," he said—a smooth command that left no room for argument.

Quamir's eyes widened, the whites reflecting moonlight. "You mean...?"

"Do you want it?"

Quamir nodded.

"Then take it," said Clark.

Quamir played with Clark. Stroked him with curiosity. Examined his length. Then, he took Scoutmaster into his mouth.

Each time Clark threw his head back, a surge built within me, threatening to break free.

"God, Mason," I chastised myself silently, "you can't do this! Get a grip!"

But there was no grip strong enough to keep me anchored, not when Clark's hands brushed along Quamir's tight coiled hair. He praised the warmth, the wetness. Scoutmaster's hips rocked, muscular calves tensing with each thrust into Quamir's eager mouth.

"Mmmmmm..." Quamir moaned, slurping and choking.

"I'm gonna cum," Clark muttered. "You're gonna swallow everything. Understand? Like you're chugging a beer."

Quamir nodded, his suction unbroken.

Clark closed his eyes and thrust two more times. "Here we go," he warned, and with a final push, he released himself into Quamir's keeping. Clark groaned with each powerful throb.

Beneath him, Quamir's face seemed agonized. His Adam's apple bobbed, barely able to keep up.

"Keep going," said Scoutmaster.

I heard the greedy swallows, saw the pleased curl of Clark's lip.

I trembled behind the tree, my every nerve alight with unspeakable desire. My hand, a traitor to my volition, worked fervently across my straining length, each pump a silent echo of Scoutmaster Clark's rhythmic affirmations. The night air pricked my skin with its chill, but the heat that engulfed me burned far fiercer than any cold could quench.

I gasped in a hushed whisper. The tree bark scraped against my hand and I braced myself, my muscles tensing, my entire being honed to the singular point of release.

In the climax of secrecy and sin, the surge—the overwhelming wave of ecstasy—broke free from the depths of my core, spilling forth in hot, frenzied jets against the stoic tree. The pulse of it consumed me, and for a fleeting moment, nothing else existed—no guilt, no shame, just raw, unadulterated pleasure.

Inside the tent, Quamir split away. He gasped for air, his mouth wide open, and he wiped his lips with the back of his hand.

"Good boy," murmured Scoutmaster Clark. "You going to be bad again?"

"Not tonight," said Quamir. "Not after that."

As quickly as it came, the intensity waned, leaving me hollow and shivering in its wake. A profound sense of dread settled in my chest, replacing the bliss that had moments ago filled me to the brim. I was lost in confusion, my body still humming from the illicit act yet my mind awash with turmoil.

I stumbled away, my steps uneven and hurried, fleeing the scene of my unraveling. The darkness of the woods closed in around me, a fitting shroud for the shadow that now clung to my soul.

Back at my tent, I fumbled with the zipper on the flap, my hands clumsy and slick with the residue of my transgression. Inside was a prison, trapping me with the knowledge of what I had done—and witnessed. I crawled into my sleeping bag, the fabric coarse against my skin, remembering the rough bark that had borne witness to my shame.

Lying there in the dark, the echoes of moans and whispers, the sounds of power and submission haunted me. Guilt gnawed at my conscience, a relentless beast that reveled in the sordid nature of my curiosity. And yet, beneath the layers of self-reproach, something else stirred—a burgeoning hunger, a yearning to understand these newfound desires that permeated my being.

"Who am I?" The question lingered in the silence, unanswered and heavy with implication.

Sleep was elusive that night. I tossed and turned on the thin cot. An hour later, I jerked off again, my head filled with images of Quamir and Clark, fantasies about being seen and included. What had begun as a quest for acceptance had led me down a path I never expected, awakening parts of me I didn't know existed. Dawn threatened to break, and I lay there, eyes wide open, contemplating the tangled web of emotions that ensnared me.

And so, amidst the chaos of my thoughts, I waited for the morning light, for the clarity that might come with it—or perhaps, the courage to explore my desires. The anticipation of what was ahead was both terrifying and exhilarating, a paradox that encapsulated the very essence of my tumultuous journey.

***

The next morning's activity was a canoe race, but the river was a beast clawing at the banks, its roar louder than we dared acknowledge. The current snarled, churning with a power that promised peril, thrashing against the rocks. Each frothy crash was a stark reminder of what could happen if any of us lost focus for even a second.

"Usually it's done in calm waters," said Scoutmaster Clark, untying the boats, "but I know you can handle it."

"Steady hands," I murmured to myself, gripping the paddle. It was more than a race; it was a test—one I couldn't afford to fail, not when validation seemed as elusive as the shifting shadows on the water's surface.

Quamir, all brawn and bravado, sat in the canoe beside mine. "Ready to eat my wake, Mason?" His voice over the rushing water was sharp and sure. "We can do this in a few years if you would rather, after you grow up some."

I wanted to wipe the smirk off his face. Though I tried not to let him bother me, he did. If I were just a little older, like Scoutmaster, or a little more developed like Quamir, maybe I could have what he had instead of hiding behind a tree and jerking off.

My thoughts clearly elsewhere, the signal to start was a blur—a shout swallowed by the river's roar. We lunged forward, our paddles slicing into the water. I watched Quamir's back work with each stroke, powerful and precise. I matched his pace, my own limbs straining, pushing past the burn that seared through them. The heat of competition ignited something wild within me.

Our canoes moved forward, swift and sleek as arrows. I focused on the rhythm—dip, pull, lift, repeat. The river fought back, its current trying to wrest control from my grasp, but I held firm, channeling every ounce of discipline I had.

"Come on, Mason! Show me what you got!" Quamir's taunt reached my ears over the cacophony, a challenge that stoked the fire in my chest.

His bluster didn't last. The river's fury was a living thing, and it had set its sights on him. Like a predator eyeing its prey, the waters nipped at the tail of his canoe, pulling it with a greed that chilled my blood. His brawny arms, which moments ago had been commanding the river with such authority, now flailed in desperate arcs in attempts to correct the course that had betrayed him.

"Quamir!" I heard my voice rise above the roar, raw and urgent. The other scouts' cries merged into a panic, their words swallowed whole by the rapids' relentless thunder.

"Left paddle! Left!" someone screamed, but the advice crumbled against the obstinate current.

Quamir was losing ground, the riverbank speeding past beside him, the perilous path to a treacherous rock bed opening like a gaping maw. Each beat of my heart was a drumroll to impending disaster.

Snatching the coil of rope that lay nestled at my feet, I leaned into my power, steering my canoe with swift precision toward the shore. The thick trunk of a maple tree loomed ahead, its roots holding tight against the river.

"Mason, what are you—" A scout's question cut short as understanding dawned on them.

Every knot I had ever learned tightened under my fingers, the rope's texture biting into my palms—a welcome pain that grounded me to the moment. With a last tug, the lifeline was secure.

I dug my paddle into the angry river; the canoe responding like an extension of my will. Water sprayed up, flecking my face. I forced my craft closer to Quamir's. His eyes widened in terror, reflecting the wild rapids that sought to claim him.

"Quamir, hold on!" I shouted, a lifeline thrown in words before the physical one that followed.

With a heave, I launched the rope through the air, muscles tensed in anticipation. It sailed between us and landed within his desperate reach.

For a moment that stretched out like eternity, I feared he would miss it. His long, defined fingers found purchase and closed over the rope—clutching it with a force born of raw survival. A fierce grunt escaped him as he wrapped the cord around his arm, anchoring himself to life, to me.

"Pull!" I commanded, straining as I reeled him in. Our gazes locked, a silent pact amidst the pandemonium.

The relief that painted his face when his canoe bumped against mine was a sight more potent than any victory. Gratitude etched into his features, and in that unguarded moment, the mask of the untouchable Quamir fell away, revealing the vulnerable human beneath.

"Thanks," he gasped, the word heavy with an emotion that transcended rivalry.

When we reached shore, Scoutmaster Clark's towering form approached, his shadow falling over us both. "Mason, that was quick thinking," he said. "Your bravery today... I'm impressed."

I nodded, still gulping air like it was my first taste of life. "Just did what anyone would've done, sir."

Inside, pride washed away layers of self-doubt. In Scoutmaster Clark's eyes, I found a glimmer of my worth reflected.

"Good work," he added, patting my shoulder with a firmness that spoke volumes.

***

The afternoon sun dipped low as I made my way back to the tent, the light through the forest canopy casting long shadows on the ground. The day had exhausted me.

I showered, then pushed aside the tent flap and found a folded piece of paper, weighted down by a small rock. A map. It was rough and hastily drawn, but unmistakably Scoutmaster Clark's handiwork; the sharp angles and precise lines mirrored his no-nonsense approach to everything. A red X marked a cabin in the woods, a place nobody had mentioned before. My name scrawled at the bottom in bold letters left no room for doubt—this was a summons.

Steeling myself, I pocketed the map and ventured deep into the woods—farther than I'd ever dared go alone. Eventually, the trees gave way to a clearing where a cabin stood, its windows glowing softly from the inside.

I pushed the door, and it creaked open. A fire crackled in a stone hearth, sending shadows across the walls. The scent of old wood and ash filled my nostrils.

"Mason," came the low, commanding voice of Scoutmaster Clark. He emerged from a corner, his presence dominating the small room. His eyes, piercing and intense, scrutinized me.

"Scoutmaster Clark," I greeted. "I got your map." It was a stupid thing to say, but I could think of nothing else.

"Sit," he instructed, pointing to a worn chair by the fire. As I complied, he began pacing, the floorboards protesting under his weight.

"Mason, do you know why you're here?" he asked, his gaze never leaving mine.

"No, sir," I replied.

"This camp... Camp Hardwood... it's more than just survival skills and knot-tying," he said, stoking the fire. "You may think being a Guardian Trailblazer is the end of scouting, but it isn't. There's one final lesson to learn—one with no merit badge or marking."

I blinked, trying to process his words. "What are you saying?"

"I'm saying that I was once like you, Mason," he continued, his voice softer now, but still laced with authority. "Supposed to be an adult; lost in the chaos of hormones and hidden yearnings. Camp Hardwood isn't for everyone, but I needed it. Do you?"

My eyes widened, my throat tightening as the implications sank in. I swallowed hard, his stare almost too much to bear. "Yes," I said, the single word holding all my trepidation and longing.

"Good," he said, a ghost of a smile playing on his lips. "Then let's begin. How do you feel about yourself? Don't be shy."

My mouth felt dry, scratchy as I tried to find the words. "I... I'm not like the others. I never developed like the other guys. I'm skinny and small and smooth. No guy wants to look like me." The confession tumbled out, every insecurity laid bare under the weight of his gaze. "And inside, there's this fear, this... heat that I don't understand."

"How so?"

"I want to like girls, but... I don't know..."

"Last night, when you watched from the woods," Clark's voice was steady, probing, "what was your body telling you?"

My heart hammered against my ribcage, betraying my cool exterior. Words failed me, and my cheeks burned with shame, realizing he knew of the moment, caught in the throes of forbidden pleasure.

The door creaked open again before I could stitch together a feeble excuse, and Quamir stepped into the dim light, his form casting a long shadow in the firelight. Our eyes met—his dark and piercing, mine wide with a storm of emotions. Apprehension knotted in my gut, curiosity pricked at the edges of my mind.

"Scoutmaster," Quamir's deep voice filled the room, edged with both confusion and possessive challenge. "Why's he here?"

Clark regarded him with a level gaze. "Quamir, Mason is on the cusp of figuring himself out. Embracing his nature Becoming a man."

"Becoming a man?" Quamir's brow furrowed, his stance protective, territorial.

"You both have needs as you learn about yourselves," said Clark.

Quamir scoffed. "I don't need no help becoming a man," he said.

"You nearly killed yourself this morning, trying to be tough," he said. "It's time you learn it's okay to be vulnerable."

"Vulnerable? Like some pussy? I'd like to see you try," Quamir taunted.

The air thickened with tension, the unspoken dance of dominance and submission playing out before me. The fire crackled, a taunting mimicry of the heat coursing through my veins, desire and fear entwined in a dangerous waltz.

"Mason? Are *you* ready?" Clark's inquiry snapped me back to the present, his presence a force that demanded an answer.

"Ready," I whispered, more to myself than to him, my resolve hardening like steel tempered by fire.

"Undress." The command was soft but irrefutable. "Both of you." Trembling, I complied, peeling the fabric from my skin, each layer discarded a step deeper into vulnerability.

Beside me, Quamir hesitated, his eyes darting briefly to mine—a flicker of solidarity in our shared exposure. "Whatever," he said, shedding his clothes and revealing the sculpted form that so starkly contrasted with me.

Clark watched us, his gaze unflinching as it swept over our nakedness. Quamir looked at me and guffawed. My face burned with the heat of a thousand suns, and I stuttered apologies. Clark silenced me, fingertips grazing the faint wisp of hair below my navel. "You're fine just how you are," he said, a declaration that held more authority than all my inner doubts combined. "You have powerful muscles, Mason. Nice arms. Nice legs."

He gestured to a soft bench that rested like an altar before the hearth and beckoned us to sit.

Quamir and I obeyed, our bare skin sticking slightly to the leather as we perched side by side—the heat from our bodies mingling in the cool air of the cabin.

"Can I touch you, Mason?" he asked.

Again, I nodded. His warm hands gripped my shoulders and ran the length of my arms; gripped my ankles and ran up my legs. Rubbed the plains of my chest. Each touch validated me. I bit my lip and became inextricably hard.

Clark's next instruction was a whisper against the crackle of the fire. "Both of you, lift your knees. Heels on the seat."

We moved as one, synchronizing without intention, our legs bent and exposing us in a way that left nothing to the imagination. "Close your eyes," he murmured, and I let the darkness behind my eyelids swallow me whole.

The moment his hand touched my hardness, it was as if he completed a circuit. Electricity surged where his fingers wrapped around my flesh, igniting a flame that threatened to consume me from the inside out. Beside me, I sensed Quamir's body react, a sharp intake of breath that matched my own.

We squirmed under the dual treatment, sounds of ecstasy escaping our lips unbidden. The bench beneath us might as well have been a raft upon tempestuous seas, our knees knocking together, fluttering like captured birds desperate for release.

"Good," came Clark's approving tone, a dark melody to the rhythm we created. "Let go, embrace this." His words were both command and benediction, urging us onward to a frontier we hadn't known existed moments before.

In the blind world I'd entered, every touch was amplified, each stroke a brush of paint on the on my senses. I could hear Quamir's labored breathing. Tremors shook his towering frame. Pheromones and manhood blended seamlessly with the forest's earthy perfume, enveloping us in a cocoon of forbidden desire.

"Feel the power coursing through you," Clark's voice grounded me. Power, control, discipline—these were the lessons imparted with every deliberate movement of his hands. I was clay being molded, raw and yielding to the sculptor's intent. And in those moments, I learned a truth that shivered through my soul: there was strength in surrender, dominion in submission.

His hands, once guiding and firm, now became instruments of a tender exploration as they shifted from the joint rhythm of our arousal to a singular focus on Quamir. Scoutmaster lowered himself between his legs. The gentle suction of his mouth, a sound so intimate and raw, filled the cabin as he lavished his attention with an expertise that was both shocking and alluring to witness.

Clark's lips hungrily devoured Quamir's long brown shaft, working up and down with an animalistic fervor. He then moved to his testicles, taking each one in turn and sucking them with a controlled yet intense force that left Quamir suspended in time.

"NGGGHHH!" Quamir exhaled, as if frustrated with himself for enjoying it.

"Good?" I asked.

Quamir grunted, the grooves of his muscular frame tightening with each pull. His eyes, dark and deep with pleasure, met mine, questioning, challenging. "You ever got sucked off, Mason?"

The inquiry sent a jolt through me, my need throbbing in response. "No," I admitted, voice shaky.

Clark released Quamir with a pop, turning his attention to me. His eyes, a piercing reflection of command, held mine as he questioned further, "Want a turn?"

"Yes," I breathed out, the word barely escaping before he descended again.

His lips enveloped my hardness, warmth and wetness unlike anything I'd known. With each movement, he cradled me, rubbing my legs in a rhythm matching his exquisite cadence. The sensations spiraled, lightning along my spine, a desire so intense it bordered on pain.

The boundaries of my body blurred. Heat pooled inside me. My breaths came in quick gasps, hands grasping at nothing, seeking a grip in a world that spun with dizzying speed. Control, the thing I thought I understood, slipped through my fingers like sand, leaving me a willing captive to the ebb and flow of Clark's mastery.

"Let go, Mason," he instructed, his arm circling my waist, pulling me in, words a balm to the chaos.

I surrendered to the pull, to the dark undertow of desire that claimed me wholly. As he drew me deeper into the depths of pleasure, whatever remained of my resistance dissolved. My body sang with a call that resonated with the crackling fire and the pulse of the surrounding forest.

Clark's voice was a deep thrum in the dim cabin, his words promising worlds untapped as he eyed us with that knowing smirk. "I've got something new for you guys tonight," he announced with a spark of mischief.

"What?" asked Quamir, a hint of defiance lacing his usual bravado. His dark eyes were alight with curiosity, his muscular chest heaving.

"Something that'll make you feel everything more intensely," Clark said, moving closer to where Quamir sat. His fingers reached out, deft and sure, pinching a brown nipple between thumb and forefinger.

Quamir jumped. "Yo—lay off my nips," he stammered, clearly taken aback. "That shit's only for girls."

"Everything feels good when done right," Clark replied, leaning in. His tongue flicked out, teasing Quamir's hardened peak. He sucked gently, teeth grazing just enough to draw a gasp, a whimper, from Quamir's lips. Quamir grew ever harder, his length an insistent presence, now glistening and moist with the evidence of his arousal.

The sight made me quiver, an echo of Quamir's desire pooling low in my belly. I watched, entranced, as Clark worked Quamir's nipples, one after the other, with a hungry fervor. This was no mere demonstration. This was worship.

Then it was my turn. Clark's gaze found mine, intense and unyielding. He approached, fingers trailing down my chest.

"I have something different in mind for you, Mason," he said, his breath hot against me. With a firm grip, he lifted my feet high. Then his tongue was there, tracing the cleft of my ass, circling my entrance in a dance so sinfully intimate I couldn't contain the scream that ripped from my throat. It was raw pleasure, a sensation so foreign and intense that my jaw chattered uncontrollably.

Quamir watched, eyes darkened with lust, his breaths coming in short, ragged pulls. "I want that..." he pleaded. Clark obliged without hesitation. Quamir's legs lifted, strong and commanding even in submission, and Clark dove in with the same fervor, tongue lapping hungrily.

Precum spurted from Quamir's cock, a bolt arcing into the air like a tribute to the carnal tableau we'd become.

Clark guided Quamir towards me. "He's never had this. Show him how it's done." He reclined me onto the soft fur on the bench. Quamir's mouth found my nipples, uncertain at first, but growing bolder under Clark's watchful eye. His lips wrapped around the sensitive flesh, sucking with a need that ignited another kind of fire within me.

Clark's hand enveloped my cock, stroking with a precision that neared divine torture. He whispered, "We're going to get those hormones flowing. Help you develop. Can you feel it in your blood? Making you stronger?"

My body squirmed in a maelstrom of pleasure. My dick throbbed in his grasp, every stroke fanning the flames higher, coaxing drips and then a gentle squirt. Fire ran through me. I was transforming, the boy I once knew twisting and writhing into something new, something powerful. My insecurities, my fears, all washed away in the deluge of surging ecstasy.

"I feel it. I feel it, Scoutmaster!" I said. "Deep inside. I feel it!"

"Let's make you into the man you're meant to be," Clark growled, his own arousal clear in the tension of his arm, the heat radiating from his body.

In that moment, in the haze of touch and taste and sound, I believed him. I believed in the wild, uncontrollable force of my own burgeoning desires, and in the strength that pulsed just beneath my skin, ready to break free.

Scoutmaster motioned for us to sit together on the bench again, our feet propped up. Quamir's broad shoulders tensed beside me, his usually cocky demeanor replaced by a quiet uncertainty that mirrored my mounting apprehension. He took a small tube from a toiletry bag on a nearby table. "This is the next part of the process," he said, his voice a soothing baritone that somehow made the unnerving situation feel less threatening. He squeezed gel from the tube, then approached us.

His large left hand disappeared behind the curve of Quamir's thigh. Quamir's jaw dropped Scoutmaster's gentle rhythm elicited a low moan, a sound that was both pained and pleasured. It was an intimate noise, one that unraveled my reluctance. Quamir squirmed, and Clark wiggled his penetrating finger gently.

When it was my turn, I braced myself for pain, but Scoutmaster's fingers were patient, coaxing my body open. The initial sting gave way to a warmth that spread through my lower half. His fingers moved inside me, touching undiscovered parts. The sensation was both too much and not enough. My breaths came out in quick gasps, my fear dissolving, like morning mist giving way to sunlight.

The cabin closed in; the walls steeped in anticipation. Wood smoke clung to the air, mingling with the musk of our arousal.

Clarks fingers continued their gentle massage. Now and then, Quamir would twitch and let out a low "uh-huh," his strong thighs lifting his legs up and down. His dark eyes glistened with an emotion I hadn't seen before and pooled with tears.

"I know I ain't no good," he whispered, his voice barely audible. "I can't help it. I can't do anything right. Ain't nothing to nobody."

Clark wiggled harder against his gland, and he let out a single sob.

Seeing him like this—vulnerable, stripped of his bravado—I had to respond. I reached out and brushed my lips against his, tentative at first, expecting him to jump back and call me a fag. Instead, we kissed.

Something shifted. Our explorations grew more fervent, our hands roaming over each other's bodies, fueled by a hunger neither of us had expected, but neither could deny.

Quamir's admission laid bare, the loneliness etched deep within him, a loneliness I recognized all too well in myself. We were two lost souls seeking solace, and in this heated moment, we found a connection that ran deeper than the physical. Our kissing intensified, becoming a language of its own—a silent conversation where every touch and caress spoke volumes of the need to be loved, to belong.

The warmth radiating from him was an unexpected comfort as I ventured further, allowing my fingers to wrap around him. He laughed, the sound warm like the embers in the fireplace, as he reacted to my touch.

"Like this," Clark guided, his hand briefly over mine, teaching me the rhythm. Quamir's foreskin moved in my fingers, foreign yet fascinating. Each slide brought forth another drop of his sticky essence, glistening on my palm.

"Shit, that feels good..." Quamir confessed, his voice husky with newfound vulnerability. He mirrored my movements, fist encircling me, a stroke that made me tremble. His words were gentle, tinged with regret. "I'm sorry for doggin' you all those times."

My cheeks flamed at his compliment, but the heat wasn't just from embarrassment—it was arousal that pooled in me, stoked by his skilled touch.

"Move to the rug," Clark directed, his presence steadfast as ever. We complied, our bodies gliding across the floor to the softness beneath us.

"Roll onto your side, Mason," he instructed next, his tone patient but firm. Quamir's hands were cautious as they turned me, a tenderness in their strength that made my heart thump erratically. I could feel his hesitation, his uncertainty mirroring my own.

"Use this," Clark said, passing the lubricant to Quamir. "A little on your dick, and some on his hole."

The slick substance was cool on my heated skin, a contrast that heightened every sensation. Quamir's touch was exploratory as he prepared us. He positioned his erection at my entrance. "Like this?" he asked.

"Deep breaths, Mason," Clark encouraged. "Let your body open up like you did with me."

The first push was a shockwave, a sharp bite. But Quamir paused, allowing me time to adjust, to invite him deeper. With each careful thrust, the pain ebbed away, and pleasure unfurled like a night-blooming flower.

Quamir rocked into me with a steady rhythm. The world narrowed down to the point of connection between us, the push and pull, give and take.

"Good, Mason," Clark praised, stroking my hair. Through the haze of sensation, I swelled with pride. My body was learning a new language—the language of desire, of yielding and claiming. And as I surrendered to it, my inner turmoil became still. I was no longer the outsider looking in; I was part of something raw and primal that connected us all.

Clark's voice faded into the background as my focus tunneled on Quamir and the connection we shared—a connection forged from power, control, and the discipline that only comes when you truly let go.

Quamir's hand slid beneath my knee, lifting my leg with a tenderness that contrasted his rugged exterior. A surge of something more than carnal desire vibrated through him; it was a yearning to be seen, to belong, just as much as I did.

"Mason," he muttered in a husky whisper, "you feel so good. So tight..."

His hips ground against mine, building in intensity as if each thrust was a pulse of raw, unguarded emotion. The initial discomfort of penetration was a distant memory, leaving only a rhythm that stirred my pleasure. I was hard—achingly so—and a strand of cum hung from me, swaying with our movements.

"Look at you two, beautiful and powerful together," said Clark. His words were fuel, stoking the fire that raged inside us. "Quamir, show him how much you want this. Mason, let yourself feel every inch."

Quamir's pace increased, his breaths coming faster and ragged. There was a new sound now, the slick, wet noise of skin against skin that echoed off the log walls. His heavy ebony balls rubbed my thighs. My moans married the rhythm, a blend of ecstasy and the sweetest pain.

"Gonna come..." Quamir groaned, pushing deeper, harder. The bed of warmth that had been growing inside me now felt like it was ablaze.

"Not yet," said Clark

Quamir tried to hold on; tried to hold back the dam while driving into me like a runaway train. "I can't!" he screamed. "It's too late!" With a gasp and a shudder, he pulled out, and a hot rush splashed across my back.

"GAAAHHHAA!" He bellowed, unloading his nuts. He rolled onto his back. "Sorry," he said, now giggling.

"It's okay," said Clark, stroking his head.

We lay on the rug, spent and panting, catching our breath. The last vestiges of doubt and insecurity melted away, leaving nothing but the raw vulnerability of two souls laid bare.

"Fuck, man," said Quamir. "Fuck." He looked down. "I'm still twitching."

Clark cradled his balls and stroked his shaft, making him shudder.

"You have more in you. There's something else you want."

Quamir wiped his hands down his face, saying nothing, trying to reject a feeling buried deep. "I... I ain't a bitch," he stuttered.

"I'm not here to make you a bitch," said Scoutmaster Clark. "I'm here to guide you and help you recognize who you are and what you want and need. To calm those restless, angry feelings once and for all."

Quamir swallowed hard.

"Do you want that?" asked Clark.

Quamir bit his lip and hesitated and finally nodded his consent.

Clark's hands guided Quamir onto his back with the ease of experience. He lifted Quamir's legs by the ankles and revealed a readiness in his stance, a solid presence like a statue carved from desire itself.

The air crackled as he aligned himself, the head of his hardness pressing against Quamir's entrance. A deep breath, a moment of suspense, and then he pushed forward. Quamir's gasp ripped through the dimly lit cabin, a sound of surrender to the overwhelming force that breached him.

It was a sight both harrowing and holy—Scoutmaster claiming Quamir with a careful dominance that left no doubt who was in control, each thrust taking them further into a realm where only pleasure and fulfillment reigned.

"Scoutmaster!" Quamir moaned, his voice raw. Clark's rhythm built steadily, each movement punctuated by the resounding slap of flesh on flesh. The sounds mingled with the crackling fire, creating a symphony of urges that filled the room.

Under Scoutmaster, Quamir was transformed. His usual tough exterior melted away, revealing the heat of his passion that surged with every stroke. His muscles tensed, his chest heaved, and he reached down to touch himself, bringing forth another sudden flood of ecstasy that painted his belly with white release.

My hand moved with a mind of its own. The sight of them, the sounds, the thick scent of arousal in the air—it was all too much, pushing me to a brink. I wasn't sure I could hold back. Panic fluttered in my chest as I let go, afraid that even the ghost of a touch would send me spiraling over the edge into oblivion.

Clark's motions inside Quamir slowed, each deliberate thrust a testament to his control. I watched, every nerve in my body alive and screaming for attention, as Clark lifted Quamir's head gently by the nape, their lips meeting in a deep, soul-consuming kiss.

Clark increased his tempo again, pressed himself deeper, pumped harder. His balls slapped against Quamir's ass, each time exorcising the demons that had haunted Quamir for years.

"I'll be good, Scoutmaster!" Quamir begged. "I can be good! I'll do whatever you say! I promise! I promise!" The last promise sounded like a broken sob.

Clark slowed. "Good boy. Are you ready?" he asked.

Quamir nodded, his longing resonating within the cavernous

space of the dim-lit cabin.

"I need you inside me," said Quamir.

Clark kissed him again. With two more thrusts, his body tensed as he honored Quamir's request, flooding his core with warmth. A hushed gasp escaped from Quamir's parted lips, his dark eyes fluttering shut, surrendering to all Clark bestowed inside him.

Then it was over, Clark's last thrusts subsiding, his release finding sanctuary within Quamir's willing form. The tremors of their climax reverberated through the air, stirring the embers of my own restrained desire.

Clark withdrew from Quamir gently, turning his piercing gaze toward me. "I know you've been waiting," he said, low and laced with promise. "I want you to come in my mouth."

My heart leapt into my throat. Wide-eyed and suddenly timid under his intense scrutiny, I felt every inch the inexperienced boy caught in the web of a man's desires. The thought of being brought to the edge by someone like Clark—the embodiment of all my unspoken yearnings—made me shake.

"M...Me?" I asked. What could I possibly offer such a man as Scoutmaster Clark?

Scoutmaster simply grinned and lowered his head. The first touch of his lips was like a spark to kindling. The warmth spread through me, igniting my senses as he took me into his mouth. Wetness filled the space between us, rhythmic and slick, while the firelight cast shadows that kept time with Clark's movements.

"God, I can feel it," I cried out, the sensation of his tongue swirling around me sending a jolt straight through my core. The power in my voice surprised even me, raw and edged with a desperation I couldn't contain. It was as if with each pull, each suck, Clark was drawing something deep from within me—fierce, untamed manhood.

My hands found his head, fingers tangling in his short-cropped hair. The urge to move, to thrust into that warm cavern, became overwhelming. I locked my legs around him, muscles tightening as I lost myself to the rhythm he set. I gasped, filling the cabin with the sound of our shared lust.

"Scoutmaster..." The name was a plea on my lips, my body winding tight like a spring. I was harder than I'd ever been. The tension built into unbearable, sweet agony. I was a bow pulled to its breaking point, and Clark was the archer, masterful and sure.

The pressure built to an apex. My entire being focused on Clark's mouth around me. Then, with a final, shuddering moan, I seized, my release crashing over me in waves. It pounded through me, pulse after relentless pulse, as I emptied myself into the welcoming heat of Scoutmaster's mouth.

He didn't pull away until I was spent, swallowing every drop with an ease that spoke of experience and control. Withdrawing, he looked up at me, his eyes softening for just a moment—a silent acknowledgment of what had passed between us.

Lying there, sprawled on the floor, our bodies intertwined, the room exhaled along with us. The fire crackled in the hearth, the air heavy with the smell of our spent desire. Our breathing slowed to match the rhythmic popping of the wood, the only other sound in the quiet aftermath.

"Thank you," I whispered, the gratitude lacing my words as I reached for Clark, needing to feel the solid reality of another person. He gathered me close, his arms a stronghold against the tremors shaking my limbs.

In the afterglow, we lay together, our emotions as naked as our bodies. Vulnerability, that raw and tender beast, crept in, wrapping around us like the smoke from the fire.

***

The first rays of dawn pierced through the canvas of my tent, rousing me from a depth of sleep I hadn't known in weeks. As I stretched, every muscle in my body felt different—stronger, infused with an unfamiliar virility. It was our last day at Camp Hardwood, and outside, the frenetic energy of packing filled the air. The rusted school bus groaned as it settled into its spot, ready to swallow us up and spit us back into the world we'd temporarily escaped.

I sat up, my mind drifting back to the secluded cabin with its firelight and musky, smoke-filled air. The memory of Scoutmaster Clark's commanding presence mingled with Quamir's smoldering gaze, stoked a blaze within me that had nothing to do with campfire.

I gathered my belongings with mechanical movements, shouldered my pack, and stepped out into the chilled morning. Mason Marcotte was no longer an average scout with a knack for knot-tying and orienteering. The night had reshaped me, my doubts seared away, leaving behind only the raw edges of newfound desire and confidence.

Boarding the bus, I claimed a window seat, my thoughts still churning. Quamir slid beside me, his once playful demeanor replaced with an intense, reflective quiet. His dark eyes, usually so full of mischief, now held a weight that mirrored my own.

"Did you see Scoutmaster Clark this morning?" he asked, his voice barely above a whisper, as if afraid to shatter the fragile silence around us.

I shook my head, the absence of our mentor leaving a hollow space between us. "No, I didn't."

The engine sputtered to life, a low rumble. As we pulled away from the leafy embrace of Camp Hardwood, I turned to Quamir, my voice laced with hope and a tinge of desperation. "Will you come back next year?"

He exhaled slowly, a soft chuckle escaping him, tinged with sadness. "We can't. We'll be nineteen."

The bus hummed beneath us, its vibrations a pale echo of the tremors that still lingered in my flesh. Quamir and I sat in silence, each lost in our own maelstrom of thoughts. My gaze wandered out the window, but I wasn't seeing the trees or the sky. I was back in that secluded cabin with Scoutmaster Clark's firm hands guiding me into realms of pleasure I hadn't known existed. My briefs became moist.

I was grateful—no, more than grateful—I was branded by the intensity of last night. The power of his mouth on me had unlocked something primal within my core. Yet, as satisfying as it was, a dark tendril of envy coiled in my gut. Quamir... he had tasted Scoutmaster Clark, had taken part of him inside in a way that I hadn't. Would he carry that with him forever?

"Was it as good for you?" I asked Quamir, the question slipping out like a shadow in the dusk.

He glanced at me, a flicker of understanding in his eyes. "Yeah," he murmured, his voice low and distant.

I wanted to ask if he felt a sting of jealousy too, but the words dissolved in my mouth. Did Scoutmaster Clark not favor me as much? It was a bitter pill, lodged in my throat.

The bus rolled on, mile after mile, while I stewed in my silent envy. But as the landscape shifted, so did something within me. A realization crept over me as quietly as dawn breaks. Scoutmaster Clark, despite what I initially craved, had given me precisely what I needed. He had ignited a transformation.

In the weeks that followed camp, my body hardened, muscles etching themselves with more definition. The hair on my legs grew thicker, and a tuft of dark hair at last sprouted between my pecs. My penis thickened, and so did my pubes. I was ready for college, for adulthood. Ready to face whatever lay ahead with the strength of a man forged in the fires of desire and discipline at Camp Hardwood.

Scoutmaster Clark had not just touched my body that night; he had awakened my soul. And for that, I would always be thankful.

Trained by Coach

The sun seared my back, and sweat slicked my skin. I pounded the trail, legs churning, breath a rhythmic gasp that matched the thud of my heart. Beside me was my best friend Emiliano Cabrera, his stride as smooth as it was swift, pushing ahead.

"Come on, Jalil!" His voice punched through my concentration, a call to arms. "You got this!"

I dug deeper, each footfall an assault against the dirt path we'd made our battleground. This was more than practice; it was a battle of wills, to the unspoken pact between us—to never settle for second best.

"Keep up, Harrington!" Emiliano's eyes flashed with his familiar, competitive glint. I couldn't help but smirk.

"Watch me." The words were a growl, torn from some primal part of me thriving on the challenge.

Coach Knight stood to the side, stopwatch in hand, a stoic sentinel marking our every move. He gave a nod, impressed or maybe just satisfied; with him, it was always hard to tell.

Coach, at 35, was the epitome of fitness. His physique was proof of his dedication and hard work, all muscle and hair and ruggedness. His strength extended beyond his physical abilities; he possessed unwavering self-assurance. None of us, including seniors like me and Emiliano, had anything close. Everyone craved his attention, especially me. Nobody else – not my dad, not my brother, not any of my uncles – would give me the time of day. They all thought I should be playing basketball, and I was forever a disappointment to them.

"Boys," he called out as we approached the finish line neck and neck, "don't make me choose who to brag about today."

"Wouldn't dream of it, Coach," I replied, breathless. Every fiber of my being burned. We crossed the line together, a photo finish that had become our signature.

Emiliano slapped my back, the sting overtaking the residual heat. "Good run," he said.

In our unspoken competition, the differences between Emiliano and me weren't simply in our running styles, but in our appearances. I was Black and stood at 5'10" with a frame that bore the marks of rigorous training: muscles well-defined under my skin, the result of four years of laps and drills. My shaved head added to my streamlined, no-nonsense appearance, the smoothness contrasting with my arms and legs—and lately chest—where hair grew thicker with each passing week.

Emiliano, you can guess, was Mexican. He was shorter. His 5'7" frame was compact but undeniably strong, especially noticeable in the powerful build of his calf muscles and arms. His long, wavy black hair often fell into his eyes, adding a touch of nonchalance to his demeanor. He'd been wishing for body hair since seventh grade when he tried to grow a mustache, but genes are a bitch and he was totally smooth. Even back in the day I told him he'd have more luck wishing for a pot of gold. Now 18 (his birthday was last week, two days before mine) Emiliano had come to peace with how it was and carried a quiet, resilient strength.

"Next time, I'll leave you in the dust," I said, the words heavy with false bravado and a silent prayer our bond could withstand the constant push and pull of our rivalry.

"Sure, Jalil. Sure." Emiliano's laugh was easy and warm and wrapped around me like a victory banner. There was respect there, in the tilt of his head, the unwavering gaze that saw through to my core.

We walked off the track, side by side, each step a silent promise to keep driving each other forward—for Coach Knight, for the team... for the unspoken truths both of us were about to face as we prepared to graduate high school.

***

The relentless thrum of rubber on asphalt punctuated the early morning. Emiliano and I were more than shadows flitting through the predawn mist; we were engines of determination. Our laughter, when it came, was breathless and laced with ambition.

"Man, this essay on *The Great Gatsby* is gonna be the death of me," Emiliano huffed, dodging a pothole that threatened to twist an ankle. "Why do we waste our time on dead white guys?"

"Stick to the themes, bro," I said. "Fitzgerald's all about disillusionment."

"Easy for you to say, Jalil. You've got a way with words that makes even Coach pause." His admiration was genuine, but I knew he'd outpace me in Calculus without breaking a sweat.

"Numbers are your game." A grin crept over my face despite the ache in my lungs. "You calculate the odds, I'll craft the narrative."

"We're Harrington and Cabrera, the golden boys of Lincoln High," he smiled.

"Golden boys who can't afford to slip," I said. The weight of expectation settled on my shoulders. We were more than just athletes;

we were the names whispered in hallways, the benchmark for every hopeful underclassman.

The halls of Lincoln High were abuzz with chatter and the shuffling of feet, a symphony of unpredictable adolescent energy we'd learned to navigate. But today, there was a disruption in the melody, a note that didn't quite fit.

"Did you see her?" The whispers snaked around lockers and lingered, a collective curiosity that tugged at my attention.

Emiliano's brow furrowed, his voice low amidst the crescendo of rumors. "Who's everyone talking about?"

"Dasani Mitchell," I said, eyes scanning until they landed on her. She was ethereal, a mirage of beauty that rooted me to the spot. I pointed her out.

"Damn," Emiliano exhaled. The flicker of accord between us had nothing to do with the finish line, for once. "New girl?" he asked, though he knew the answer.

Dasani was impossible to overlook—her confidence an aura that challenged every stare, her grace a dance that defied the rigid lines of our small-town norms.

"She's like something out of a dream," he said, echoing my thoughts.

"Or a challenge," I added. The familiar stir of competition surged, but this was different—a hunger that wasn't sated by distance run or races won.

"Careful, Jalil," Emiliano warned, a mix of jest and caution. "Girls aren't trophies."

"Who said anything about her being a prize?" I shot back, my gaze lingering on her retreating form. But beneath the bravado, uncertainty tightened my chest—a knot I couldn't untangle.

He clapped a hand on my shoulder with the weight of solidarity. "I know that look. You're intrigued."

Emiliano understood more than I gave him credit for—the unsaid desires that lingered long after the locker room lights dimmed.

"And you aren't?" I asked.

He smiled, a challenge written large on his face.

***

Steam billowed around us like cloaks as the hot water cascaded over our tired muscles. The locker room was empty except for Emiliano and me, the echo of our breathing fusing with the hiss of showers. I leaned against the cool tiles, letting the water rinse off the sweat and grime from another grueling practice. A small silver crucifix and some *Católico* medallion with a weeping santa somebody slapped his chest.

"Dasani," Emiliano said, breaking the silence, a low hum beneath the roar of water. His tone carried weight, a hidden depth that made my pulse quicken.

"Yeah?" My response came out more like a challenge than I intended, a voice roughened by exertion and something darker, unspoken. I turned my head just enough to catch his silhouette through the mist.

"You were right. I can't shake her image from earlier," he confessed. "That smile, it's like she knows secrets about you before you've even spoken."

I scrubbed a hand along my scalp, tension filling my gut. "She's got that allure—damn magnetic, for sure."

"What do you think it'd be like... with her?" Emiliano's question hung between us, daring and provocative.

"Imagination's a dangerous playground," I replied, trying to sound dismissive, but he had planted the seed. Visions of Dasani's lips, the curve of her waist, the promise in her eyes—they ignited something that had no place in the cold tiles of the shower.

"Picture this," Emiliano said, oblivious or indifferent to the shift in my stance. "A late-night rendezvous, just you and her, no boundaries, no holding back..."

I choked back a surge of desire, images swirling, vivid and intoxicating. Dasani's laughter, a whisper in the dark; the feel of her skin, warm and yielding under my touch. My knees grew week, my brain urging me toward fantasies best left unvoiced.

"Sounds like a dream," I managed, voice tight, betraying the storm raging beneath the surface. "But dreams have a way of turning on you."

"Maybe," Emiliano conceded, his own breath catching, a subtle signal I recognized all too well.

A primal urge surged through me, a heaviness flooding my lower body. My muscles tensed as I fought against the rising heat, trying to contain my thickening. If I got hard, I'd never be able to live it down with Emiliano.

"First one to get hard looses," I heard him utter, his back to me.

"Huh?"

"You heard me," he said. "Don't think about her. If you do, you get hard, and if you get hard, you lose."

"Jesus," I said, rolling my eyes. The shower was always strictly business, and we had never before played games. Emiliano and I even had a bro-code in the shower. We established it in 9th grade. Eyes above the chest.

But had I seen his dick?

I won't lie. I'm sure we both caught glimpses. We were both cut. My dick was thicker and bigger by an inch, which would shut him up in any contest he wanted to start, but he had a suitable length and no reason for shame.

As our bodies developed, he grew soft, wavy pubes like on his head; mine came in tight and curly. I wished my hair was more like his. His dick didn't look like it was coming out of a jungle. I hit some sort of growth spurt and was growing out of control, but didn't know what to do. It's not like I could ask my barber for a shape-up down there, or ask my parents for a private set of clippers. My dad would kill me if I used his to tame my crotch.

We fell into silence, each lost in our reverie of Dasani's imagined touch, her scent woven into the steam. I clung to the image of her dark eyes, fierce and soft all at once, as they beckoned me from across a chasm of longing.

His voice shook me out of my thoughts. "You lose," he said.

I looked down. He was right. My dick was like an iron mast and pointed to the wall. The only thing that kept me from becoming defensive was him. His turgid dick shot straight up above a taut sack.

"You're no better," I said.

"Yeah, but yours got hard first," he said.

"I wasn't watching. How do I know you aren't lying?" I asked.

He only laughed and threw a handful of water at me. His eyes moved down and went wide. "Jesus, you're big!" he said. "You got some nice balls on you, too."

"*Nice?*"

"I mean huge. You could make a baby with those things."

Not knowing what else to do, I cradled them and pulled them forward.

He continued, "They look like coach Knight's."

"When did you see his balls?" I asked.

"I didn't. But you can tell he's got big balls," said Emiliano.

I smirked. "I guess. Yours will get the job done. They're just tight cuz you're horny for Dasani."

"Yeah," he said. "Turn around. I'm gonna get some release."

"Seriously?" I asked.

"I have to," he said. "You can, too. I won't look."

Before I could protest, he turned his ass to me—a firm, tan bubble. The water poured over him, and his shoulders bobbed up and down as he stroked himself.

I did the same. What was I thinking? Anybody could walk in and see us. My body's needs fast overtook my reservations.

"Different when you're not alone, isn't it?" Emiliano's voice cut through the mist, low and knowing.

"Everything is," I managed. I fueled every stroke with the image of Dasani's smile, but my recent conversation with Emiliano kept interrupting my thoughts. *You got some nice balls on you.*

"What are you thinkin' about?" he asked.

"Her boobs under my hands," I lied.

"Her nipples are so hard." Emiliano's silhouette shifted against the tiled wall, movements deliberate, shadowed hands mirroring my own.

"I'd cup her titties and circle her nips with my thumbs," I countered, my breath shallow. The closeness of him, the shared fantasy... "Think I'd fit in her pussy?"

He inhaled sharply. There was nothing but the noise of the shower for a few seconds.

His crucifix caught the light. "Is it wrong, what we're doing?" He dared to ask what we both wondered, the question hanging between each ragged exhale.

"Who cares?" I asked, truth laced with defiance. This was uncharted territory, a line crossed without a single step taken. But the thrill, the raw honesty in our joint act, it bound us tighter than any cross country run ever could.

My soapy fingers now ran up the length of my dick, gripping the head and circling it before pulling back down. My balls churned and my lips parted.

"Close," Emiliano gasped, every fiber coiling, ready to snap.

"Me too," I admitted, locked in the gravity of the moment, the inevitability of surrender.

We strained toward an invisible finish line, chasing release. Our groans harmonized, a chorus of restraint coming undone.

My hand gripped my throbbing erection with savage force, my body contorting as waves of intense pleasure crashed over me. His hand beat hard, and from the corner of my eye something else: one of his fingers snuck behind and grazed his hole, eliciting a whimper.

"Her pussy's so wet," he muttered. "Gonna cum inside it."

Thoughts of her getting fucked somehow became thoughts of him fucking her. No time to ask why. My cock pulsed and strained against my grip, aching for release. With an animalistic grunt, I let go and watched in awe as thick ropes of hot, white cum shot out, splattering on the ground and cascading towards the drain.

Emiliano's heavy breathing filled the room, followed by a battle cry as he reached his own climax just moments after me, his thick white load striking the wall.. There was solace in the simultaneity, a silent acknowledgment we'd crossed a threshold together.

"Damn," he sighed. "Ain't never come that hard before." I nodded, still panting, unable to articulate the enormity of what had just transpired.

In an instant, the charge of our friendship morphed into something deeper, something neither of us had words for yet.

***

The water trickled to a stop, droplets echoing in the cavernous space of the locker room showers. Emiliano twisted the faucet with a finality that reverberated off the tiles. My hand followed suit, movements mechanical, the chilly air raising goosebumps.

"Dasani," he leaned back against the slick wall, his gaze distant. "She's something else."

"Out of our league," I acknowledged, more to myself than to him.

"Speak for yourself," he shot back, but his smile didn't quite reach his eyes.

I wrapped a towel around my waist, the rough fabric bringing me back to reality. Emiliano followed, mirroring my movements, the two of us in this dance we hadn't rehearsed but performed flawlessly.

"Today...this..." I struggled to find the words, the gravity of our shared moment weighing heavy on my tongue.

"Who care?" Emiliano finished, his voice steady, but I caught the briefest tremor in his hands as he raked them through his hair.

"Right," I said, the lie sitting uneasily between us. Everything had changed, the axis tilted, and yet we stood here, pretending the earth was still flat beneath our feet.

"Race tomorrow..." Emiliano said, snapping his towel onto his shoulder.

"Win it for her?" I ventured, the challenge implicit in my tone.

"Win it for us," he corrected, and there it was—the spark that ignited our competition, the flame that now burned with a different hue.

We moved to our lockers, the clatter of metal and the rustle of clothing filling the silence.

"See you at the start line," Emiliano said, slinging his bag over his shoulder.

"Wouldn't miss it," I responded, the edge in my voice softened by the warmth that lingered from our shared moment.

He paused at the doorway, looking back at me, and in that glance, I read a thousand unspoken thoughts. Then he was gone, leaving me alone with demons of desire that clung to the steam-filled air.

***

The next afternoon, the scent of fresh-cut grass and sun-baked rubber clung to my skin. I slammed my locker shut in the hallway. Emiliano and I had just spent lunch doing running drills and barely had time to change before science class. We were still simmering with adrenaline, muscles loose and minds sharp. Neither of us had said anything about the day before.

"You know, for a numbers genius, you really botched your science project," I said, elbowing him.

"I didn't see your vinegar volcano erupting anything other than yawns," he said.

"Touché."

"Besides," Emiliano said, "science is about trial and error. And speaking of trials…" His voice trailed off, eyes tracking something—or someone—behind me.

"Speaking of—?" I turned, following his gaze.

Dasani Mitchell approached, her stride a blend of assertion and grace. Like yesterday, she owned the hallway—and every breath we took. She wore confidence like a second skin, her smile not quite reaching the guarded depths of her eyes.

"Dasani," I greeted, my voice more gravelly than intended. "Settling in okay?"

"Hi, Jalil. Hi Emiliano," she said, the sound of my name in her voice sending a current down my spine. "Just fine. Where have you two been?"

"Drills. You going to come watch us at the meet?" Emiliano asked, his tone light, flirty. I shifted weight from one foot to the other, feeling the heat rise in my cheeks.

"Can't," she said, chin tilted up in mock arrogance. "We're still moving in. I'd wish you luck, but you don't need it, right?"

"Never hurts," Emiliano said, laughing.

"It's gotta be a pain, moving to a new school a few months before graduation," I said. "By the time you make a friend, we're all on to other things."

"I'm just trying to get through it," said Dasani.

Emiliano forced himself in front of me. "Hey, the school is having its annual springtime bonfire tomorrow. You going? It's gonna be lit—in every sense of the word. Last one before we graduate, and a good chance to make some short-term friends."

"Wasn't planning on it, but..." She glanced between us, a decision teetering on her lips.

"Come on," he pressed, "it'll be fun. Plus, you'll get to see this guy try not to burn his marshmallows," he said, nudging me again.

"Fine, I'll be there," Dasani conceded, her eyes now directed at me. "Just to make sure Jalil doesn't singe his eyebrows off."

"Guess I'm saved then," I said, forcing laughter. "See you there."

"Great," Emiliano said, saturated with victory as Dasani gave a small wave and walked away.

I leaned against my locker, watching Dasani's retreating form with a knot in my stomach. Emiliano's laugh echoed too loudly in my ears, his smile too wide for comfort. He clapped me on the back, his eyes alight with a thrill I couldn't share.

In science class, Emiliano couldn't stop talking about his minor victory.

"Man, you saw that, right? She's into it," he said, oblivious to the churning storm inside me.

"Sure," I said, the word sharp and clipped. "Dasani's... something."

"Something? Bro... And I think you're just pissed you didn't shoot your shot first." There was a sting in his words.

"Jealous? Of how you cut in front of me to get your words in?" I scoffed, raking a hand through sweat-damp hair. Jealousy was such a flat word for the maelstrom that raged within. It was more than Dasani, more than the bonfire—I didn't quite know what.

"Whatever, man," said Emiliano. The periodic table swam before my eyes, each element blurring into a smudge of color and letters as I directed my attention to anything but the low thrum of unease.

Emiliano leaned close, his voice dropping to a conspiratorial whisper. "She's old enough to pick who she likes? You sure you're not just a tiny bit envious?"

"Envy's a sin," I said, more to myself than in response. "And I'm no sinner."

I excused myself, claiming a headache, and made my way to the sanctuary of the locker room.

***

The oddly comforting smell of musk and disinfectant met me when I opened the locker room door. Steam rose like a specter from the showers nearby. I needed space, air—anything to dampen the fire that licked at my insides. A twenty minute run. Ten minutes. Anything.

I slipped off my shirt, the fabric sticking slightly to my skin. My movements were mechanical as I pulled on a thin tank top, the fresh fabric cool against my heated back. I shimmied into a pair of short-inseam running shorts and laced my shoes, desperate for the rush of wind against my legs, the promise of exhaustion to dull the edges of my thoughts.

Were Emiliano and I, at the end of our high school career, about to fight over a girl?

I stepped toward the exit and passed the showers. Inside, Coach Knight soaped himself, water cascading over his broad shoulders, his back turned to me—a mountain of a man outlined in mist. The sight should have been innocuous, routine even, but something in the way his muscles shifted and flexed held me captive.

I stood, frozen, on the threshold between the changing room and the showers. He hadn't heard me come in. Water traveled down the valleys of his muscles. Rivulets traced the contours of his form, over lats that someone could have chiseled from stone, down glutes and legs that rippled with each subtle movement. Lower, between his thighs, my gaze snagged, unbidden, on the swell of his manhood—large enough to be seen from behind.

Heat flushed through me. A conflagration. It wasn't just his size—it was his unabashed masculinity, the primal certainty in every line of his body. He turned. Under hard abdominals, his large penis hung heavy, the formidable testicles beneath a testimonial to virility itself.

"That you, Harrington?"

His voice, a low rumble, shattered the trance. My head snapped up, eyes meeting his. There was no accusation there, just a glint of something unreadable.

"Coach, I—" The words lodged in my throat, guilt and something far more dangerous warring within me. "I wasn't—"

He turned the water off and wrapped a towel around himself. "Come to my office," he said, an implicit command that brooked no argument.

I followed him, each step with an irrational yet inescapable dread. His office was close quarters, crammed with trophies and plaques that spoke of victories both personal and shared.

"Sit." He gestured to a small sofa against the wall. He took his place behind a desk, the fortress of his authority.

"Coach, about the shower—I didn't mean to..."

"Stop." He held up a hand, and I obeyed, the silence thick between us. "Shouldn't you be in class? What brings you here?"

"Everything," I confessed, the words tumbling out.

"Talk to me."

"Emiliano—he's..." I struggled to articulate the maelstrom of feelings, "He can just charm anyone. The new girl, Dasani. And I'm just... here."

"Jealous?" His eyebrow quirked.

"Maybe. I don't know." The admission was a weight lifted, but it left me exposed. "It's more than that. I'm lost. Like I don't even know who I am or what I want anymore. No matter how much I accomplish, it's never good enough. For four years, all people tell me is how much better I can do. I can compete with Emiliano on most things, but he's got that wavy hair and that Latino swagger going on that girls love. Maybe I *can't* do better on some things, especially if I'm just a regular, ugly Black kid."

I smirked, hoping to lighten the mood with a little self-deprecation, but Coach took it at face value. Maybe he was right to do so.

"Attraction is complicated," Coach Knight said, softening. "And we can't tie our self-worth to who wants us—or who we want."

I kept my head down, unable to meet his gaze.

"Believe me, Jalil, I've been where you are. Wrestling with desire, with identity—it's part of life."

"Does it ever get clearer?" My hands were fists, knuckles white.

"It does. But it starts with being honest—with yourself, first and foremost."

Honesty was like a blade, sharp and threatening. But in the safe confines of his office, with his steady presence grounding me, I edged closer to the truth that clawed within.

"Look at me, Jalil," he said, his voice steadying the chaos. He waited until our eyes met. "You're one hell of an athlete. Your dedication—it shows in every sinew, every muscle."

I swallowed hard. The weight of his gaze, like sunlight on my skin, was warm and somehow validating. "More than that," he continued, leaning back in his chair, his eyes never leaving mine, "you've got a fire in you. It draws people to you. You're not some ugly Black kid. There are some ugly Black kids in this school. You're not one of them."

I laughed. "It just doesn't feel that way, lately. I went all the way through high school and never had a girl. Now one shows up, and it becomes a competition with Emiliano like everything else, and I'll be honest, I don't even know if I want her. I only know I have to compete."

"What *do* you want?"

I shrugged.

He shuffled some papers. "There was cum all over the shower yesterday. It clogged the drain. Know how it got there?"

His question cut through the air, sharp and direct.

I dropped my gaze to the floor, again. Heat flushed my cheeks. "I... we... sorry..."

"Don't worry about it," said Coach. "The school will pick up the plumbing bill.

"We were thinking about Dasani. That's all. I swear."

"You clogged a drain thinking about a girl you don't even like?"

My hands clenched in my lap.

"It's okay. Attraction isn't something we choose, Jalil. It happens. And sometimes it surprises us." His tone was gentle.

"Surprised is...one word for it." I said.

"Tell me," he urged, "how did you feel when you saw *me* in the shower just now?"

My throat became as dry as the Sahara. Blood rushed to my face.

"Just say it," said Coach.

"I didn't want to stop looking," I confessed, the truth a razor's edge. "Confused, I guess. Because... well...lately with Emiliano..."

"Ah," he nodded, understanding coloring his features. "That's a tough knot to unravel."

"Impossible," I said.

"Nothing's impossible."

"I hate it. It isn't normal. I'm sorry for looking. I need to be more respectful and professional..."

Coach Knight stood, closing the distance between us. His presence was a force field, somehow comforting. "You need to be yourself. You just turned 18. Can I show you how the world sees you—the strength? The charisma?" His voice was a low thrum, resonating within my chest.

"Show me?" I echoed, unsure.

"Only if you want." His eyes searched mine for permission. "If not, that's okay, too."

My mind screamed caution, but my body yearned for affirmation. After a taut moment, I nodded. The silent acquiescence was like stepping off a cliff.

"Stand up," he instructed.

"Yes, sir," I obeyed, rising to my feet as he circled me, his gaze appraising. Then his hands were on me, firm and insistent, skimming over clothed skin. Each touch sparked a current that traveled the expanse of my nervous system.

"Take off your tank top" he commanded.

The fabric whispered against me. I lifted the shirt over my head, exposing my torso to the coldness of the office. His fingers traced the lines of my abs, tickling gently.

"See?" he asked, his breath hot on my neck. "You're powerful. Desirable."

"Coach..." My voice was a strangled sound, overwhelmed by sensation and a dawning realization of self. I could feel myself getting thick, and concentrated on not getting a full-on boner in front of coach.

"*You* need to feel it, Jalil." His hands were relentless, mapping territory and staking claim. "Believe in your worth."

My mouth fell open as his thumbs brushed over my nipples, sending shockwaves down to my groin. My resolve crumbled, replaced by aching need.

I leaned into his touch, my skin humming with newfound electricity, each caress rewriting my doubts into something bold and affirming. My breaths came in shallow gulps as I teetered on the brink of understanding, the heat of his hands a brand upon my awakening flesh.

"Shorts off," he said, "if you want to continue."

My head dipped and I shook my head. "Coach, I don't know..."

"Don't be ashamed."

"My hair's been growing out-of-control lately, is all," I said. I kept my eyes forward and dropped my shorts and underwear.

He cradled my nuts and ran his hand over my beefy length sending a charge through me.

"You're a big boy," he said. "You've never used your gifts?"

"Not with someone else," I confessed.

He nodded. "You don't like your body hair?"

"Emiliano's isn't all messy like this."

He retreated to his desk, opened a drawer, retrieved a pair of cordless clippers, and set them humming. He moved my balls up and down and my dick left and right. My coily pubes fell to his floor. When he finished, my prick looked like a salami hanging in the deli.

"Nice and fresh," he said. "Sit."

The cool leather of the coach's couch creaked beneath me. Coach sat down close, his body heat a stark contrast to the chill in the air.

"Close your eyes," he said in that same soft command that had stripped me of my shirt. "You're warm and thick."

"Trying not to get hard," I confessed.

"Let yourself go," replied Coach. "It's okay."

I obeyed, flinching slightly as his hand traveled up my thigh and closed around me. I became steely and twitched. With a steady yet forceful grip, he explored every inch of me, igniting a fierce heat that spread through my being. My pulse rushed with a frantic intensity, my heart thudding against my breastbone. His expert movements sent shivers down my spine. He worked his hand up and down my shaft, unleashing an overwhelming surge of pleasure that left me trembling in his grasp.

"Try thinking about her now," he coaxed. "Dasani."

Her name conjured up her image—her confident strides, her laugh echoing down the hallway. I tried to focus on that, on her, but the visions flickered and waned like a candle in the wind. The pleasure building was distant like a storm on the horizon. "Coach, I can't..." I started, the frustration evident in my voice.

"Shh," he soothed, "Try."

His hand moved with practiced ease, but my thoughts scattered like confetti, my arousal stubbornly muted. It was no use; Dasani's image dissolved into the ether, untouchable. I softened and withdrew.

"Can't," I admitted, breathless with the effort of chasing an elusive climax.

"Let's try something different." His words came out low and knowing.

Before I could respond, he shifted, his intense presence enveloping me. His hand disappeared and in its place was something far more intimate and arousing. The electrifying sensation of his mouth around me was a bolt of lightning that kindled my desire. In mere seconds, my cock was pulsating as he sucked, his skilled tongue traced tantalizing circles around me and driving me wild.

I closed my eyes and threw my head back. "God, Coach..."

"Let it happen, Jalil. Dare to think about what you really want."

Suddenly, there he was—Emiliano—in my mind's eye, replacing every fractured fantasy of Dasani. His smile, his easy laughter, the way his skin glistened with sweat after practice. I released my breath at the realization, my body responding to the truth my mind had been denying.

"Emiliano." The name slipped from my lips like a sacred vow.

"Good," he praised. The warmth of his approval was nearly as potent as the wet heat of his mouth. "See, Jalil?" Coach said, a steady anchor pulling me back from the edge. "You know what you want. Let yourself have it."

Coach's mouth was a crucible, forging a new truth from the raw ore of my need. The rhythm of his head bobbing, the slick sounds filling the air - they tethered me to the moment.

"Relax into it," Coach said teasing my tip, his hands gripping my thighs with a firmness that anchored my drifting senses. He moved his lips up and down and sucked with just the right amount of pressure.

"Coach," I moaned. "You're suckin' me so good."

The heat of him wrapped around me was a reassurance, a confirmation my feelings were tangible and real. It was a physical connection that transcended the boundaries I'd built around myself, walls erected to keep out desires I couldn't name until now. Suddenly, my brain got in the way.

Coach paused. "What is it?"

"Yesterday, when Emiliano was... you know... in the shower. His finger went behind him and he played with... I dunno. Nevermind."

"Do you want me to play with your ass?"

"No way," I said. "No, no, no. I was just noticing. I mean, I never thought about... *that*... as a pleasure zone." I hesitated. "Is it?"

Coach smirked and went back to sucking me, this time drawing his hands up to cup my ass. HIs index finger moved into my crack, and I gasped. I never knew there were so many nerves down there. I thrust my pelvis a few inches off the sofa, and he slipped a finger in. Not far, maybe to the first knuckle. It itched and burned, but set my teeth on edge in a way I'd never known.

My hips bucked involuntarily, fucking his mouth, seeking more of his maddening friction. Each time I rocked, his finger went deeper. I was fascinated and horrified by my lack of control, as if my body belonged to someone else—someone braver, someone who dared to want what I'd buried deep.

"Feel good?" he coaxed, looking up at me through lashes wet with effort.

"Y-Yeah," I stuttered, the admission dragged from me by the undeniable pleasure.

"Think about him," Coach said, his hands now cradling my hips, guiding me.

I did. I thought of Emiliano's laugh, the electric touch of his skin against mine, the look in his eyes when we shared a private joke. It was Emiliano's presence that filled my senses, not Dasani's vanishing figure. Emiliano's essence enveloped me, a balm soothing the ache of years spent in silent yearning. I thought of the shower yesterday. His hard prick. How we came together, and the trail of sticky jizz he left on the floor.

"Show me what that big dick can do," said Coach.

Coach gripped my cock at the base and sucked, pumping me

faster and faster. My legs kicked and flailed, then locked behind his back at the ankles.

A primal roar burst from my lips as the tension consuming me reached its breaking point. "Coach!! Coach, I'm gonna... I'm gonna..."

A wave of ecstasy crashed over me, pulling me under in a riptide of pure release. My hole clenched tight around coach's finger. My body convulsed and my dick pounded mercilessly in his mouth. Every nerve ending flared to life only to be extinguished in the next second by another hurricane of intense sensation. It wasn't only my cock blasting cum, but a rough pulsing inside me, against his finger, that I'd never experienced. I didn't know which way to twist and turn and screamed out loud.

"GAAAAAAAAH!"

When I quieted, he looked at me with satisfaction, swallowing the proof of my lust. "That's it," he said. "Good." My dick became sensitive and he swabbed me with his tongue, making me giggle and twist. "You gave me quite a load," he said, laughing. "You could knock up the whole town with that thing.

I giggled, gasping for breath, my pulse thundering like the roar of victory on race day. But this was an unconventional kind of triumph, one that bore no medal or accolade, only the stark revelation of my own hidden truths.

"You can't hide what's inside, Jalil." Coach wiped his mouth with the back of his hand and stood, his eyes locking with mine. "It's okay to want something, or someone. It's human."

"Emiliano..." I said, barely audible, still riding the aftershocks.

"Maybe he needs you to be honest, to help him find his own truth," Coach said, his tone softer now, almost contemplative.

"Me? Help Emiliano?" I questioned, my voice weak but laced with incredulity. "He's straight as an arrow with a dick for Dasani that won't quit."

"Sometimes, we don't see our own reflection until someone shows it to us," Coach said, his words heavy with an understanding that spanned lifetimes.

"Reflection..." The metaphor settled into my thoughts, blending with the newfound clarity that ran through me.

"Admit what you want, Jalil," Coach said, "at least to yourself. Then, consider helping Emiliano do the same."

Honesty was a concept both foreign and familiar, like a language I'd forgotten I spoke. My chest tightened with the magnitude of the task ahead, but for the first time, it wasn't insurmountable. With Coach's guidance, I saw a path forward, one where honesty wasn't just a mumble, but a shout into the daylight.

"Thank you, Coach," I said, firmer than before. And in that thanks was not just gratitude for the experience he'd given me, but for the permission to seek the truth of who I was—and whom I desired.

***

The flames from the bonfire licked the night sky, casting a flickering orange glow over the athletic field. A huddle of 75 students encircled the blaze. In the light of the fire, everyone there felt the moment, if not the blaze, would burn forever. Not me. The future crept toward me, like a demon lurking in the shadows. Naturally, Emiliano was thinking the same thing.

"Can you believe we're done, Jalil?" The logs crackled.

"Hard to imagine," I said. "No more races, no more school... just what comes next." My eyes drifted across the crowd, catching sight of Dasani. Her laughter was a melody that played a dissonant chord. Turning eighteen hadn't brought clarity; instead, it left me grappling with the uncertainty of a life beyond these school gates, of a future where I wanted—no, needed—Emiliano by my side.

"Hey man, don't sweat it," Emiliano said. "We'll figure it out. We always do."

"Right." I forced a smile as hollow as the empty stands around us.

"Dasani's looking fine tonight, huh?" He nudged me, his eyebrows raised suggestively. I followed his gaze. A knot tightened in me. She was leaning back, her silhouette against the fire painted her in mystery and allure.

"Definitely," I said. The word left a bitter taste in my mouth.

"Watch and learn, Jalil." Emiliano strutted towards her, his confidence rolling off him in waves. They locked eyes, and something electric passed between them—an undeniable chemistry. Her laugh tilted towards a flirtatious giggle, her hand brushed his arm.

"Charming as ever," I said under my breath, jealousy coiling around my spine like a serpent. Their banter flowed effortlessly, and even from this distance, I could see Dasani's eyes glinting with interest.

"Want to get out of here?" Emiliano's lips moved, the question meant only for Dasani.

"Thought you'd never ask," she said, her voice carrying just enough for me to catch the excitement laced within.

They slipped away, shadows merging with darkness, and disappeared under the stadium bleachers. I stood alone with the fire's heat on my face and a cold emptiness swelling inside my chest.

"Dammit," I hissed, my hands clenching into fists. The conflicting emotions swirled—a storm raging. Desire for what Emiliano had, jealousy that it wasn't me he wanted, fear of losing him to someone else, and a longing so deep it ached. I threw a stick into the fire, watching it splinter and crackle, wishing I could burn away these feelings consuming me.

"Get a grip, Harrington," I scolded myself. But the truth was, I didn't know how to let go of the one thing I wanted most—to have Emiliano in my life, not just as a friend, but as something more. Something deeper. The thought was terrifying and exhilarating, and I couldn't push it away any longer.

***

The bonfire's embers dulled to a soft glow, and the night's chill crept in as I stood alone on the edge of the athletic field. Emiliano swaggered back from under the bleachers, a wolfish grin plastered across his face.

"Damn, Jalil," he said, wiping his lips with two fingers, "Dasani's lips are like plush velvet, man. And her body... it's fire." His eyes glinted with a wild hunger that made my heart sink.

"Really?" I managed, tight-lipped, the image searing into my mind like a brand.

"Her tits, bro," he said, mimicking the shape with his hands, "You could cut glass with her nipples." He laughed, but there was an edge to it—a hint of something unfulfilled.

I shifted uncomfortably, the heat in my cheeks betraying more than I wanted. "Sounds like you had fun," I said, trying to keep the bitterness from leaking into my voice.

"I'm still hard" Emiliano said, his breath coming out in a heated rush. "Wanna hit the showers?"

"Showers?" The word echoed strangely in my ears.

"Yeah, the locker room's empty. Come on." He tugged at my sleeve, his urgency palpable. "I need release, like the other day. Paint a picture with words. You talked me into a frenzy last time. It's what

I need."

I wasn't sure what to say, but he pulled me through the empty school. We navigated the dimly lit hallways, our footsteps echoing off the lockers, resonating with the thundering pulse in my veins. Inside the locker room, the air smelled like always—bleach and sweat and stale cologne. We peeled off our clothes.

"Bro!" he said. "What happened?" he said, pointing to my junk.

I tensed, not sure what was wrong. "Oh," I relaxed. "I trimmed up."

"It looks good."

"*Good*?"

"I mean, it makes your junk look huge." I watched Emiliano's body move—confident, unashamed—as he stepped into the shower.

"Turn it on," he barked, and I complied, reaching for the metal handle. Water cascaded over us, steaming hot, and I shivered despite the warmth.

"Think of Dasani," Emiliano said, closing his eyes, his hand gripping himself. "Imagine those perfect curves, that smooth skin."

My own hand moved of its own accord, my head filled with different thoughts. My throat was dry, words lodged there like stones. "Yeah," I said, the scene unfolding in my mind, but it was distorted—blurred by another image, one I tried to suppress.

"Her moans, man," Emiliano groaned, his movements growing frenzied, "like music."

"Music," I echoed, the sound hollow. Emiliano beside me, his pleasure building, became the melody I hadn't known I craved. I matched his rhythm, stroke for stroke, the tension ever tighter in my core.

"Fuck, Jalil," he panted, "thinking about what just happened under the bleachers gets me so close."

Each word, each confession, entwined us further, binding us in this act that was as intimate as it was desperate.

The steam clung to us, dense and humid. Our heavy breaths competed with the relentless drumming of water against tile. I glanced at Emiliano; his eyelids fluttered with the tempo of his hand, and something fierce and possessive awoke. My hand abandoned my own need, reaching out, seeking him, and made contact with his hardness.

"Wha—Jalil?" He stuttered, eyes shooting open. His confusion was clear as my fingers wrapped around him. His hesitation was palpable, thick as the mist filling the room. Had I just made a colossal mistake?

"Let me," I pleaded, eyes locked with his, while my grip tightened. "I want to."

He searched my face, his own features a storm of conflict and desire. For a heart-stopping moment, he resisted, but then his body yielded, leaning into my touch. A slow exhale escaped his lips, his muscles relaxing as pleasure drew taut the line of his jaw.

"The fuck, Jalil..." My hand moved with intent across his light brown skin. He rocked into my grip, and I took it as permission to continue. I stroked him firm and fast, twisting on each upstroke. His breaths grew ragged, and when I swiped my thumb over the head of his cock, his eyes rolled back.

"You like it?" I asked, emboldened by the way his body pressed into mine.

His only response was a low moan, lost in the cascade of water. Encouraged, my other hand ventured further, exploring the dampened expanse of his body until my fingertips grazed the cusp of his ass.

"Wait—" Emiliano tensed, his voice cracking like the brittle surface of ice.

"I know what you like," I said, my touch tentative, coaxing.

But as my finger pressed lightly against his entrance, Emiliano recoiled sharply, like a spring unwound. He stumbled back, putting distance between us, his expression contorted with a mixture of panic and rage.

"Fuck, Jalil! What the hell?" His rejection was a jagged knife, tearing through the fog and the moment we'd shared.

"Emiliano, I—" I started, my mind reeling, trying to bridge the gap his words had created.

"Since when were you a fag?" His accusation sliced through me, a searing heat that burned hotter than the steam. He kissed his crucifix and rattled of something in fast Spanish.

"Emiliano, no, it's not like that," I said, scrambling for words that wouldn't come, an explanation that might soothe the raw edges of what had transpired.

"I'm not like that! Jesus!" His anger was a live wire, sparking dangerously.

"Please, just listen—" I reached out, but he was already on his way out of the shower, leaving me with the fallout of his anger and the cold bite of rejection. Then, the slap of bare feet on wet floor sounded through the haze. Coach Knight stood at the entrance, his broad frame wrapped in nothing but a white towel, clinging to his waist by sheer will.

"Back inside, Emiliano," he said, voice firm and unyielding.

Emiliano froze, his hand on the cold tile. He looked like a deer caught in the headlights, eyes wide with fear and defiance.

"Coach, I—"

"Didn't ask for an excuse, son. Inside." Coach's tone brokered no debate, and Emiliano shuffled back, shoulders slumped.

"Care to share why you're fleeing?" Coach folded his arms across his chest, towel stretching taut over muscles carved from years of training.

"Nothing, I just—"

"Cut the bullshit." Coach's gaze bore into him. "You were enjoying it until you weren't."

I flinched at Coach's bluntness, water still streaming down my back, mixing with unease. What might he do?

"Look," Emiliano stammered, "I'm not gay, okay? It's not right." He touched the cross around his neck.

"Right according to whom?" Coach leaned against the wall, his jaw set, a challenge in his stare.

"I might feel some things I shouldn't, but it doesn't mean anything," Emiliano's voice was a strained whisper, his protest weak. "Not if I can be normal."

"Coach..." I didn't want Emiliano to face this interrogation alone, but Coach raised a finger and silenced me.

"Let him speak, Jalil."

My tongue was heavy, useless. I watched Emiliano struggle, watched the internal war play out across his face—the same battle I'd been waging in secret for years.

"I mean, I was just with Dasani! Feeling up her tits!"

"That's fine," said coach. "As long as you're not denying yourself something you might like better."

Emiliano looked at me, open-mouthed. His eyes dropped to my junk, curious, then returned to my face. "You don't like her?" he asked.

"I like you," I said, a hint of apology in my tone. "I didn't know it until the other day. Now, it makes me crazy when you're with her. I can't help it."

Emiliano's gaze dropping to the slick floor. "Coach, I don't know if I can. My parents. My relatives. *Abuelita*."

"Can't or won't?" There was a knowing edge to Coach's question, one that hinted at his own ghosts. "Confront what scares you."

"Coach, is this because—"

"Because I've been there?" Coach cut me off, his words crisp. A silence bloomed, thick with unspoken truths. "Yeah, it is. And if I had someone to tell me it's okay, maybe things would've been different."

Emiliano's eyes met mine, the storm in them quieting to uncertainty. Coach's words echoed through the steam and the doubt, carving out a space where fear had less of a foothold.

"I've known you boys for four years. It's time you two explore a new kind of competition." He nodded toward our bodies with a tilt of his chin. "Start with the basics. Get to know what makes each other tick."

"Do you want to?" I asked Emiliano.

He stuttered. "I dunno... I mean... Can I...."

I waited for him to get the words out.

"Can I see what your balls feel like?" Emiliano asked at last. "I keep thinking about them. Ever since the other day."

I inched forward. He played with my nuts in his hand and caressed my shaft, and the room swirled around me.

"Can I feel you again?" I asked.

"Yeah," he said. "It was nice, earlier."

My hands trembled. I reached out, Emiliano's body heat seared into my palms. We locked eyes—his, a deep brown that always held a spark of mischief. My fingers dipped below his waist. His cock was hot, alive under my touch, and I swallowed the lump in my throat.

"Like this, Coach?" I asked, trying to mask my uncertainty with bravado while we felt each other.

"Exactly," he said. "Good. Now keep going."

I explored Emiliano more boldly, my touch growing firmer. He gripped me in turn, his hand sending jolts of pleasure up my spine.

God, it was good, better than anything I'd ever admit out loud.

Without warning, Emiliano bridged the gap between us, pressing his lips against mine. The kiss was a shock of warmth, an undercurrent of desire threading through my insides. It wasn't gentle or hesitant—it was a claim, one that I found myself leaning into, craving more of his taste, the press of his body against mine.

"Shit!" I said. "I guess you like it?"

"I guess so," Emiliano exhaled and gave me another crushing kiss that left no room for doubt.

I let my hand trail lower, thumb sweeping across his hole, the motion eliciting a sharp intake of breath from Emiliano. Every nerve ending in my body sang with a foreign sort of urgency, a need I couldn't name but knew I wanted to chase down to its very end.

"Keep...keep doing that," Emiliano urged. His voice carried a raw edge of pleasure that sent a surge of pride through me.

"Here?" I asked, circling the rim, teasing him, testing the waters of this newfound intimacy.

He didn't reply, instead pushing back against my hand, his body demanding more.

I reveled in his response—how he opened up under my ministrations. It was a dance of give and take, a rhythm we were creating together, forging something beyond the competitiveness that had always defined us.

"More, Jalil..." Emiliano's plea was a siren call, pulling me deeper into the intoxicating tide of sensation and connection. And I, lost in the moment, gave in willingly, diving headfirst into an ocean of desire that threatened to swallow us both whole.

Naked, we left the shower and moved toward the benches in the locker room. The fluorescent lights hummed overhead.

"Alright," Coach Knight's voice was firm, yet there was an undercurrent of something softer in it. "I can show you how to take this further if that's what you both want."

I met Emiliano's gaze, his dark eyes shining with nerves and excitement. He nodded, and I mirrored the motion, our silent agreement hanging between us. "Yes, sir," I said, my steady voice opposing my nervous energy.

"Good," he replied. "First thing's about being comfortable. Make sure he's ready for you, and go slow. It's about connection, not just the physical act."

Emiliano lay back on the bench, his chest rising and falling with shallow breaths. I trembled and positioned myself between his smooth thighs, spreading them gently. His skin was warm, inviting—his trust in me palpable.

"Like this?" I asked Coach.

He nodded. "Use your fingers first, get him open for you." His instruction was clinical, but necessary.

I did as told, watching Emiliano's face for any sign of discomfort. But there was only pleasure there, and a hunger that matched my own. With each careful movement, Emiliano opened to me, and walls crumbled in both of us—ones we hadn't even known we'd built.

"More," Emiliano murmured, and I obliged, adding another finger, stretching him, preparing him. "Jesus!" He groaned. "I've never felt this stretched out."

"Okay, now...slowly," Coach instructed, a grounding presence in the haze of desire.

I lined myself up, the head of my cock nudging at Emiliano's entrance. The push was tentative at first, uncertain—but then there was a give, and a warmth that enveloped me whole.

Emiliano gritted his teeth, wincing through the pain, pulling at me to keep going.

"Fuck..." The expletive slipped as I slid home, buried within him.

The tightness, the heat—it was overwhelming, consuming. This wasn't just sex; it was a merging of souls who had been orbiting each other, denying gravity until now.

"Move when you're ready," the coach prompted, his tone softer than before.

I found a rhythm, guided by the tightening grip of Emiliano's hands on my hips. Each thrust carved out a space inside me that was raw and new, filling me with a sense of wholeness I never knew I lacked.

"God, Jalil..." Emiliano said. Hearing my name on his lips like that—it was like a key turning in a lock. I leaned down, capturing his mouth with mine, sealing the silent promise that he was safe and this was just the beginning. "Your dick is so fucking perfect."

Coach put his hand on my ass and helped me pump. With his quiet affirmations in the background, I lost myself to the sensation, to the moment, to Emiliano. We moved together, a dance of flesh and need that was more than lust. It was understanding, acceptance, and intimacy that we could create only through shared vulnerability. In that space, on that bench, with Emiliano and the coach bearing witness, I discovered a part of myself that had remained hidden, a part that only they could bring to light.

The heat from Emiliano's body merged with the steam lingering in the air, cloaking us in a haze that made everything surreal. Coach Knight removed his towel and moved into the space we'd created, his own naked form a study in confidence and raw masculine appeal. The sight of him—the contours of muscle under skin, the shadowed lines of age and experience—set a thrumming pulse through our veins.

"Good, Jalil," he rumbled in a cadence that matched the rhythm of our breathing. "You're doing great."

Emiliano shivered beneath me at the sound, and I echoed that tremor, both of us drawn to the coach's presence like moths to a flame. It was the strangest blend of guidance and participation, a dynamic that shouldn't have worked but somehow did.

"Emiliano," I whispered against his neck, tasting salt and desire on his skin. "He's... he's joining us."

"Let him," Emiliano breathed out, his hands roaming over my back in approval.

Coach's hand found mine, sliding it down to where Emiliano and I connected, urging me to take in every detail of what was happening between us. His other hand rested on Emiliano's chest and grazed his nipples, a silent solidarity in this shared exploration.

"Feel each other," Coach instructed over the slick sounds of flesh meeting flesh. "This is about connection."

My hips moved with a mind of their own. My thrusts became rapid, each one punctuated by Emiliano's moans and the encouraging pressure of Coach's guiding hand.

"I... I'm... my body... I'm gonna..." I shivered, pummeling Emiliano faster and deeper, my balls slamming against his ass with every push.

"Inside him," whispered coach. "Big thrust."

With a final burst of strength, I plunged into Emiliano's body and propelled myself over the edge, pouring myself into him. I fought to keep my balance and remain inside him while my dick beat like a drum. It wasn't just release—it was a bonding. We were here together, discovering uncharted territories within ourselves.

"Jalil!" Emiliano shouted, his insides filling with my seed. The raw edge in his voice pulled a shuddering breath from my lungs.

"Beautiful," Coach said, a testament to what we'd shared.

We disentangled slowly, still riding the high of our climax, and turned our attention to Coach. He stood before us, every inch the authority figure we knew.

"Your turn," Emiliano said with a grin, a playful challenge in his eyes.

I took Coach's cock in my hand, the weight and heat of him unfamiliar yet curiously right. Emiliano joined me, our hands and mouths working in tandem, learning the shape and taste of the man who had ushered us into this new realm of being.

"Ah, guys..." Coach said. There was a note of surrender in his tone that thrilled me.

Emiliano sucked him deep, eyes glinting with mischief and something softer, a display of the trust we'd built. I watched for a moment, memorizing the tableau, before taking my turn, letting the heady scent and flavor of arousal fill my senses.

"Like that, yeah..." Coach's hand cradled the back of my head, guiding without force, his approval sparking another kind of warmth in my chest.

We passed him back and forth between us, sharing him as we'd shared each other. I thought he might come, but instead, with a naughty smirk, he lay me back where Emiliano had been minutes earlier.

Coach's weight shifted behind me, heavy with promise. His hands—those large, capable hands—slid along my waist, grounding and real. I turned my head, seeking his gaze; he met it unflinchingly, the silent question in his eyes clear as his intent.

"You want this?" His voice was gravel, low and resonant.

"Show me how," I managed, the words more a breath than sound.

Coach's fingers traced my spine, a shiver chasing their path before settling at my hips. It was more than touch—it was ownership, direction, safety. He positioned himself, and the blunt pressure at my entrance forced a gasp from my lips. Emiliano's hand found mine, squeezing in silent solidarity.

"Relax," Coach said, "I've got you."

I exhaled slowly, nodding my consent. The push was firm but unhurried, respect for my boundaries woven into every inch he gained. My muscles yielded, and he slid home, filling me wholly. A moan clawed its way out, raw and needy.

"Coach..." It wasn't a plea; it was acknowledgment. Of him, of this, of us.

"Feel that, Jalil?" he asked, his pace steady, each thrust pushing me further into a haze of heat and light.

"Every... every inch," I stuttered, my voice breaking on waves of sensation. My world narrowed to the fullness inside me, the slide of his skin, and the relentless pressure building in my core.

My thoughts became a tangle, a mess of desire and submission. But there was clarity too, in the way he took command, the way he guided me through this labyrinth of sensation. I surrendered to it, to him, letting go of everything but the moment.

His pace quickened. Pressure built inside me like a raging storm. A delicious pain tore at my backside. His unit crushed against that little part of my insides he touched with his finger the other day, making my jaw chatter. Tears of desire filled my eyes.

Emiliano felt my chest... my nipples... he kissed me deep with assurance.

Coach held the underside of my leg, pushing it toward my chest. His climax hit like a thunderclap, ricocheting through my limbs, leaving me breathless and boneless. My toes curled. He swelled, the pulsing heat marking me deep.

Then, he was gone. He had removed himself from inside me, unfulfilled. A terrible feeling consumed me: abandonment, like everyone else in my life. It didn't last. He bellowed in release. His warm, sticky semen covered my hole in heavy bursts before he smashed back inside me to finish, his warmth spreading, a tangible sign of our connection.

"OH!" I screamed in genuine surprise.

We stayed locked together, the remnants of our passion ebbing. His hand stroked my smooth scalp, a gesture as tender as the ferocity we'd shared. I lifted my eyes to meet his, finding an emotion there I hadn't expected, a vulnerability that echoed my own.

"Good boy," he said.

"Coach…" I said, recognizing the gift for what it was. The satisfaction nestled, profound and true. This wasn't just about pleasure; it was about trust, about barriers broken and new ground forged.

I turned my attention to Emiliano. He stood there, a statue carved from desire. His cock remained a proud declaration of unfinished business. It was my turn now, my chance to explore the landscape of his pleasure.

"Come here," I said. My voice heavy with need.

Emiliano stepped forward, the predatory grace of his movements stoking the fire inside me.

"You gonna do it like Dasani would?" he asked.

"I'm gonna do it better than she would," I replied.

He clasped the back of my neck in his hand and gently guided me down.

"Show me what you've got, Jalil," he said, a challenge wrapped in velvet tones.

My lips closed around him, and I tasted the salt of sweat, the bitter hint of pre-cum—flavors of raw, unexplored maleness. His groan vibrated through me as I took him deeper, our connection tightening like a twisted rope.

"Fuck, yes," Emiliano's hips bucked instinctively. "Just like that."

The warmth of him on my tongue, the pulse against my lips—I was lost in the cadence of his pleasure. My hands roamed over his brown calves and thighs, the power of his muscles evidence of countless miles run side by side. This wasn't just physical; it was the culmination of every race, every shared glance across the track.

"Keep going," he urged, his voice strained with the edge of release.

I swirled my tongue with determination, unrelenting in my pursuit, then pulled him deep into my mouth until my nose met the softness of his hair.

"Unghhh..." He twisted. "Your lips..."

I couldn't let Dasani take him away from me. My lips sealed tightly around the base of his throbbing shaft as I sucked with voracious hunger. My tongue danced teasingly along its length. His hardened member twitched, each time gifting me a sweet preview of what was to come and building a fiery anticipation.

When Emiliano at last hardened for a final burst, I made sure I was ready to receive all he had been holding back. He tried to pull away, but I wouldn't allow it.

"Jalil! Bro!!" he screamed. He flooded my mouth with the proof of his ecstasy, moaning and trembling. I swallowed every drop. The moment was ours. It was more than sex; it was an affirmation of everything we'd been too afraid to admit.

"Jesus, Jalil," Coach said from where he watched, his voice laced with admiration. "You're a natural."

We collapsed onto the benches, our bodies slick and spent. The silence settled around us, filled only by our ragged breathing synchronizing—a trio bound by the secrets of skin and sweat.

"Guys..." Emiliano's voice sounded almost reverent. "That was... shit, I don't even have words."

"Words are overrated," I said. The corner of my mouth lifted into a smirk, but inside, something akin to wonder filled me.

Coach nodded, his eyes softening. "What matters is this—the trust, the openness."

"Dasani, man," said Emiliano. "She's a lifetime ago. Like test driving a used car and thinking it's the one until you get behind the wheel of a Mustang."

I laughed. "So you're saying you like me better?"

He grabbed my hand and pulled me up from between his legs. "You know this changes things, right?"

I nodded, unable to look away from the intensity in his gaze. "Yeah. It does."

His arm went across my shoulder—a gesture so tender it threatened to undo me. "We've always been about competition, pushing each other to be better. But now..."

"Competition's not going anywhere," I flicked my hand at his hip. "It's just... different now."

"No more chasing after girls to prove something. We've got nothing to prove. Not to them."

"Right. Just to each other."

"Good." Emiliano's lips quirked up at the edges. "Because I'm not done with you, Harrington. Not by a long shot."

"Wouldn't dream of calling it quits now," I said, the challenge sparking something feral.

Our laughter mingled, a shared secret against the backdrop of emptied lockers and fading adrenaline.

"Let's get out of here," Emiliano said, standing and pulling me up with him.

"Lead the way," I replied, but before we could take a step, he pulled me into a fierce, affirming kiss.

Coach was on his way to the shower, and we bid him a good night.

"Night boys," he said. "Good job today."

As we left the locker room behind, stepping into the dimly lit corridor, I couldn't shake the anticipation coursing through me. This was only the beginning, and I was eager—starved, even—for every lesson, every touch, every whispered confession in the dark.

Together, we walked toward an uncertain future, but the certainty of our connection was a beacon that would guide us through whatever lay ahead.

Capturing the Finish

My lungs burned as I cleared the last hurdle, legs pumping across the finish line. Jeff was right beside me, stride for stride. We slowed to a jog, chests heaving, sweat dripping off our brows.

"Nice run," Jeff panted, clapping me on the back. "Almost beat my personal best."

"Almost," I grinned, still trying to catch my breath. "I'll get you next time."

Jeff laughed. "In your dreams, shorty." He playfully shoved my shoulder as we walked towards the locker room.

"Size doesn't matter," I quipped back with a smirk.

Jeff and I had a routine - we always stayed late to squeeze in some extra training. It was only us left after practice, like it had been in high school. Only four months ago we graduated Campbell High. Class of 1976. We'd be the first graduating class of the new decade at Oakwood College, 45 minutes from home. Neither of us had much direction, but we had track scholarships that didn't earn themselves and parents who couldn't pay for school.

"I don't know how I'm going to afford books this year," Jeff said as we entered the locker room. "My carburetor won't pass inspection, either, and Erica wants me to take her to homecoming back at Campbell."

"That's what happens when you date a younger girl," I smiled, peeling off my sweat-soaked shirt. "Anyway, I feel your pain. I've been saving up for months, but I'm still short. Hard to find a girl when you're broke."

"Hard to find a girl when you're short," Jeff ribbed. HeJ pulled down his tall socks, lines from the elastic etched into his skin. "I don't have time to work a regular job, with year-round track conditioning."

"Well, unless you want to sell test answers, we're shit outta luck," I said, stuffing my sweaty clothes in my gym bag.

My eyes flicked over to him briefly, before I focused on tying my shoes. Jeff, with his sandy brown hair, had an athlete's body - all lean muscle and clean lines. Back in sixth grade, when the cold weather broke and we returned to wearing shorts, he was the first guy I ever noticed with leg hair. I still envied his thick, hairy thighs, broad chest and cut abs. I worked as hard as he did, but could never seem to bulk up. After five years of running I had a tight body with strong quads and calves, but I was ten pounds lighter and three inches shorter and had boring black hair. Girls always looked at him first.

Jeff sighed. "Maybe I'll start a dog walking business or some shit. Or, maybe the rumors about Coach Kinger are true." Jeff's voice was low, but there was a twinkle in his eye.

Coach Kinger was an assistant coach on the track team. He was a grad student, maybe 25 or 26. If Jeff had the body I wanted, Kinger had the body Jeff wanted. The guy was ripped. He held several track records at the school and nearly went to the Olympics for shot put.

I wiped the sweat from my brow with the back of my hand. "What about him?"

"Rumor has it Kinger got paid for doing a porno back in his college days." said Jeff. The way he said it, like he was commenting on the weather, made me want to laugh it off. Instead, there was a weird churn in my gut.

"A movie? Or a magazine?"

"Dunno."

"That's gotta be bullshit," I said, trying to sound more convinced than I felt. An image of Coach naked, his biceps straining against his shirt as he demonstrated proper form flashed across my mind. Unwanted. Intrusive.

"Sure, sure," Jeff replied. His smirk saying he didn't quite buy my dismissal. We ran into Coach Kinger on our way out of the stadium and fell into step behind him. My gaze lingered on the man's physique. His shoulders were powerful and his legs like tree trunks. Through the fabric of his short track shorts, the definition in his glutes was unmistakable. A flicker of something akin to curiosity sparked within me, but I shoved it down fast.

Once he was out of earshot, Jeff asked, "I wonder how much money Coach made for doing porn? Think we could get in on that action?" he laughed. "We could make our own."

"He didn't really do it!" I said. "And why would I make one with you?"

"Not with me, asshole. Anyway, I'm messing with you," said Jeff. "Pastor Ed would send me right to hell."

Jeff grew up in an evangelical church where his pastor, Pastor Ed, made sure he was straight as an arrow and clean as a whistle. Once a month he went home just to go to church. It didn't hurt that Erica was there.

What would it be like to do a movie like that? No. Not now. Not ever.

The autumn air bit at my flushed skin as I paced the familiar route home. My mind was a tangled mess, thoughts racing faster than my heart after that final sprint. Jeff's words echoed in my head, teasing out a curiosity I don't want to acknowledge.

"Make our own film," he'd said, as if it was nothing. Yet there I was, playing with the idea like a forbidden fruit, tempting and sweet. I shoved my hands into my pockets, fingers trembling. I wouldn't know how. I'd never even been with a girl.

My house was empty when I got there, silence greeting me like an old friend. My bag hit the floor with a thud, heavier than usual. Upstairs, my room waited, the door ajar, a sliver of sanctuary from the chaos in my head.

I kicked the door shut behind me and collapsed on the bed, my chest heaving. The urge was sudden, insistent. I needed release—a distraction from the maelstrom of what-ifs and maybes. Fingers fumbled with my belt, urgency fueling my movements.

Pants around my ankles, I closed my eyes, letting fantasies take over. Images of girls from high school, their laughter and soft curves, danced before me. But they faded, replaced by something else—someone else. Coach Kinger whispered in my ear, telling me exactly what he wanted me to do.

"Push yourself, Thompson," his voice said, but it wasn't about running anymore. It was about taking risks, exploring edges I've never dared before.

My hand moved of its own accord, guided by the phantom pressure of his words. Each stroke was a challenge, each breath a gasp of possibilities. I chased the pleasure, driven by the image of his powerful body, the authority in his stance.

"Harder," he ordered. I obeyed without question, my hand racing. I remembered the look of his arms jutting from his tank top and his thighs extending from his shorts, all muscle and coarse hair.

The rush built, a crescendo of heat and desire that threatened to consume me. With a final command from the coach in my head, I shattered, ecstasy ripping through me that left me breathless and spent as warm goo struck my shoulders and neck.

Lying there, panting, I wondered what it meant.

***

Two days later, sweat clung to my skin, making my shorts stick. It had been a long day at practice, with a film guy there to shoot reels for analysis. "I'm here to capture the finish," he said.

The air in the locker room was thick with the musk of exertion and the faint clang of distant weights. I told Coach Kinger I wanted to talk for a few minutes. Now, he sat on one of the benches, a clipboard in his lap, looking every bit the part of the seasoned coach who'd seen too many hopeful kids sprint their hearts out.

"Mike," he said, nodding slightly, his eyes locking onto mine with that familiar intensity, "what can I do for you?"

I perched on the edge of the bench opposite him, my heart pounding from more than the practice run. "Coach, I gotta ask you something," I started, the words stumbling out. "Expenses are adding up fast here at school and I have to pay the bursar next week." My hands twisted the hem of my shirt, damp with sweat. "Thing is, I'm strapped for cash. I don't know if I can make it past next semester, even with my scholarship."

Coach leaned back, his gaze never wavering.

"Heard from the grapevine you found a way to make money when you were a student," I added, a hint of desperation seeping into my voice. I couldn't believe I was even saying this.

Coach Kinger's lips curved into a knowing smile, and he set the clipboard aside. "We all find ways."

"How?" I asked. "Not that I want to. But If."

"I can arrange it," said coach. "How does two hundred dollars sound, if you're interested? I started off as talent, but now I direct."

My mouth went dry. I blinked, unsure if I'd heard him correctly. Two hundred dollars would be more than enough to take the edge off, but the gravity of what he was implying hit me like a ton of bricks. "You mean, like... you would make the film?" I managed to choke out.

"Exactly," he affirmed, leaning forward, elbows on his knees. "I've made a lot of films with guys from the team. You have the right body for it." I blushed. "We'd start you with a solo film. For clients in California. Nobody here would see it."

The locker room was suddenly ten degrees hotter, the scent of aged sweat and metal flooding my senses. This was Coach Kinger, the man who was training me, who knew my limits on the track—but this? This was a different kind of limit altogether.

"So I'd..." The words caught in my throat with disbelief and... something else. Something wild that I couldn't quite name. My mind spun, scenarios playing out at lightning speed.

"Jerk off," Coach said, breaking into my thoughts. "Think about it. No pressure. But the offer stands. Everything's discreet. Professional. Your face won't be plastered anywhere."

My heart thudded against my ribcage. Could I trust him? Or myself?

"Meet me tomorrow after practice if you're interested."

***

I thought about the offer every moment until practice the next day. Each stride on the track was heavy.

"Hey, Mike! You good?" Jeff clapped me on the back as we walked off the field, his usual grin in place.

"Tired," I lied, watching as he turned toward the parking lot.

"Catch you tomorrow, man."

"Take it easy!" His voice faded as I veered back to the gym, alone now, the evening air chilly.

The changing room hummed with an unfamiliar energy after hours. Fluorescent lights buzzed overhead, casting long shadows on the lockers.

Coach Kinger approached from the corridor. "Mike," he said, the cameraman from the other day trailing behind him. "This is Chuck."

A nod was all I got from the guy—a silent professional armed with his 16mm camera, its lens cold and unblinking. A fuzzy microphone hung above, ready to capture every sound. My pulse quickened.

"You've decided?"

"Two hundred, right?" I asked.

"Correct."

"And nobody will know?"

"Not unless you say something."

"Okay," I said. "I... there are other guys on the team who are better looking... have nicer bodies..."

"Shhh," said Coach, stopping me. "You're perfect for this. Let's get started," Coach said, clapping his hands once, the sound sharp in the quiet room.

"Right." I licked my dry lips, watching the cameraman load the film with practiced ease, the click and whirl of the mechanism slicing through the tension. This was real. This was happening.

"Remember, Mike," Coach's voice was softer now, somehow more intimate. "It's you, your body, your pleasure. We're not even here."

He laid out the plan. "This will be easy. We'll be shooting only one scene." His eyes met mine, reading my nerves like an open playbook. "You sit on that bench," he pointed, "do your thing, finish on yourself. All your clothes come off except your socks. They stay up to your knees.

I tugged at them to make sure they were in place.

"When you're done, wipe yourself off with your tank top. Are you okay with this?" Coach's question sliced through my haze of thoughts.

"Yeah," I managed, my voice a stranger in the quiet between us. "Yeah, I'm good."

"Remember, consent is key. You call the shots. If at any point you don't want to do this, let me know and we'll stop."

I nodded.

He stepped back to give me space, like the distance could somehow ease the intimacy of what I was about to do.

I sat on the bench, the cold of the metal locker room bench seeping into my skin—the same bench where I'd tied countless cleats and slapped congratulatory hands. Now, it was my stage. I spread a terrycloth towel next to me.

"Take your time," Coach encouraged.

I closed my eyes for a moment. The click of the camera and the soft hum of the fluorescent lights faded away, leaving only the thud of my pulse in my ears. My hands trembled as they hovered over my body, an admission of vulnerability I'd never shown before. A part of me wanted to bolt, to keep my clothes on and pretend this offer had never been made. But another part—a deeper, braver part—whispered that this was another hurdle to leap.

I palmed myself through the thin fabric of my track shorts. I stirred. The blood rushed south. My heart was a trapped bird in my chest, slamming against its cage, seeking escape.

"Relax, Mike," Coach's voice cut through the fog of my hesitation. "Like you're alone. Take off your shirt."

I whisked my tank top over my head and rubbed my pecs, then

took my hand under my shorts and gave my balls a squeeze. I coaxed life into my flesh, my hand working with growing confidence. It was a strange dance, one of self-discovery played out under watchful eyes. A bead of perspiration trickled down my temple, not from exertion, but from the heat of the moment.

Finally, firmness asserted itself, demanding attention. I drew in a deep breath, hooked my fingers into the waistband of my shorts and briefs and slid them down. They pooled around my ankles.

My bare skin met the rough texture of the towel when I sat. It was alien, yet somehow right. I leaned onto a row of lockers behind me. The chill of the metal against my back contrasted with the warmth spreading through my core. Legs open, I was vulnerable and exposed, yet something inside twisted with anticipation, with the desire to be seen.

The camera whirred a soft mechanical growl.

Coach spoke from behind the camera. "Good, Mike. You have a nice penis. Let your hand explore it."

I grew warm at coach's praise. I wrapped my fingers around myself, a tentative grip that morphed into something more assured with each rhythmic stroke. The touch was both familiar and new, guided by the subtle tilts of Coach's head, his murmured commands that urged me to find a rhythm and pace entirely my own.

"Try circling the head," he instructed, and I obeyed, thumb brushing over the sensitive skin, sending jolts of pleasure radiating through me. It was an education, this slow dance of self-pleasure under his watchful eye—teaching me ways to coax out sensations I'd never unearthed alone in the dark confines of my bedroom.

"Play with your hole." His directive was gentle but firm, pushing boundaries that I never approached before.

I paused. I'd never touched my asshole. "Exit only," Jeff would say. It was certainly not a place for fingers. Yet, the curiosity stirred, and

I didn't want to hesitate. I brought my knees to my head, exposing my pucker to the camera. My fingertips grazed the untouched rim, and a shiver of something forbidden coursed through me.

"Press inside," Coach encouraged. I pressed a little deeper, exploring the ridges and folds. A foreign sensation bloomed—tingling, surging into a potent mix of shock and pleasure that set my jaw chattering. It was a revelation, the discovery of a hidden trove of nerve endings that responded eagerly to my tentative touch.

Slowly, slowly, I slipped past the second knuckle, gasping at the fullness, the stretch. I became lost in it. Each tender probe sent waves crashing against the shore of my restraint, urging me toward a precipice I never knew existed.

"Like that, Mike." Coach whispered. His words were a balm, soothing over any lingering doubts. I delved deeper, driven by the forceful urge to unearth every last drop of gratification from the depths within.

I smashed my other hand up and down over my prick, which ached with hardness. The pressure mounted, an undeniable force. My body tensed, each muscle wired tight with anticipation. The room faded, sound dulled, and only the pulse of blood in my ears remained, throbbing in time with my racing heart.

"Good... almost there..." Coach's voice was a distant anchor, grounding me as I teetered on the brink. "You have a great body, Mike. Abs nice and tight. Solid arms. Your calves are like boulders under those socks."

Coach's approval was making me lose my mind. I wanted to hold it in for him—to keep going longer and prove my stamina—but my fist pumped up and down without control.

"Let it go!" said Coach. "Show me what your body can do."

With a final, determined stroke, the dam broke. I raised my legs and pounded my hole with my finger. My toes curled. A surge of heat rocketed through me, pleasure cresting into a blinding white crescendo. I cried out, unashamed, as release washed over me in shuddering waves, cum striking my chest and streaking down toward my abs.

As I quieted, guilt gnawed at the edges of my mind, a reminder of the line I'd crossed. Yet it was entwined with a deep-seated satisfaction, the kind that comes from fulfilling a primal need. Beneath it all was the sweet undercurrent of having pleased Coach Kinger, of earning that look of approval in his eyes.

I relaxed, spent, breathing hard. My chest moved up and down, splattered with the evidence of my abandon, strangely satisfying against my skin.

"The tank top," Coach reminded me. I gathered it from the floor and wiped away the stickiness, my movements slow.

"Cut!" He presented the envelope, heavy with the weight of the promised cash. His fingers brushed mine as he handed it over, a fleeting touch laden with unspoken understanding.

"Good, boy," he said, and the words resonating deeper than they should. They're simple, yet they validated something within me I hadn't known needed acknowledging. Nobody in my family had ever said it.

The Cameraman silently packed his equipment, the click and clack of metal on metal a quiet punctuation to the charged silence. The 16mm camera was now silent, the fuzzy microphone stowed away, the remnants of the moment captured in spools of film waiting to be developed.

The deal was done. I wrapped a towel around my waist, clutching the envelope. What had I done? The question lingered, but drowned out by the echo of Coach's praise and the rustle of paper that promised a continued future at the school.

My shaky legs found strength as I dressed. Every movement was a step back to reality, to who I was before this room, before the offer, before the camera's invasive eye. But I couldn't undo what had been done. I couldn't unfeel the thrill.

"See you at practice tomorrow, Mike," Coach called out as he headed for the door. "Let me know if you ever want to do more."

"See you," I replied, the envelope secure in my pocket.

***

The next day after practice, Jeff plopped down beside me on the bench in front of our lockers. We were both catching our breath.

"Think the bursar is still open?" I asked casually, trying to divert my mind from the secret that weighed upon me.

"You came up with the money to pay?" Jeff raised an eyebrow, a smirk playing on his lips. "How?"

I hesitated, my heart racing. Was it time to tell him? I took a deep breath, my voice wavering as I began to reveal my experience. "Well, you see... I filmed this... thing with coach Kinger. Turns out the rumors are true."

His eyes narrowed, curiosity and concern mingling in their depths.

"Coach asked me to do a... jerkoff video." My cheeks burned hot with embarrassment.

"Ha!" Jeff burst out laughing. "Seriously?!"

"Shut up!" I snapped, vulnerable. "I got $200, and so what? Nobody will ever see it."

"Alright, alright," he said, his laughter subsiding. "So, how was it?"

"Terrifying," I admitted. "I shouldn't have done it, but the pleasure mixed with guilt was... intoxicating."

Jeff's expression softened, and his mocking tone vanished. It was replaced by a new understanding, as if my words had struck a chord within him. He looked at me thoughtfully, his eyes searching mine for something unspoken. He hesitated for a moment, then leaned in closer to me, his voice barely above a whisper. "I... I did one too."

My eyebrows shoot up in surprise, and we exchanged glances, a silent understanding passing between us as we realize the depth of our shared secret.

"Really?" I said, still reeling from his confession.

"Yeah," he admitted, his eyes cast down. "Same reason as you. A few weeks ago. I wasn't going to say anything."

"That's how you knew about him!" I exclaimed.

What did his film look like? I'd seen Jeff naked in the showers. He had huge balls under a big dick, and the fantasy of him pumping his it into his fist with his eyes closed caused a rush of heat between my legs. I inhaled sharply and turned my mind to other things.

My voice grew softer. "What if someone finds out? What if people talk?"

"Kinger promised me that no one who matters will ever see the film. I believe him," said Jeff. "Hey, what did you think of Kinger when... you know... directed you." He trailed off, not needing to elaborate on the experience we both shared.

"Um, well..." I said, unsure how much to reveal. "That confidence, that authority... it's hard not to be drawn to him. His commands sort of made me cum harder."

"Same. I wasn't expecting it," Jeff said, quiet against the echo of falling water nearby. "Did you catch a look at his thighs? His arms?"

"Huge," I said.

"Not that I'm queer or anything," Jeff added.

"Of course not," I quickly chimed in, echoing his sentiment. "Me neither. Just think of all the girls who are gonna watch us in

California."

"Did he tell you about other opportunities?" Jeff asked.

"He mentioned it," I said.

"How much more money could we make, and what else would we have to do?" he asked. "I mean, it's easy, and even kind of fun. I was thinking maybe I could fix my car if I did it a few more times."

"We could put or money together and get an apartment," I said. "Live off-campus. Party it up. Want to ask him?"

Jeff and I dressed quickly and hurried to Coach Kinger's office.

***

Coach's office smelled like pungent linament, even from the door. Jeff knocked, and we heard a gruff "Come in" from inside.

"Afternoon, coach," I said.

"What can I do for you boys?"

"Well," Jeff started, then paused.

"We wondered if you had more work for us, coach," I said. "If other people needed more films."

"It doesn't have to be solo, if you know what I mean," said Jeff.

Coach smiled. "I was just thinking about you two. I have another proposition." He paused, eyes lingering on us for a beat too long. "I'll pay you each $1,000 if you have sex on camera."

"With girls?" asked Jeff.

"With each other," said coach.

"What?!" Jeff's eyes went wide, mirroring my own shock.

"Think about it," Coach Kinger said, leaning forward, his fingers tapping on the desk. "It's easy money, and, like last time, no one ever has to know."

"Coach, this is…I mean…" I stammered, my mind racing. A thousand dollars could help with college expenses, but this... was it worth it? Could I even go through with it?

"Take some time to discuss it," Coach said, sitting back again, "then give me your decision."

Jeff and I searched each other's faces for answers. Wordlessly, we left the office, not yet ready to face the choice before us.

We made our way to the wooden benches in the locker room where we sat not fifteen minutes earlier, seeking solace in their familiarity. I looked over at Jeff, his brows furrowed.

"Man, this is crazy," he said, running a hand through his wavy hair. "What do you think we should do? Do you think he'd give us the chance with girls instead, if we asked for $500?"

I sighed, my eyes scanning the empty room before settling on the metal lockers that lined the walls. "A thousand dollars is a lot of money, but... with you?"

"Right?" said Jeff. "That's some sick homo shit, right there."

We were quiet for a few moments.

"Did you ever fuck a girl?" asked Jeff.

"Did you?" I asked back.

"I mean, Erica..." said Jeff, "after prom."

"I never got lucky, even like that," I said. "I was hoping college would turn things around."

My mind was again a whirlwind. The idea of having sex with Jeff was making me nervous, not disgusted. What would I do with him if I had the chance? Would he find me attractive? And... what did it mean that I was even considering it? It was the money. It had to be. I might do it for a grand, but Jeff would never. Not with a girlfriend back home. Not with pastor Ed in his life. Not with...

"Nobody has to know, right" Jeff replied, his gaze locked on mine. "If we do it, we keep it between us."

"Are you okay..." I asked softly, "with... doing that?"

He hesitated, shifting on the bench uncomfortably. "We've known each other forever, and I know you don't have the clap or some shit."

"True," I admitted, the tension in my body beginning to ease ever so slightly. "But this is different, isn't it?"

Jeff bit his lip. "Think about it, Mike. This could be our chance to pay off everything, and even have some left over. We could do it and get it done. It wouldn't have to mean anything. It's not like we're in love."

"I know," I whispered, my mind racing with the possibilities. "But, what will we have to do to each other? Will it hurt? Can we even get turned on?"

"Close your eyes and pretend. It's a grand. We'll make sure we shower first. I'll just think of girls to get hard before they turn the camera on."

My chest tightened as I searched for the right words. My response stood to define our friendship forever.

"Wanna go for it?" he pressed.

"Okay, but remember," I continued, locking eyes with Jeff, "it's for the money. It's not like we're really gay or anything." The words were strange on my tongue but provided a sense of reassurance.

"Yeah," Jeff responded, his cheeks flushing a deep red as he began tugging at his shorts.

The wooden floor creaked beneath our feet as we again approached Coach Kinger's office, our steps echoing down the empty hallway. A mix of nerves and anticipation flooded through me. I glanced at Jeff and wondered what lay ahead for us.

"Ready?" Jeff asked, his voice barely audible above the pounding in my ears.

I nodded. "As ready as I'll ever be."

We pushed open the door to find Coach Kinger seated behind his desk.

"Boys," Kinger's voice broke the silence, deep and certain. I didn't miss the way his eyes held us, like we were at the starting blocks again, waiting for the signal to sprint. We'd been here before, for pep talks and strategy sessions, but never with the air this heavy, this charged.

"We'll do it," said Jeff.

"Take a seat," he said. The chair beneath me groaned as I settled into it.

Coach leaned forward, hands clasped on the desk, the light casting shadows that made his features seem even more imposing. "Here's how it'll start," he began. "You two will undress. Then, you kiss."

Undressing? Kissing? My jaw chattered. "Hope you've got your game face on for this, Harding," I said.

He shifted, a muscle twitching in his jaw. "I can pretend anything."

The room seemed to shrink, walls inching closer as Coach Kinger leaned forward, elbows on the desk, eyes sharp and unyielding. "Mike," he continued, voice a low rumble, "you'll be giving Jeff head."

Those words, so blunt, so stark, sliced through the haze of nervous energy. I watched Jeff's reaction. His eyes stretched wide, a flash of white around his blue irises. His chest rose sharply.

A shiver ran down my spine. Cold fear and something warmer. The full weight of what we were about to do pressed down on me.

"I know you're both scared. You've never explored like this. But, it's about trust. It's about chemistry, and I know you have it," said Coach.

I nodded. Chemistry. We've always moved together with an ease that said more than our words. But this... this is a dance of a different kind.

"Jeff," Coach continued, his voice dripping with intensity. "You'll be fucking Mike. Mike, I want you to jerk off while he's fucking you."

The words fell from Coach's mouth like a hammer, slamming into my chest and stealing the air from my lungs.

Jeff's eyes turned to me, burning like branding irons. The weight of his gaze drowned out any other thoughts or sounds in the cramped office. Panic swelled in my stomach.

"In his ass?" asked Jeff.

"It'll be warmer and tighter than anything you've ever known," said coach. He turned to me. "It's a little bigger than a finger, but you can get used to it."

The idea of Jeff being my first was both terrifying and exhilarating. "We can figure it out," I rasped, my own desires and fears bubbling to the surface.

Coach Kinger's eyes gleamed, satisfied, as if there was never a question we'd reach this point before we did. He leans back, hands clasped behind his head, the picture of confidence. As if he's choreographed every move we're about to make. "Let's move."

***

The custodian had made his rounds in the locker room, and locked the doors. I turned the lights back on. We took quick showers, barely noticing each other, and dressed again in our uniforms, per coach's instructions. When we returned, Chuck the cameraman was there.

"Scared?" Jeff asked at last, pulling his socks to his knees.

"Terrified," I admit. "Did coach have you play with your hole when you did your jerkoff film?"

"Yeah," said Jeff.

"It wasn't bad, right?" I asked.

"It was weird. It hurt, then I got used to it. That's probably what... what it's like," said Jeff. "Anyway, how are we going to do this? How am I going to get it up?"

The cameraman's movements—the mechanical clicks and soft shuffles of his expertise—echoed as he set up his equipment. His hands moved with precision, adjusting the tripod, fine-tuning his lens with an artist's touch.

"Ready," the cameraman murmured, more to himself than to us.

"You'll start by exploring each other's bodies," said Coach, "and take it from there. I promise it won't be hard."

"I promise it won't be hard, too," Jeff mocked.

The mockery hurt a little—the idea Jeff didn't like me and would never like me stung. Something deep within my core took it as a challenge.

"Action," said Coach. His command, firm and devoid of hesitation, hung heavy in the air. It was the starting gun at the track, the signal to release every pent-up emotion and let the physical take over. I fixed my eyes on Jeff, letting all else fall away.

Jeff's hand hovered, tentative, then landed—a soft brush against my cheek. My skin prickled with each feather-light contact.

"Like this?" His whisper cut through the thick silence.

"Cut," said Coach. "Start again. No talking. Just do it."

Nodding, Jeff retracted his hand. It was a reset, but the energy didn't dissipate. It built, it swirled, it pushed at the space that no longer existed between us.

He reached out once more, silent now, fingertips tracing the curve of my jawline. I leaned in, craving that touch—it's comfort and fire all at once. Our eyes locked, and for a heartbeat, we're only Jeff and Mike—no camera, no coach, no locker room.

A nervous giggle bubbled up from deep within him. "This is weird," he said, laughter in his words.

"Keep going, boys," came the encouragement from behind the lens. Coach's words were a lifeline back to the scene. "Like at a meet, focus. You trained for this."

He was right—not the act, but the discipline, the drive to push through the weirdness, the unexpected.

Jeff's laughter died. He clearly had little experience initiating a kiss.

"Trust me?" I whispered.

He nodded. Our lips touched, soft, uncertain—tender at first, a gentle inquiry before it deepened and grew bold and insistent. The world narrowed down to the taste of him, the sweep of his tongue against mine.

"That's it," said coach.

Heat bloomed within me, spreading like wildfire through my veins as our mouths moved together with growing urgency. There was no giggling now, no space for anything but this—Jeff and me, and the raw need that pulled us closer. I was growing tight in my shorts, but what about Jeff? Was this anything but some cynical, mechanical exercise to him?

Suddenly Jeff's hands, strong and sure, skimmed down my sides. Our breaths mingled, ragged, syncing with the pounding of our chests.

With every second, his movements became less tentative, more deliberate. His fingers hooked under my tank top, and the fabric lifted, cool air kissing the skin he warmed with his hands. We broke our kiss long enough to strip away the barriers—two tank tops tossed aside, discarded like the last remnants of hesitation between us.

His chest was a landscape of muscle and sinew I've watched in motion countless times, but never like this—never close enough to explore, to worship. My fingertips started their own journey across his torso. Each ridge and valley under my palms sent a silent promise of what was to come, and the thought alone was enough to tighten my breath.

"I always wanted pecs like yours." I whispered, tracing the cut of his pectorals.

"You're really strong, too," he replied. "I make fun of you for being short, but those quads... I wish I had them."

"Jeff, have a seat on the bench. Mike, sit on his lap, facing him," said Coach.

We sank onto the bench, the wood creaking beneath our combined weight. His thighs were firm against mine. His heat pressed against me, undeniably stiff, and I smiled. The hardness was for me. I was doing that to him. Our mouths met again, a crash of lips and tongues that sends our pulses racing.

We Kissed. Breathed. Pressed closer. Every shift, every moan was a language we'd always spoken, only now we understood its true depth. There was no holding back—the urgency between us demanded everything.

Heat from Jeff's lips seared a path along my neck. His kisses ignited tiny fires all over, leaving shivers in their wake. His mouth was warm, insistent, staking claim with every press of skin on skin.

He stood. My fingers found his waist, tracing the line of his shorts before gripping the fabric. I had a moment of hesitation, a fleeting second where doubt and desire collided. Then, I pulled. The material gave way, revealing him—hard, throbbing, the very essence of my cravings. His length stood proud against the dim light.

"Suck me," he said. "I need it."

Still seated, I leaned forward. He was bigger than I had remembered from past glimpses. The scent of him, musk and desire, filled my senses as I took Jeff into my mouth. His sharp intake of breath was my guide, the sound fueling my courage. My tongue teased the sensitive head, probing the texture, the taste. His pubes tickled my nose, and his balls tightened against my chin.

"Fuck, Mike..." His moan filled the space between us, a low rumble that vibrated through my core. "This is amazing. Better... better than..."

I knew how he wanted to finish his sentence, and it drove me wild. My hands steadied on his hips. I lowered them, exploring the power of his runner's build, his stony thighs, his hard calf muscles twitching under his high socks. Firm, solid, a testament to discipline and strength—and yet, yielding to me in this moment of raw need.

Jeff's fingers threaded through my hair, a gentle pressure urging me closer. The lockers faded. The world was only us. I looked up, and our gazes locked—a silent conversation of shared secrets and unspoken promises.

"I'm gonna cum if you keep sucking me like that." He gasped. His eyes reflected a plea, a battle within. The grip in my hair tightened, and we settled into a rhythm we both understood.

I focused, determined to draw out every shudder, every breath. His length pulsed on my tongue, and I committed to memory the way he felt, the way he tasted. It was more than physical. Jeff surrendered to the moment, to me.

I stood and found my way back to his lips. His eyes darkened. His fingers trailed down my sides, coaxing a shiver from deep within.

"I never thought... I always... a girl, you know?" said Jeff. "But this is unreal. You're unreal."

I flushed and smiled, and gave his dick a stroke. It was as stiff as a barbell.

"I need to put it somewhere," he whispered into my ear. "Bad."

He lay me back on the bench. I faced the ceiling. A tug at my waistband forced my hips toward the sky, and he whisked my shorts past my feet, exposing my dripping length. He slid his hands down the backs of my legs, through my scant hair, taking my socks.

His touch was gentle at first, probing, promising. My body tensed, then yielded, the sensation of him exploring me both unfamiliar and intoxicating. The hands that knew only the fierceness of competition were now learning the contours of desire.

"Your dick gets pretty big when you're hard," he said, jerking me.

"Raise his legs," said Coach. "Put them on your shoulders."

Jeff did as coach commanded, trying not to look at my exposed hole.

"Good Jeff," said coach. Now, press yourself against his entrance. Don't be afraid of it. Watch the tip go inside."

His grip tightened on my hips, a silent anchor in the storm he was about to unleash. The pressure built as he pushed, but I was too tight, and he slipped out. Coach threw him a bottle of something slick.

"Smear it on your dick, and put a little on his hole, and try again."

This time, my body yielded. Jeff entered me, inch by deliberate inch. It was a slow burn, an exquisite stretch that melded pain with a pleasure so intense it blurred the lines between the two.

"Mike..." The sound of my name on his lips was both plea and promise. "Holy shit."

Our bodies connected and synced in a rhythm both new and as old as time. His thrusts, hesitant at first, grew bolder, each one pushing deeper into me.

"Better," he gasps out, "better than... anything. You're so fucking warm inside."

His words, raw and honest, wrapped around me, more intimate than the act itself. He gave me his truth, his revelation, and it stirred something deep. It was no longer simply physical; we're crossing lines drawn by every guy in sports, erasing them with every shared breath and thrust.

Tears pricked my eyes, a mix of sharp pleasure and aching tenderness. "Harder," I whispered, chasing the edge, needing him to lose control with me.

His movements became more insistent, driving us both toward the precipice. He forced the air from me, pleasuring himself on my insides, enveloping me in a tide that swept me away. When I was certain he had forgotten about me, lost in his own bliss, he kissed me. Stroked my hair. Stared into my eyes.

His face contorted, beads of sweat rolling down his forehead. He leaned closer, taking my nipple into his mouth and sucking gently, sending a shiver through my body. His fist pumped my dick.

"I'm so close, man," I panted, my hands gripping his muscular shoulders.

"Me too," he groaned, moving faster now. "Want me to...?"

"Yeah," I nodded. "Inside me. Don't stop."

With one final thrust, Jeff climaxed, his eyes locked on mine. Warmth flooded my core. I, too, lost control, my gland throbbing against Jeff's prick as streams of jizz streamed over my head and onto the floor.

"Cut!" Coach Kinger's authoritative voice sliced through the room like a knife. "Good job, boys."

"I'm gonna grab a coffee," said Chuck, the cameraman, leaving the room.

As Jeff pulled out, his erection subsiding, uncertainty washed over his face. He stumbled back, stunned.

"Oh, shit..." he said. "I... I...."

I looked up at him. Coach looked from behind the camera.

"I didn't mean it," Jeff said. My chest cratered. "I mean... it was for the money. Right, Mike? Like we talked about." He looked at coach. "I'm no homo, coach. I swear. I do it with Erica all the time. I'm normal, like every other guy on the team."

In the middle of passion, I was already imagining doing it with Jeff again. I liked the way he took me. I needed him to want me, to dump Erica, and a mixture of sadness and anger bubbled up. I had him inside me. I meant something to him. Now, he was falling apart fast, guilt and insecurity overtaking him.

"Just... give me the money. Let's pretend it didn't happen, or whatever," said Jeff.

Coach moved from behind the camera and approached. "It's okay to be scared, Jeff, but it's time to be honest with yourself instead of scared. Your body knows what it wants. What it needs. Do you feel the same things with Erica when you fuck her?"

I remembered the way Jeff's hands gripped my muscles; how he wrapped his arm around the small of my back; how he raised my legs and plunged into me with abandon.

Jeff's bottom lip twitched. "None of this is right. My first time with Erica should have been like with Mike, and my first time with Mike should have been like with Erica. I'm so fucked up. Pastor Ed says Christians control their urges and desires, and I'm going to have to. I can't be this way."

The atmosphere shifted, a palpable tension settling between us. Coach Kinger locked eyes with both of us.

"I want to fuck you, Jeff," he said. "You need the completeness, the fullness, of a man to understand yourself. Will you let me?"

I thought for sure Jeff would turn away. Instead, he stared. His blue eyes became moist. He looked away and back again.

Without breaking eye contact, Coach removed his clothing, revealing a taut, muscular body that put both of us to shame. His large, stiff erection drew our gazes instinctively. "Can I touch you?"

Jeff stood paralyzed, and replied with a brief nod in the affirmative.

Coach's hand reached out and caressed Jeff's penis, still thick and sticky from our lovemaking. Jeff shivered. His body responded instinctively to the man's commanding presence. He was hardening again. Watching them, my arousal grew, too.

"Look at you, Jeff," Coach Kinger murmured, his fingers tracing his shaft. He changed his grip and tightened around Jeff's balls. "So innocent with those big blue eyes and that sandy blond hair, but these big babymaking balls aren't empty yet, are they? They aren't satisfied."

Jeff swallowed hard. "No, sir," he whispered.

"Good," Coach Kinger replied, guiding Jeff towards the bench with a firm yet gentle touch. Jeff willingly followed, frightened and alive. I stood back, my eyes fixed on the scene unfolding before me, torn between my desire to join them and the fear of entering uncharted territory.

Kinger's strong hands moved over every inch of Jeff's muscular body. Jeff's moans filled my ears, soft and needy, and I couldn't help but let my own desire intensify.

"Mike, don't be shy," Coach Kinger called over his shoulder, his tone both inviting and demanding. I hesitated, my pulse quickening, before taking a step closer. The room was charged with anticipation. There was no turning back.

"Relax, Jeff," Coach whispered, leaning down so that his lips brushed against Jeff's ear. "It's okay to want this." The words seemed to have an immediate effect on Jeff, who arched his back in response, offering himself completely to coach.

Jeff's erection grew harder than ever. God, how was it possible for him to be even more turned on? My own arousal was becoming unbearable, and I silently cursed myself for staring. My brain took notes about what to do to Jeff, later. What he liked. What made him moan or squeak or cry.

"Feels good, doesn't it?" Coach asked with authority. Jeff nodded, his eyes glazed with lust. Heat radiated from them, and I longed to be part of their intimate exchange.

Coach took his time with Jeff, licking, sucking, and rubbing his erection with skill. Jeff's pleasure built, his groans growing louder and more desperate.

"You have a nice, hairy chest, Jeff," said coach. "Furry legs. Quite a young man."

Unable to resist any longer, I reached down and gripped my throbbing cock, giving it a few tentative strokes.

Jeff gasped between moans, "Mike, come here."

The desire to give in to my fantasies warred with the last vestiges of caution in my mind. But the sight of Jeff, so completely lost in rapture, tipped the scales.

I stepped forward. My legs quivered, but I moved closer until I was standing by the bench. Coach gave me an approving nod, and I positioned myself next to Jeff, our bodies pressed close together. The heat radiating from him was intoxicating. My arousal spiked.

"Take control, Mike," Coach urged, guiding my hand to Jeff's throbbing erection.

The moment my fingers made contact with Jeff's heated flesh, I heard him inhale. Waves of pleasure seemed to ripple through his body, and I reveled in the power I had over my best friend. As I stroked him, the look in his eyes told me I was doing everything right.

"Good," Coach murmured, before sinking down to his knees in front of me. His warm breath ghosted over my erection. Without a word, he took me into his mouth.

The sensation was indescribable. Coach's skilled tongue worked its magic, teasing and caressing me in all the right ways. My body shook and my legs cramped as the pleasure built higher and higher. I focused on Jeff, the connection between us only growing stronger as we shared this intimate moment.

"It's amazing," I moaned. Jeff's eyes filled with lust and understanding and something else. Jealousy? Did he not like to see Coach pleasuring me?

"Kiss him, Mike," Coach Kinger's voice was low and commanding, urging us to continue exploring our newfound intimacy.

As I rubbed Jeff's arousal, coach backed away and Jeff reciprocated with a purpose he didn't have before. Our hands moved in sync, stroking each other with determination. We were lost in each other, our bodies close enough to be one.

"Fuck, you two look so good together," Coach said, his voice heavy with undisguised lust. He watched us intently, his own desire reaching its apex.

Sensing the mounting urgency in the room, Coach made his move. He positioned himself behind Jeff, gripping his glutes possessively. I could see the anticipation on Jeff's face, mixed with a hint of nervousness. Was this really happening?

"Relax, Jeff. This is going to feel incredible," the coach assured him, lubing himself, his tone simultaneously soothing and authoritative. "You don't want to take your socks off?"

Jeff shook his head no.

With a slow and deliberate motion, Coach Kinger gripped Jeff's legs at the ankles and raised them high. He ran his nose up the sole of Jeff's foot, and Jeff squirmed and giggled. He sucked on his toes through the tight fabric.

"NNNNNnnnnnhhh!" cried Jeff.

"You like that?" asked Coach, repeating the motion on the other foot while Jeff lost his mind.

Jeff splayed his toes as Coach Kinger repositioned and placed his cherry dick head against Jeff's hole. "Ready?" asked coach.

"Go slow?" Jeff panted.

Coach entered him, their bodies merging in a powerful union.

The room filled with the sounds of bliss - Jeff's moans mixing with my gasps as I bore witness.

The stretch from Coach's tumescence shattered him with a magnificent pop. "Gaaaaaah!" Jeff cried,

"Just relax," said Coach.

"It will feel good soon," I said to Jeff.

Tears streamed down Jeff's face. He gripped my hamstring. First I thought it was for stability—for comfort—but he guided me to his mouth and began licking and sucking me, his lips and tongue working in perfect harmony. My body trembled. My balls hardened, and a wash of precum escaped.

"Jeff," I moaned, my voice barely audible over the sounds of our passion. "Holy shit bud. You like it?"

Jeff answered by sucking harder. Swirling his tongue. Pulling me further in. My eyes rolled back.

"Keep going, boys," Coach Kinger said. His grip on Jeff's hips tightened, his thrusts growing more forceful as he fucked him with unrelenting determination. With every thrust, Jeff bellowed a grunt or a moan. "Coaaaaach!" he croaked. "More! All the way!"

Coach planted his fiery brand as hard and as far as it would go inside. His balls slapped Jeff's backside.

Jeff's dick twitched hard in my fingers, and mine in his mouth. "I can't... I'm gonna..." Jeff cried.

"Me too," I replied. My chest tightened. The pressure built within me.

"Show me what you're made of, boys," Coach Kinger said.

We reached our peak simultaneously, our cries echoing throughout the locker room. My body spasmed as I shot my load into Jeff's mouth. He eagerly swallowed three, four, five times. Bobbing his head. Lapping his tongue. His prick tightened in my fist and a second later exploded like a battleship cannon, streams of hot cum splattering across Coach's chest.

Coach Kinger's thrusts grew more powerful, his body tensing with the anticipation of release. Jeff's eyes strained as he struggled to hold on. Suddenly, Coach let out a guttural moan. He pulled out and squirted his first two shots against Jeff's hole, then plunged back in to finish, his body shuddering and releasing his scorching seed.

As our bodies trembled from the aftershocks of our climax, I marveled at the intensity of what we'd experienced.

"Damn," Jeff breathed, his own body still trembling from the aftermath. "Coach... that was..."

"Amazing?" Coach Kinger grinned, pulling out and stepping back, his chest heaving as he tried to catch his breath. "I told you boys you had it in you. Still scared, Jeff?"

"Not anymore, coach," said Jeff. He looked at me. "You had a lot of cum," he laughed. "I wasn't expecting it from a little guy." He leaned closer. "I like having your sperm inside me. It makes me feel stronger."

As we wiped ourselves down with towels, the reality of what had happened began to sink in. This wasn't some fantasy or dream - we'd actually gone through with it, crossing a line that could never be uncrossed. My thoughts raced, anxiety bubbling up inside me.

"Hey," Coach Kinger called out, reaching into his locker and pulling out a stack of cash. "You've earned this. Both of you."

Jeff and I exchanged a glance, uncertainty flickering in his eyes. Did we really want to accept money for what had transpired? It felt dirty, somehow, like we were cheapening the experience.

"Coach, we, uh..." I stammered, glancing at Jeff for backup. "We don't want your money."

"No?" The coach raised an eyebrow, clearly surprised by our response.

"Maybe," Jeff hesitated before continuing, "we can work something else out?"

"Like what?" Coach Kinger asked, curiosity piqued.

"Let's do it again," I blurted, my heart pounding in my chest. "It's a long track season."

A slow smile spread across Coach Kinger's face as he considered our proposal. "You've got a deal, boys."

As we left the locker room that night, my life had changed forever. We'd forged a bond with each other - and with Coach Kinger - that would carry us through college. We looked forward to exploring the depths of our newfound connection, unsure of where it would lead but eager to find out.

The End.

THE NUTCRACKER PRINCE

The cold bit at my skin as I stepped off the bus, the icy breath of an Illinois winter greeting me like an old adversary. I pulled my coat tighter around me, my breath visible in the early evening air, small puffs of warmth against the city's skyline. I had just finished my fall semester and faced four weeks of freedom before school resumed. With suitcase in hand and anticipation threading through every step, I trudged toward the Majestic Theater, the Jewel of the Chicago Ballet.

The grand edifice loomed ahead, its towering presence demanding my full attention. Its ornate architecture—a blend of intricate stonework and regal columns—stood defiantly against the gray backdrop of downtown bustle. Stepping closer felt like entering another era, one of opulence and spectacle, and I paused, allowing myself to be dwarfed by its splendor. The Majestic was not just any building; it was a sanctuary for grace and beauty. I stood on its hallowed threshold.

As I pushed through the heavy doors, the chill gave way to the theater's welcoming warmth. Golden light spilled from chandeliers, their crystals twinkling with the memories of countless performances. A symphony of soft music played somewhere in the distance, a haunting melody seeping from the very walls.

"Mr. Everly?" a voice called out, breaking through my thoughts.

I turned to see the theater manager, a man whose face bore the lines of many seasons spent behind the curtain. He extended a firm handshake and handed over a set of keys. "We're happy to have you here. Our custodian is gone for the holiday. His mother passed away. It's a hell of a time for it to happen—it's Nutcracker season. You seem awfully young. How old are you?"

"Nineteen," I replied. "I just completed my first semester of college."

"Are you from here?"

"Racine, but my grandparents lived here from about…"

"Do you have custodial experience?" he interrupted.

"Plenty," I assured him. "And in theater, too. My dad worked as a custodian at the Orpheum. He'd bring me along and sneak me into shows. I never cared much for ballet, but this venue…"

"Very nice," he waved me off. "We need to hang the greens for Christmas this week, so I hope you're good with a staple gun."

"The job comes with an apartment?" I asked.

"Top floor," he said, gesturing toward a staircase shrouded in shadows. "Can't say it's much."

"Thank you," I replied, my voice steadier than I felt.

"Not going home for Christmas?" he asked.

"Not this year." I had recently come out to my mom and dad, and it did not go well. For several weeks, before I found this job with its meager apartment, I was not even sure where I might live when school dismissed for the holiday. No time to get into all that.

My boots echoed along the narrow corridors adorned with posters that whispered tales of ballets past. Each step took me deeper into the heart of the Majestic, into a realm as fantastic as the candy cane sets onstage.

I unlocked the door to my apartment. The room was simple—a bed, a sofa, a table, and a window that looked out over the city. But it was mine, a place of refuge and solitude. A smile crept across my face, a sense of independence blossoming within me. With a deep breath, I braced myself for the night's work ahead.

I again descended into the theater, moving like a shadow onstage among a horde of performers. Even with my limited knowledge of dance, their movements appeared surreal, bodies weaving stories in the air. I watched, unseen, absorbing the rhythm of this place, making quick rounds to empty bins while storing the layout in my mind.

The footlights beckoned me from the shadows of the wings. A Korean dancer graced the stage, a vision of restraint and fluidity. It was hard to determine his age, but his movements sliced through the air with the precision of someone molded by the strictest rigors of ballet. His jet-black hair absorbed the spotlight, casting his face in sharp relief, while his expressive eyes seemed to pierce the unseen horizon, simmering with intensity. Two older adults, likely his parents, watched him with stoic pride. Victor Hargrove, the show's artistic director, scrutinized every movement.

I approached a nearby ballerina. "Who's the dancer?" I asked.

"You don't know? That's Kwang-Sik Kim," she replied. "They imported our Nutcracker Prince from Korea this year. He was some kind of child prodigy." Rolling her eyes, she added in a lower tone, "The way his parents manage him, it looks like nobody got the note he grew up."

"Remarkable," Victor muttered, his steely voice cutting through the air. He stood with Kwang-Sik's parents at the edge of the stage, his posture rigid with expectation. "He truly embodies the Nutcracker Prince, doesn't he? Talent like his is rare."

"Indeed," Kwang-Sik's father replied, pride etched across his features.

"Your son has traveled far to be here," Victor continued, each word deliberate. "I assure you, it will be worth it. His name is already known, but this... this will cement his legacy."

Kwang-Sik remained expressionless.

I lingered, half-hidden behind a curtain. The conversation faded, and the clatter of my bucket echoed louder than I preferred. Moving to another part of the theater, I sensed a shift in the atmosphere.

Ryan Thompson, the dancer playing Cavalier, boomed, "Look at these legs, huh?" He lounged against the barre, his lean body showcased in tights that left little to the imagination, flexing his quads. I briefly debated whether he had dropped a potato down the front of his dance belt, then turned away to avoid staring. It was real.

"You could break a walnut with those thighs," Marcus Johnson chimed in, slapping Ryan's ass with a sharp crack. Equally endowed, Marcus's presence dominated—even without the grandeur of his Mouse King costume. The surrounding ballerinas tittered, glancing sideways with flushed cheeks and coy smiles.

"Our Nutcracker finally arrived today with his mommy and daddy," Ryan mused, his tone a mix of jest and something darker. "I don't know why management went overseas. A local boy would've brought the house down."

"He's supposed to be practiced and ready," Marcus said, shaking his head. "Still, an Asian prince? How does that fit in with anything?" His words hung heavy in the air, a discordant note in the otherwise harmonious space.

"Says the Black Mouse King," Ryan laughed.

Tension crackled as Kwang-Sik approached Ryan and Marcus, extending his hand in a gesture of professionalism that felt out of place against their smug postures. "Hello, I am Kwang-Sik Kim," he said, his accent drawing out the syllables.

I watched as his gaze drifted over Ryan and Marcus, landing briefly on the bulges in their tights before snapping forward, avoiding scrutiny.

"Kwang-who?" Ryan quipped with a smirk. Marcus snorted, leaning back as if the weight of his own ego might topple him. He turned his attention to a performer onstage practicing the Chinese Dance. "Aren't you better suited for that role?" he asked.

Kwang-Sik didn't respond or even face Marcus. He withdrew his hand and moved to the other side of the stage.

Ryan snickered, his eyes lingering hungrily on Kwang-Sik's tight costume. He turned to the ballerinas gathered beside him and said, in a stage whisper, "Asian men are good at ballet because their dicks don't get in the way."

The girls giggled, reveling in the cruelty. Kwang-Sik stood still, but I was sure he heard.

"I'm serious!" Ryan scoffed. "Did you see his? No nuts to crack."

"And look how fat his calves are" Marcus remarked. "He might make it in China. Not here." He plucked a Christmas bulb from a prop box, but it slipped from his fingers and shattered on the floor.

"Janitor!" Marcus called out. "We've got a mess here!"

My name wasn't 'Janitor,' but I held back my formal introduction and grabbed the broom.

"Shit!" Marcus exclaimed. "There's really a janitor here? I was just joking!"

The dancers barely noticed me, their attention focused on more important matters—like themselves. Their laughter rang out, a dissonant melody that grated against my nerves.

"Thomas Everly," I finally said when a break came, extending my hand to them. Their cocksure smiles didn't waver as they shook, dismissing me as quickly as they'd acknowledged me.

"Right. Thanks for cleaning up, Tom," Ryan said, patting my shoulder with a condescension that lingered like an unpleasant aftertaste.

"Keep up the good work," Marcus added, his voice dripping with insincerity.

"Will do," I murmured, turning away from their self-assured grins to finish my shift.

It didn't matter to them that I was a biochem major with a minor in physics, or that I loved history and culture. I had watched my dad—an honest-to-god janitor—take crap from people like them my whole life, and anger surged through my veins.

The theater quieted as actors and dancers departed to places where janitors like me couldn't follow. Alone in the dimming light, I climbed the narrow staircase to The Custodian's Loft, my muscles aching and my mind replaying the sharp divides of this new realm.

In my studio apartment, the night stretched out before me—a canvas painted in shadows and city lights. I sat on the bed, the springs creaking under my weight, thinking of Kwang-Sik's concealed pain, Ryan and Marcus's careless cruelty, and the beauty and brutality woven into the world of professional dance.

***

The next day, an ancient curtain pulley creaked under my touch, obstinate as I oiled it and coaxed it back into duty. From my perch atop the ladder backstage at The Majestic, I became just another shadow among the whispers of tulle and satin.

Kwang-Sik took the stage, and once again, the world stilled. He spun and leapt—every motion a testament to his graceful defiance against gravity. I couldn't take my eyes from his solid glutes. Hargrove nodded with approval, offering only a few notes.

It didn't take long to hear Ryan's comment. "The boy prince is at it again," he whispered sharply. Marcus snickered beside him, their arms crossed over chests puffed out with poorly veiled jealousy. "How do you think he keeps his dance belt from sliding down his tiny dick?"

Marcus mimed a minuscule gap between his thumb and forefinger, and the ballerinas stifled giggles behind painted hands.

Power continued to play its cruel game here, but my job required me to remain invisible. I wanted to know Kwang-Sik's story, to understand the weight he bore with such apparent ease. My grip on my wrench tightened.

The performance ended, the magic dissolved, and reality rushed back in harsh waves. I descended, taking up my tools of trade: mop, bucket, the scent of lemon cleaner cutting through the heavy perfume of sweat and rosin.

I navigated the aftermath, a specter among the living set pieces of the theater. There was a rhythm to the cleanup, a cadence to the chaos that I had learned from my father.

Ryan's laughter bubbled through the crowd, flirtatious banter woven between the clatter of scenery being struck. Girls fluttered around him like moths to a flame, drawn to the danger, the warmth. The same went for Marcus, with his ocean eyes and careless charm.

I left to polish the brass railings in the lobby.

An hour later, I returned. The stagehands had gone home. The orchestra pit lay like a graveyard of forgotten notes and silent echoes as I descended, the feather duster in my hand sweeping away the last remnants of dust and lint. The theater was quiet now, and by the time I finished, nobody remained in the house.

Or so I thought.

A soft rustling drew my attention—muffled whispers slithering through the stillness from stage left. Peering around an idle timpani, I caught sight of Ryan and Marcus, their figures bold against the dim backstage light, still clad in their dance tights.

I ducked behind the timpani to avoid interaction.

"You got it?" Marcus asked.

"In the mail today," Ryan murmured, his voice low yet laced with excitement. With a magician's flourish, he revealed a rubber sex toy – a woman's torso, twin openings promising forbidden pleasures.

"Damn..." Marcus's eyes sparkled, a smirk curling his lips, revealing both interest and arousal. "Wonder what it feels like?"

"It's modeled after Jenna Teas, the porn star." Ryan's fingers explored the edges of the synthetic flesh, pressing and prodding. The front of his tights stretched forward, his imagination running wild. "It's supposed to be like the real thing."

"Only one way to find out." Marcus's voice carried a challenge, a dare thrown down in the face of decency.

"Think you could handle it?" Ryan taunted.

"I'll tear that thing in half." Marcus's bravado filled the space between them, electric anticipation crackling as his arousal became evident. He glanced left and right. "Don't let the ballerinas see me doing this," he hissed.

"Nobody here but us," Ryan replied with a dismissive wave, his eyes never leaving the rubber form before them. He slapped it waist-high onto a prop bench.

With that reassurance, Marcus fumbled with his tights, pushing them down to reveal his generous endowment, thick and eager against the cool backstage air. He positioned himself over the toy, brow creased in concentration. As he thrust, the torso wobbled and slipped on the polished wood of the table, like a fish too lively to be caught. His curses echoed softly, frustration etched into every failed attempt.

Ryan repositioned himself, gripping the rubber masturbator near his waist, steadying it against his own burgeoning need. "Try it now."

Marcus nodded his thanks, and with a grunt of effort, he aligned himself and pushed into the opening. He found his rhythm and shuddered, the latex flesh yielding to his size.

The sight and sensation flipped a switch in Ryan. Holding the object for Marcus, feeling the friction of the toy brush against him with each thrust—kindled something deep within. "I want to fuck it, too," he growled, his voice edged with a hunger I hadn't heard before.

In one swift motion, Ryan mirrored Marcus, peeling away the tight fabric to bare himself. He was impressive, his length straining for contact. Carefully, he maneuvered to the other side of the toy and, with a sharp intake of breath, pressed into the second opening. The torso squished between them, a bridge connecting their desires.

Their movements were awkward at first, a clumsy ballet off-stage. The toy scrunched and stretched, accommodating both men as they found a shared pace. "I can feel your..." Marcus began, only to be interrupted by a sharp "Shut up, just keep going" from Ryan. The brush of flesh against flesh within the confines of the device was unmistakable, a connection neither had expected but both craved.

As their thrusts grew more urgent, initial hesitance melted away under the heat of raw pleasure. Their hands, initially meant to steady themselves, roamed with purpose, clutching at hips and buttocks, pulling each other closer. The sound of skin slapping against rubber echoed in the empty space, mingling with labored breathing and low moans that filled the air.

"Harder," Ryan gasped, fingers sinking into Marcus's flesh, urging him on. Marcus responded in kind, his grip tightening as their bodies moved in frenzied harmony. In the darkened theater, hidden from the world, they chased release, their climax building like a storm on the horizon—inevitable, intense, and all-consuming.

The heat between them intensified, a fire that demanded attention. Marcus's hands explored the contours of Ryan's back as they embraced, their foreheads touching, each craving the other.

Their bodies, charged with an electric current, pressed hard against the latex that connected them. They fucked the toy with a ferocity born of desperation, their groans merging into a raw harmony. At last, they reached the edge, teetering before plunging together, their bodies bending into one another, cocks pounding and filling the rubber with their intertwined release.

In the shadows of the orchestra pit, I found my hand wrapped around my arousal through my pants, caught in the voyeuristic grip of the scene unfolding before me. Just as I began to process my feelings, movement on the opposite side of the stage drew my attention: Kwang-Sik, hidden behind a curtain, his body language a mix of curiosity and shame.

He had changed into street clothes—a hoodie and an oversized ball cap. The fabric of his lightweight track pants betrayed an arousal he struggled to contain. I could only imagine the storm of emotions raging within him, the confusion over the desires he was witnessing and the longing he felt for the older guys who had been mean to him.

I remained discreet, observing rather than intervening. In the silence of my mind, empathy blossomed for Kwang-Sik. He carried secrets heavy with complexity, and my chest tightened—a yearning to offer support, to let him know he wasn't alone in this tangled web of longing and discovery.

"Holy hell," Marcus panted, his voice breaking the stillness.

"Shit," Ryan agreed, his tone thick with satisfaction and disbelief at what had just transpired.

Sweat trickled down Ryan's neck as they awkwardly tugged at their tights—wet fabric clinging to flushed skin.

"What the hell was that?" Ryan muttered, tearing his gaze from Marcus's still-glossy lips.

"Your idea, bro," Marcus shot back, his voice sharp but laced with confusion. He yanked his dance belt up over his hips, the force suggesting anger at more than just the garment.

"Was not," Ryan retorted, though his denial lacked conviction. "You're the one who wanted to use the toy."

"Fuck you," Marcus spat. Their eyes locked for a moment, and something unspoken passed between them—a secret that drew them closer despite the tension.

"Whatever. How do we clean this thing?" Ryan gestured at the soiled toy lying abandoned on the floor, cum dripping from it in a grotesque monument to their shared climax.

"Dump it," Marcus decided, as if disposing of evidence. "Trash it before anyone sees."

"Right," Ryan agreed too quickly. They both understood the stakes of discovery in this place. "Let's just forget this happened, okay?" His tone became pleading, seeking reassurance from Marcus.

"We're not fags or anything. It was just a rubber toy turning us on." Marcus's agreement was terse, yet his glance darted back to Ryan, revealing a flicker of doubt.

"Just don't talk about it," Ryan said.

The two exited, straightening their costumes and their egos, while Kwang-Sik's shadow melted away from behind the curtain. His departure was a frantic rush—the result of a mind overwhelmed by emotions too complex to name and, I'm sure, a fear of being caught. His face burned, not from exertion, but with the raw heat of shame, embarrassment, and a terror born of desire. With each step, he seemed to echo the frantic beat of his heart.

I did my best to regain my composure, performing a quick once-over of the orchestra pit with a dust mop. The dressing room needed cleaning, but the sharp exchanges between Ryan and Marcus carried through the wooden door. I had no desire to catch their barbs, so I lingered, waiting for their storm to pass. My footsteps echoed as I made my way to the entryway of The Majestic to secure the front doors.

In the dimming opulence, I found Kwang-Sik, a solitary figure seated on the grand stairway. His frame quivered with muffled sobs. I approached, my footsteps whispering on the plush carpet.

"Hey," I murmured, my voice low. "Are you okay?"

His red, swollen eyes met mine before darting away, as if direct contact might crack open a terrible confession. He scrubbed at his face, erasing tears with the heel of his hand, and muttered an apology, explaining he was waiting for his parents.

"I have to lock the doors," I offered with a half-smile, hoping to cut through the heaviness. "But I'll wait. Wouldn't want you stuck here all night with the two idiots you have to dance with."

Kwang-Sik snorted a laugh, breaking the ice.

Kwang-Sik bristled, labeling them perverts who were nothing but cruel.

"Perverts?" I asked, feigning ignorance.

"I won't repeat what I saw them doing together," he replied.

"They're cruel," I countered, "but maybe not perverted. When you can't express what you feel and who you are, you either withdraw from life or become mean, and the truth manifests in strange ways." My words hung in the air between us, giving Kwang-Sik pause. "Anyway, I'd like to know more about you. What's your life like?"

His shoulders rose and fell, as if lifting the burden of his world was too much. Sensing my intrusion, I almost retracted my question.

"Nobody ever asks," he said, drawing a deep breath. "I've been dancing since I was three." His narrative sounded less like a life and more like a regimen, his eyes distant.

"Your parents pull the strings?" I ventured gently, probing the edges of his controlled existence.

"Pull the strings?" I had lost him in the euphemism. He looked straight ahead, as if watching the ghost of his childhood dance across the opulent lobby. "They wanted a prodigy. Mom... she saw herself in me—the dancer she never became."

"Do you have friends? A girlfriend? Anyone?" I asked, though I could guess the answer.

"Friends are distractions. Girlfriends... my parents won't expect me to have one until I'm older. After dance. After school, perhaps."

"Sounds lonely."

"Doesn't matter." He shrugged, but his eyes betrayed him—they screamed for connection. "Ryan, Marcus. I see their kind everywhere I go. Unfocused. Not serious." His disdain was palpable, a bitter taste on his tongue.

"Maybe not everyone needs to be serious all the time," I countered. "Life isn't just about control and precision. It's also about the messy, chaotic bits that make it real."

Kwang-Sik fell silent, lost in thought. I nudged again, steering us toward what had broken him earlier. "Ever been intimate?" I pushed, perhaps too far, but the question lingered between us.

His jaw went slack. "None of your business," he snapped, though his protest felt weak, half-hearted.

Outside, headlights swept over the theater's façade. A car idled into view.

"Nobody likes me," Kwang-Sik whispered, so low I almost didn't catch it. "So there's your answer about intimacy."

"I think you're cute," I said, standing and brushing my hand against the door handle.

The color that bloomed on his cheeks was fierce and defiant. "Stop it!" He glanced anxiously toward the glass doors. "I'm not... that way."

"I am," I replied with a smirk, twisting the lock open. "Lighten up."

He hesitated, caught between two worlds. Then, without another word, he slipped out into the evening where his parents waited, unaware.

***

The following night, The Majestic Theater buzzed with a static charge of anticipation, mirrored in the fluttering hearts backstage. I leaned against the cool wall, observing as dancers stretched and preened, their costumes vibrant against the dull backdrop of the wings.

Kwang-Sik stood apart, enveloped in his Nutcracker costume. His hands trembled slightly as he adjusted his jacket. The dark circles under his eyes revealed a night spent restless, anticipating the performance ahead.

The crowd's murmur swelled to a crescendo, and the orchestra's first notes sliced through the tense air. Drosselmeyer presented a doll to a little girl. As the moment approached, Kwang-Sik moved into position, but faint, hesitant steps marred his usual grace. He resembled a ghost of the dancer I had watched the day before, each movement an echo rather than a bold statement.

As the ballet unfolded, Kwang-Sik danced mechanically. Then it happened—a misstep, subtle yet jarring. A collective gasp rippled through the audience, a wave of shock that lapped at the stage.

Whispers flitted between the dancers. Marcus turned to Ryan. "Tomorrow night, important people are coming. Members of the press and recruiters from reputable dance schools. If he dances like this, it might make *us* look good."

"Be ready to pick up any money that kid drops," Ryan replied.

The final curtain fell, and applause thundered, hollow and undeserved. As the cheers faded, disappointment settled over the stage like a heavy fog. Victor Hargrove's scowl pierced through the dissipating crowd, his glare fixed on the young dancer.

Kwang-Sik's parents joined the silent tribunal, their faces etched with disapproval, mirroring Hargrove's discontent. The air soured. Hargrove's voice boomed about money wasted. Harsh Korean syllables slashed the space between Hargrove and the parents.

Kwang-Sik stood like a statue amidst the chaotic flurry of voices, palms slick with sweat, his composure cracking. Tremors coursed through his frame, a subtle quiver betraying the turmoil beneath his stoic exterior.

The shouting continued—at him, around him—and at last, he broke. In a moment that shattered the illusion of control, Kwang-Sik's facade crumbled like fragile porcelain. A guttural cry erupted from his throat, echoing through the theater. His outburst revealed a kaleidoscope of pent-up frustration and self-doubt unleashed in a torrent of emotion. It was a side of him that none had seen before.

"Shut up! All of you! I hate this! I hate all of it!" He had never dared to break the chains of years of obedience, but his rebellion was short-lived; his father's hand struck with the weight of a lifetime's expectations.

The impact reverberated through the quiet theater. He fell to the floor, tears streaming down his cheeks, carving rivers of misery as the troupe melted away, leaving him in despair. Hargrove turned away.

Perfection had crushed Kwang-Sik. Alone under the stage lights, his sobs became a haunting coda to Tchaikovsky's masterwork.

Kwang-Sik's father glared down at him. "Get yourself together. Don't come back to the hotel until you do."

His parents left.

The stage stood empty, a cavernous void illuminated by a single light. The echo of applause had long since faded. Kwang-Sik huddled like a forgotten prop in the vast silence of The Majestic Theater. His shoulders trembled with sobs that seemed to draw from the depths of shattered dreams.

I approached from the wings. "Hey," I murmured. Tentatively, my hand found its way to his back. "Come on."

He didn't look up as I led him away, his body compliant yet fragile under my touch. My apartment loomed at the end of our journey. I slid the key into the lock, the tumblers clicking. When I pushed the door open, a hush enveloped us.

Kwang-Sik paused on the threshold, his face a canvas of conflict. Fear sketched lines across his brow, while relief softened the curve of his mouth. I stepped aside, giving him space to choose.

"I don't even know you..." His voice was a thread, barely audible.

"Thomas," I replied.

Kwang-Sik glided to the sofa, each step deliberate, as if the floorboards might crack beneath his ballet flats. He settled in, hands clasped so tightly that his knuckles turned white. I took a seat beside him, leaving a noticeable gap on the couch.

"Your parents," I began. "The pressure, the dancing... it's a lot to handle." My words hovered around him, hoping to draw out the man hidden within the dancer.

His eyes flickered up briefly before darting away, unable to meet my gaze. I could see the weight of expectations in that moment, the burden of perfection pressing down on him.

"Look," I said. "You're right. You don't know me, and I don't know you. We spoke for just five minutes last night, and I made you blush. Maybe it's better that way. Nothing you say or do will ever get back to anyone. No one I know would recognize you or care. So, what happened tonight? Why did you seem so off?"

Kwang-Sik's gaze shifted, and he fidgeted with the hem of his shirt. For a brief moment, he hovered on the brink of sharing his thoughts. Unspoken words lingered in the air, doubt clouding his expression and emotions swirling behind his eyes. He turned away, silent.

"Ryan and Marcus?" I pressed.

He lowered his head, refusing to elaborate.

I felt the distance grow. "If you don't want to talk..." I started.

"I don't want to think about them..." he interrupted, his voice barely above a whisper. "I can't stop. It's ruined my focus... I didn't think two boys could..."

Silence enveloped us once more.

"I saw them being physical. Intimate," he mumbled.

"It's a lot to process," I offered gently.

"Last night you said you were... you know..." he hesitated.

"*That way?*" I replied.

He ignored my teasing. "Help me. My body keeps reacting to the memory of what I saw. I can't face them. How can I stop this?"

"Embrace what you feel. Maybe try... you know, jerk off while thinking about them for a few nights. It'll pass."

His cheeks flushed, and he turned his gaze away. "I would never," he said firmly.

"Think about two guys when you jerk off?" I asked.

"Abuse my body like that," he shot back.

I shifted in my seat. "Wait. You don't...?"

"Gross," he replied.

"You *have* done it before, right?"

He fell silent again.

"What the hell? Never?" I started over. "How old are you?"

"How old are *you*?" he countered.

"Nineteen," I said. "Almost twenty."

"I'm old too. I graduate from high school next summer," he replied.

I nodded, absorbing his words. "But you never...?"

"No."

As Kwang-Sik sat across from me, his demeanor a mix of vulnerability and defiance, the differences between us felt palpable. His cultural background, steeped in traditions and expectations I could only begin to understand, clashed with my more relaxed upbringing. The chasm between his elite ballet world and the pressures from his family felt insurmountable. Perhaps I should have stopped trying to bridge that gap. Some divides are too vast to cross.

"Never mind," I said. "You should head back. Your family is probably waiting."

I eased forward from the sofa, but he grasped my arm. "What does it feel like?"

"What?"

"What we were just discussing. Can you... show me?"

"Show you?" I asked, surprised. "You want me to...?"

"Show me how," he insisted.

He genuinely didn't know, hadn't dared to explore the depths of his own body. His innocence lay bare before me, a thing both sacred and yearning.

I leaned closer, the fabric of my jeans brushing against the worn rug beneath us. "I'm going to explore your body," I said in a low voice, "from your ankles to your abs. Then, when the front of your tights strain, I'm going to make you come. Do you understand?"

He inhaled sharply.

"Understand?" I repeated.

He nodded, his face a mixture of anticipation and anxiety.

"No tears, either," I added. "It's time to start being a man. You're old enough."

He nodded again, stretching his legs out and bracing himself.

My fingertips traced the contours of his muscular calves through the sheer material of his tights. He shuddered, a testament to the storm brewing within him. His body was a hesitant chord, straining against the melody I intended to compose. As my hands persisted, confidence woven into each motion, Kwang-Sik's resistance melted into curiosity—a flower bud trembling on the verge of bloom.

I moved my palms higher, gliding over the hills and valleys of his thighs. I could sense him clinging to the edge of something wondrous and terrifying.

"I hate my legs," he confessed. "Dancers are supposed to be lean."

"I like your muscles," I replied. The air thickened, heavy with unspoken needs.

"Thomas," he sputtered.

"Relax," I whispered back.

An unmistakable growth stretched the front of his tights. Kwang-Sik's hand darted down, an instinctive attempt to shield his burgeoning need from the world.

"It's okay," I said softly, gently catching his wrist.

He looked at me, eyes wide, a battle raging within them. Fear collided with longing, each vying for dominance.

"Let go," I urged. After a moment suspended in time, he did. His hand fell away from the bulge that begged for attention, and he shifted from apprehension to surrender.

I stood and slid beside him, my arm curling around his frame.

At first, my touch was a whisper—gentle, questioning. Then it grew firmer, more insistent. Each stroke drew a ragged breath from Kwang-Sik's lips, each caress a silent plea for more. His body tightened, heart drumming a frenzied rhythm against my chest. He grew even harder, his erection pressing against the elastic confines, a visual symphony of forbidden pleasures.

"Thomas…" The word escaped as a choked gasp, his head tilting back, exposing the vulnerable line of his throat. His toes curled into the tattered carpet, and every muscle in his body seemed to spasm with the electric sensation of my hand moving over him. "Are you hard, too?" he whispered.

"Feel and find out," I responded, an invitation laid bare between us.

He reached out, tentative at first, then bolder as he discovered the solid length of me. A shiver ran through him, and a soft moan slipped from his lips. He was exhilarated, exploring with an innocent curiosity that ignited heat in my gut. My arousal was undeniable under the press of his palm, spurring him on, emboldened by the shared intimacy of our secret.

"You're huge," he said, his voice laced with awe. "I'm…"

"You're fine," I interrupted. "I like it."

His breath caught. Moisture darkened his tights, a spot of pre-cum that spoke of his sweet naivety. "Am I orgasming?" Kwang-Sik asked, trembling.

"You've really never had one?" I probed, my voice barely above a whisper.

"Maybe," Kwang-Sik murmured, the word escaping like a secret confessed in the dark. "I don't know. How does it feel?"

"You'd know," I said, choosing my words carefully. "It's like a buildup of pressure that demands release, a sensation so intense it takes over your entire body. You lose control, and then… there's this powerful rush, a wave of pleasure."

His eyes widened with a blend of terror and curiosity, his chest rising and falling with quickened breaths.

Without another word, I slipped my hand under the thin, stretchy nylon, my fingers brushing against the heat of his hard flesh. He squirmed at the contact, a gasp escaping his lips, his body tensing and then relaxing into my touch.

"Okay?" I asked, and he nodded, eyes fluttering shut.

We worked together to strip away the barriers between us. He lifted his shirt over his head and peeled his tights and dance belt down to his thighs. His erection sprang free, and I couldn't suppress a low murmur of desire at the sight.

Kwang-Sik's manhood was an emblem of innocence, a testament to his untouched purity. His cock, though modest, stood erect with an intensity that belied its dimensions. His balls were taut orbs of youthful vigor, firm and round, as if sculpted by some divine artist. A soft thicket of pubic hair crowned his groin.

My hands began their gentle work. I drew them down on his tight, flat abs. One encircled the base of his shaft while the other glided along the length, exploring the texture and contours with reverence. Kwang-Sik giggled nervously at first, then snickered, a sound that morphed into soft moans. His body responded in honest jerks, kicks, and squirms—a dance of pleasure under my orchestration.

"Does it… always feel like this?" he panted, his question punctuated by a shudder as I squeezed his balls, noting their fullness, ready for release.

"Only when it's right," I replied. He surrendered to the sensations, to the needs of his body and the ministrations of my hands.

I stroked him with purpose. The tension in Kwang-Sik wound tight, like strings of a violin pulled to the brink before a symphony. I felt every pulse, each beat a harbinger of the storm that brewed within him as my hand continued its steady motion.

What must this be like for him? This was his first time, his body deciphering a brand-new language of pleasure and desire. Every shudder, every gasp, every desperate clutch at the fabric on the sofa was a testament to this exploration. I could only imagine the thoughts racing through his mind—questions, fears, sensations—all colliding and intertwining as he discovered his body drawing closer to a release he had never known.

"Thomas..." he gasped, the word barely escaping his lips as if he was afraid to break the spell we wove together.

"Try to make it harder, Kwang-Sik," I urged, my voice soft but insistent. "Can you?"

His dick twitched. He tremored, a crescendo of emotion as the spiraling tension inside twisted tighter, veering out of his grasp. "Mmmmmm!" he moaned.

"Again!"

His knees drew toward his chest. He throbbed again, an uncontrollable force that frightened him with its intensity. "Unnnn-nnngh!" he cried. "It's so hard!"

"Once more!" I instructed. "You're going to do it!"

Tears brimmed in his eyes, spilling over as his body tensed one final time. His eyes went wide. "I can't stop it! Thomas! It's cramping!" With a shudder that racked his frame, he bent forward and released. A mighty orgasm tore through him, and he cried out, raw and unbridled. His dick pounded with ferocity, releasing its pent-up tension, warm wetness seeping between my fingers. Every muscle contorted and spasmed as his young gland pumped his thick essence into the air and onto his stomach and chest.

"Aaaaaaaaaah!" he screamed, his head thrashing.

As he stilled, I held him close, my arms wrapped protectively around his trembling form. His lips sought mine, pressing against them in a desperate kiss that tasted of salt and surrender. Warm stickiness painted his belly, marking the culmination of his revelation—the acknowledgment of desires long suppressed, emotions never permitted to surface.

His breathing slowed, and I brushed away the dampness from his cheeks with my thumb, watching the transformation that unfurled.

A peace settled between us, an understanding that transcended words.

"You liked it?" I asked.

He whimpered and shook, and I kissed him again.

"What about you?" Kwang-Sik's voice was fragile, yet there was a newfound curiosity that flickered in his gaze.

"God, I'm so close," I admitted, my desire tightened by the sight and sounds of his pleasure. "You turn me on so bad."

"Do it here." His finger traced a line through the mess on his abs, a daring invitation that sent a jolt of heat surging through me.

I stood and quickly lowered my pants and underwear, releasing my aching need. Kwang-Sik's hands joined mine, his touch electric and igniting my senses, driving me toward the edge with reckless hunger.

"Let me," he said, taking control.

"Kwang-Sik," I groaned, feeling my release approach. His soft fingers wrapped around me, moving up and down my shaft and it took no time for me to lose my mind. "I'm gonna jizz."

I seized and spilled over him, my climax mingling with his, my body shaking in the aftermath.

"I could feel your sperm pumping out," he smiled as my breathing slowed.

"Told you—you're cute," I said. He giggled.

Afterward, we lay there, breathless and wide-eyed. Kwang-Sik's expression reflected awe and unspoken freedom. I smiled at him, conveying without words that he was safe and accepted in the space we shared.

"Thank you," he sighed.

"Your parents are waiting," I reminded him gently.

He dressed in silence, his movements slow and deliberate. As he reached the door, he paused and looked back at me, vulnerability tugging at my chest.

"Another performance tomorrow," he said, a faint smile gracing his lips as he stepped into the night, leaving behind the sanctuary of my apartment—a place where he had dared to reveal both his soul and body.

***

The next morning found me on my knees again, this time the worn fabric of the auditorium carpet pressing into my skin as I tightened a loose bolt on an ornate seat. The musty scent of old wood and varnish filled the air, mingling with the lingering traces of last night's encounter. My hands moved mechanically, but my mind replayed Kwang-Sik's touch, a stark contrast to the cold metal beneath my fingers.

Christmas greens adorned the theater, and white lights twinkled among the pine needles.

The murmur of approaching dancers swelled in the grand space, their voices echoing off the high ceilings. They gathered and stretched, and the soft thud of ballet slippers against the stage heralded the evening's performance.

Kwang-Sik entered, his presence cutting through the chatter. He exuded confidence, moving with a quiet assertiveness that hadn't been there the day before. His eyes, usually downturned in contemplation, now held a steady gaze that met the world head-on. This subtle shift resonated loudly.

"Kwang-Sik!" Ryan's voice sliced through the newfound silence, sharp as a blade. "Ready to stumble through another night?"

Next to him, Marcus snickered, his lean body coiled with mocking anticipation. They resembled predators circling prey, but the

Kwang-Sik standing before them was no longer the same dancer they had taunted.

"I've perfected the sequence," he replied, his voice steady. The weight of his words carried an unfamiliar confidence.

Ryan and Marcus exchanged a glance, their arrogance faltering. The surrounding dancers paused, the atmosphere charged with the crackle of a power shift. Their dismissive smirks wavered, replaced by the dawning realization that the hierarchy they knew was crumbling.

"Right," Ryan managed, his tone lacking its usual bite. "We'll see what the audience thinks."

As Kwang-Sik strode toward the stage, I sensed the company tracing the lines of his back, reading the story written in the set of his spine. He stood poised, ready, and unyielding. Whispers filled the void, a chorus of curiosity and respect humming beneath the surface. Ryan and Marcus fell silent, their earlier bravado reduced to uncertain glances and uncomfortable shifting.

From the shadows, I watched, fingers still wrapped around the wrench. Pride surged within me, fierce and protective, yet tinged with fear.

Showtime neared. The audience arrived. The house lights dimmed. The auditorium pulsed with a silent, thick anticipation. I lingered in the wings, where I could see Kwang-Sik against the backdrop, his frame a shadow poised on the brink of revelation.

He closed his eyes, embracing a ritual of stillness amid the storm of whispers and shuffling programs. The audience, a sea of silhouettes, remained oblivious to the metamorphosis happening mere feet from their prying gaze.

I slipped down into the house, into an empty seat. When the moment arrived and the music surged—a lush cascade of strings and brass—Kwang-Sik blossomed into motion. His body became the melody, each line and curve echoing Tchaikovsky's orchestral bloom. He leaped without hesitation, landing with fluid certainty, lost in his craft.

My breath caught in my chest. He spun with such grace that gravity seemed a mere suggestion. His limbs extended with the precision of a master calligrapher, painting strokes of movement into the air. The arc of his leg in a grand jeté sliced through space, a testament to countless hours of sweat and perseverance now made manifest.

In the dim theater, gasps mingled with applause, creating a soft, reverent murmur that swelled with each pirouette. Women leaned forward in their seats, pearls glinting at their throats, while men adjusted their ties, striving to regain composure in the presence of such striking beauty.

"Remarkable," a voice from behind me breathed, edged with surprise.

"Indeed," another replied, softer but purposeful. "He holds promise."

I didn't need to turn around to identify them. Vincent Laurent, a writer for the prestigious *Echelon Dance Review*, had a reputation for discovering rising stars in the ballet world. Gabrielle St. Claire represented the esteemed Harmony Ballet Academy in Chicago, known for nurturing exceptional talent.

"Watch him—there," St. Claire murmured as Kwang-Sik executed a series of entrechats, his precise movements defying the laws of physics with an effortless grace.

"His lines... impeccable form," Laurent noted, the scratch of his pen against paper providing a quiet rhythm beneath the music's swell.

My heart raced, torn between elation for Kwang-Sik and a cold grip of something resembling grief. Under the spotlight's glow, I sensed the fragile fabric of our shared moments thinning, ready to tear with the slightest tug. After tonight, he would be famous. I stood as an unseen witness to a star's ascent and the quiet, inevitable fading of our brief connection.

The theater erupted into a cacophony of applause that echoed off the gilt-edged walls. On stage, Kwang-Sik stood, chest heaving slightly, his gaze unwavering as he absorbed the adulation like sunlight warming the earth. The light enveloped him in a celestial glow, transforming him before an audience that had become disciples of his art.

I remained hidden in the crowd, shrouded in darkness, witnessing the metamorphosis of a man into a deity through the eyes of those around me. Victor Hargrove stood at the edge of the stage, hands clasped over his heart as if holding back a surge of pride. His stern facade softened, revealing a rare smile as he nodded to Kwang-Sik, an unspoken blessing from the high priest of ballet. Meanwhile, Ryan and Marcus stormed off to the dressing room, consumed by jealousy.

Laurent and St. Claire navigated through the standing ovation, their expressions intent. They paused at the stage, waiting for the sea of admirers to part. When they finally reached Kwang-Sik, their faces transformed into genuine admiration.

"Brilliant performance," St. Claire declared, her voice rising above the thunderous crowd. "We haven't witnessed such raw talent in years."

"Kwang-Sik, isn't it?" Laurent asked, extending his hand. "Your grace on stage is matched only by your evident passion. We would be honored to discuss your future in dance."

Kwang-Sik nodded, his eyes sparkling with ambition and newfound confidence. "Thank you," he replied, his voice barely audible over the clamor. "I'd like that."

His words carried the scent of dreams, opportunities that could reshape his life and take him to places I could not follow. My heart thudded painfully against my ribs, each beat growing louder with every passing moment.

I made my way backstage. Shadows stretched and deepened as the bustle began to fade. Crew members moved past, their voices a distant hum while I stood frozen.

Onstage, a circle formed around Kwang-Sik, a barrier of bodies adorned in sequins and sweat, each reflecting his success back at him. He had become the nucleus of this new world, a world spinning faster than the pirouettes he executed with such finesse.

I retreated, each step toward the exit pulling me deeper into the cool stillness of my existence. The city's pulse beckoned from beyond the heavy stage door, but inside me, silence reigned—a void where the echoes of our heat had once thrummed.

I slipped out of The Majestic Theater's back door, the last echoes of applause lingering in my ears. I felt like a ghost haunting the corridors. A group of cleaners I was to manage passed by with barely a nod. They were fine on their own. The buzz of Kwang-Sik's success thrummed through the walls.

Chicago's streets greeted me with a harsh winter bite. The wind sliced across my cheeks, replacing the lavish scents of polished wood and fresh flowers. I pulled my jacket tight around me, trying to ward off the chill.

My breath misted before me. I hurried toward a familiar diner two blocks away, seeking solace in the mundane expectation of coffee, but found none. The shop stood closed, its windows dark, chairs upturned on tables. My heart sank—a tiny defeat.

Returning to the theater, I retreated to the hidden loft that served as my refuge. My fingers trembled as they fumbled with the keys. Emotions swirled within me—a cocktail of pride for him and despair for myself. The key finally turned, and I stepped inside.

As I closed the door, the click echoed too loudly in the hollow space. Leaning against the solid wood, I pressed my forehead to its cool surface. Eyes shut, I fought to calm the storm within me, striving to silence my racing thoughts.

What was happening? Why did I care so much? Just 48 hours ago, I hadn't even known Kwang-Sik. Now, I felt like a lovesick girl.

The room, with its four walls closing in, transformed into a chamber of echoes. My place in his life—was it etched in stone or scrawled in sand?

I sat on the edge of my creaking bed, resolve sparking in my eyes and piercing the veil of melancholy. That moment we shared, as fleeting as it was, I would hold sacred. In the grand tapestry of his ascent, I was a thread—perhaps minor, but woven into the whole. In the quiet I found consolation—not in the physicality of passion, but in the silent acknowledgment that I was there, a witness to the beginning of Kwang-Sik's journey. That had to be good enough.

I faded into a fitful sleep. Twenty minutes in, a knock on the door jolted me from my thoughts. Probably a cleaner, wondering where I was. I jerked up from the creaky bed, my mind still clinging to the haziness of daydreams. Hesitating, my hand hovered over the doorknob, my heart thumping against my ribs like a caged bird desperate for release.

"Who's there?" I called, my voice rougher than I intended.

"Nutcracker Prince," came the gleeful reply.

I swung the door open to find Kwang-Sik, still dressed in costume, his eyes wide and fixed on me. His lips parted as if to speak but pressed together again, as if words had fled, leaving him stranded between silence and revelation.

"Come in," I said, stepping aside.

He crossed the threshold, and the air thickened with unspoken emotions, heavy and charged.

"Did you see the show?" he asked.

"You were amazing," I replied.

"They were there tonight, at the theater. A critic... and a recruiter," he said.

I nodded, leaning back against the peeling paint of the door frame.

"The recruiter wants me to study here, in Chicago. And the critic..." He swallowed hard, his Adam's apple bobbing. "He believes I can be a star."

"Congratulations," I managed, my voice a low murmur in the quiet. "What are you going to do?"

His question floated softly, yet it carried the weight of the world. "If I study here... can we be together?"

My heart raced at his words. I stepped closer, closing the distance between us. His vulnerability tugged at me, an unspoken plea. I cupped his cheeks, noticing the flicker of hope in his eyes. Without hesitation, I pressed my lips against his.

The kiss transformed everything. The outside world faded away; only we existed in that moment, our breaths mingling and our bodies radiating warmth. His lips felt soft yet demanding, and we melted together—two souls merging in an electric instant.

When we finally pulled apart, the intimacy lingered, our foreheads resting against each other in silent understanding. "Let's celebrate," I murmured, my voice low and husky, as I guided him toward the couch. My touch offered reassurance, a safe haven amid the tumult of emotions swirling around us.

As he settled onto the couch, a tremor coursed through him—a tantalizing mix of nerves and anticipation. His trust enveloped us like a palpable force. Kwang-Sik looked up, his question suspended in the charged air.

"Are we going to do what we did the other night?" he asked, his voice a blend of innocence and longing.

"Even better," I assured him.

I watched as Kwang-Sik slowly removed his shirt. His movements were tentative yet eager, his dark eyes shimmering with a mix of curiosity and desire.

He reclined, assuming the position he had taken the previous evening, his length already straining against the fabric of his nylons. I slipped my hand beneath the waistband, circling the head of his erection with my thumb, coaxing a shiver from him that sent waves of pleasure through me. I began with familiar motions, but tonight was about exploring new heights of ecstasy.

I stepped back to remove my shirt, and he ran his hands through the hair on my chest, intrigued. I reciprocated by exploring his smooth pecs, teasing his dark nipples until they hardened under my touch. I licked and sucked each one, eliciting soft gasps from him.

He unbuckled my pants, letting them pool on the floor. I wore a pair of black CK trunks that left little to the imagination, and he ran his hand across my bulge.

We pressed together, our bodies aligning—me in my underwear, him in his tights, nestled between his strong thighs. The friction ignited a fire within me, and I felt the slickness of precum forming. Kwang-Sik whimpered, thrusting against me, unable to contain his desire.

"I always wanted to do this. I never thought I would," he moaned. "Keep rubbing together!"

I did for a time, then withdrew. Consumed by desire, I yanked his tights and dance belt down to his knees, exposing his throbbing arousal.

"W...What...?" he stammered.

I said nothing, lowering my head to envelop him. The warmth of my mouth drew a gasp that shattered the silence. I savored his taste—sweet musk and salt—working my lips down his velvety shaft. He tensed at first, then surrendered to the sensation, losing himself in the moment.

Kwang-Sik's body reacted beneath me, a canvas of pleasure. His toes curled against the frayed couch, grasping for something solid. His calves flexed like marble pillars with each swirl of my tongue. I reveled in the power I held over him, drawing forth such primal, unguarded responses.

I lifted his legs, bending him like a figure from his ballet program. His entrance beckoned, uncharted territory whispering promises of raw intimacy. I lowered my head, paying homage to his testicles first. The tender skin beneath my lips elicited a string of low moans that reverberated through my apartment.

I savored the weight of each ball, teasing and playing with them with my tongue. In his early teenage years, Kwang-Sik had neglected them, but now they tightened, ready to fulfill their natural purpose.

"Thomas... the pressure when you suck," he muttered, his words half-lost in pleasure. He was all tightness and need under me, every touch magnified by the surrounding silence.

I trailed lower, letting my tongue wander, and with a careful intent reached his virgin entrance, circling it gently at first, feeling him spasm with each flick. His fingers clawed at the sofa. He gritted his teeth, and his head thrashed, lost in a cosmos of sensation.

I pulled back slightly, catching my breath. My gaze locked on his flushed face. "I want to fuck you," I declared, my voice thick with a hunger that echoed in the tightening of my loins.

"Will it hurt?" The vulnerability in his question made my heart clench as much as it made my desire spike.

"Only at first," I answered, kissing him deeply. My fingers trailed down, circling his entrance before gently pressing one inside. His body became taut, the warmth engulfing my finger in a tight grasp.

"Relax," I whispered against his lips, adding a second finger, scissoring slowly, carefully. Kwang-Sik's breathing turned hard and ragged, pain and pleasure etched into his features.

"Ready?" I whispered after a moment.

He nodded, sweat beading on his brow. "My body needs it."

"Let's give your body what it craves," I promised.

I lined myself up, the head of my cock brushing against his quivering entrance. His eyes became wide with fear and want. I pushed in gently, so damn slowly, against the resistance of his untried hole.

"Ah..." Kwang-Sik said in a ragged whisper, an exhalation of both tenderness and pleasure as he adjusted to the intrusion. Pain etched his brow, but beneath it was something else—a wellspring of bliss beginning to surface.

"Deep breaths," I murmured. The heat was intense, almost scalding. Inch by inch, I eased forward, watching every flicker of emotion cross his face.

His legs trembled as they wrapped around me, the muscles in his thighs stiff. He pulled me deeper, his heels pressing into my back, urging me on without words. Once fully sheathed within him, we paused, our breaths mingling, hearts racing. For a moment, neither of us moved.

The shift in him was palpable, from the tightness of uncertainty to the unfolding of acceptance. His hands roamed over me, no longer seeking reassurance but now claiming, possessing. There was power in his touch, a silent declaration that he was ready, willing—no, eager—for this.

"Do it," he breathed out, and those words were all the permission I needed.

I withdrew slightly, only to return, setting a rhythm that was both relentless and reverent. Kwang-Sik's face reflected raw sensation, each thrust painting strokes of ecstasy across his features.

"Are you—" but my concern faltered as his expression twisted, not in discomfort, but sheer bliss.

"More," he gasped, and I obliged, driving into him harder, deeper. Our bodies slapped together, the sound obscene in its intimacy—a testament to our act.

I could feel it building, the pressure in my groin signaling the imminent release. "Kwang-Sik, I'm going to—"

"Inside," he begged, his fingers digging into my skin. "In me, Thomas."

With a few more thrusts, I spilled into him, my orgasm ripping through me, leaving me shuddering and spent. I collapsed atop him, both of us slick with sweat, panting, the room spinning.

I slid out from Kwang-Sik's warmth, breathless, suspended in the afterglow. My voice was rough with desire as I looked at him, his body still quivering from the intensity of our connection. "Now, what are we going to do about you?" I asked.

Without waiting for his response, I descended on him again. My mouth enveloped his tight erection while my fingers sought his tender entrance. The shock of pleasure made his back arch.

"Thomas..." he moaned, his hands tangling in my hair, urging me closer. His hips bucked into my mouth, seeking release while my finger fucked him.

"Tell me when," I murmured, my tongue swirling around him.

"I'm so close," he stammered, panic lacing his voice. "It's like last time, only worse... I'm scared, Thomas! My body... I can't... I'm gonna..."

In one swift, powerful motion, I took him completely, savoring all of him. He kicked his legs in the air, squirming and gripping my head. His body strained with pleasure, his heartbeat racing. A deafening cry escaped his lips, echoing through the room as he released himself into my mouth. Each pulse filled me with ecstasy. The taste was warm and bittersweet, driving me to swallow every drop with insatiable hunger.

Afterward, we lay tangled in the sheets, limbs entwined. The air thickened with fulfillment, each breath a shared testament to our union. Our hearts throbbed in harmony, grounding us in the moment. Silence enveloped us, a blanket of serenity. Outside, the city hummed, but in our loft above it all, time stood still. We drifted toward sleep, bodies entwined, daring to dream of tomorrow together.

***

The next morning, the world seemed to hold its breath. I scrubbed the stage of The Majestic Theater while Kwang-Sik faced his own daunting performance, steeling himself outside his parents' hotel room. He later told me what happened.

"Kwang-Sik, where have you been all night?" his mother asked, worry and authority etched across her face.

"Out," he replied, the word hanging heavily between them. Though his stance remained unwavering, a storm brewed inside him.

"Out?" his father echoed, disbelief sharpening the single syllable into an accusation.

But Kwang-Sik stood firm, a truth demanding to be heard, even if it trembled on his lips. "I've been thinking about the offers made to me last night," he declared, his voice soft yet resolute. The confession lingered in the air, raw and unadorned.

"Here? In Chicago? You're meant for better things. Think about the Bolshoi." His mother's brows knitted together, concern painting her features. His father folded his arms, a barricade of skepticism.

"This is where I need to be," Kwang-Sik pressed on, each word heavy with the weight of dreams long confined. "I met someone."

"Met someone?" his mother asked, surprise flickering in her eyes.
"Some ballerina?" his father scoffed.
"They're all trouble," his mother added.
"A custodian at the theater," Kwang-Sik replied.
His mother gasped in horror.

His parents' eyes reflected resistance, steeped in cultural expectations and parental fears. Yet as Kwang-Sik spoke, something shifted. They stood on the brink of understanding, teetering between the world they knew and the one their son inhabited—a world woven from discipline, grace, and an all-consuming love for ballet.

His mother's hand fluttered to her chest, as if warding off an unseen blow, while his father's jaw worked silently. In that moment, acceptance began to seep through the cracks of their disbelief.

"But your dreams..." his father muttered, the words grudging and strained. "You're too close to greatness to throw them away..."

Kwang-Sik inhaled sharply, a tentative peace settling over his features. "They're mine to chase."

His parents fell silent. It wasn't a victory won by force; it was an armistice brokered by love—a tacit acknowledgment that while they might never fully embrace his life, they wouldn't stand in his way.

"Thank you," Kwang-Sik whispered, his voice barely audible but saturated with unspoken gratitude and relief. The tension that had cocooned the room dissolved, replaced by a fragile hope that things could be different. There would be no jubilant fanfare or celebratory embrace, just the quiet knowledge that, for now, the battle was over.

A Salvation Army bell ringer stood by a kettle outside the hotel, her Santa hat perched jauntily atop her head. Kwang-Sik walked toward me, his shoulders lighter and his gait more assured than when he had entered. The crisp air hinted at change, invigorating and alive.

As he approached, I noticed the weight of expectation lifting from him, like fog dissipating under the warmth of the morning sun.

With purpose, he navigated the streets, each step drawing him closer to his dreams—and to me.

He pushed open the doors of the Majestic Theater.

"Thomas," he breathed, a mix of disbelief and hope coloring his voice. Our eyes locked, and the world around us faded, leaving only the space between us.

"Kwang-Sik," I replied, my voice a gentle caress as I wrapped my arms around him. Our embrace spoke volumes, a silent exchange filled with joy that resonated through our entwined bodies.

"Did you...?" My question lingered in the air, unspoken yet palpable.

"I did." Triumph colored his tone, and pride swelled within me. "They'll never truly understand, but they won't stop me."

"Then nothing will," I vowed, sealing my promise with a kiss that hinted at a shared future and battles fought side by side. Our lips met in a tender clash of hope and desire, and I felt the strength of our connection.

"Your dreams start now," I whispered against his mouth, "and I'm here for all of it."

"And I've got your back, too. Through school, through everything," he replied, determination shining in his eyes. "Let's conquer it all."

I knew we would, together.

Friarhaven

"Focus, Aiden!" Sir Tristan's voice sliced through the haze of heat that had settled over the kingdom of Aranthia for weeks.

Castle Friarhaven's stone spires cast long shadows across the lush training field, the sun's relentless glare as harsh as the weight of expectation on our shoulders. No rest awaited us today or tomorrow. War raged in the East, dragons invaded from the West. Many knights had fallen; we stood as the last line—all barely old enough to wield a sword, too inexperienced to fight.

Sir Tristan, a striking man in his early thirties, was one of the few knights who had endured over two seasons since the world turned bleak. Now, he led us. Every command shaped the air into submission. I squared off against Lucas, my wooden sword an extension of my shaky resolve. Each clash, each parry, felt like a revelation of my shortcomings.

Lucas moved with a confidence that belied the seriousness of our training, his body a blend of strength and fluidity. Broad shoulders blocked the sun; his tanned, hairy legs anchored him firmly to the ground. I struggled to match Lucas's form—the way he swung his blade, the cleverness of his footwork—but my strikes wavered, and my defense crumbled. Sir Tristan called it—Lucas emerged victorious.

"Exemplary form, Lucas," Tristan said. The other squires nodded, admiration evident in their eyes. On the castle's parapet, Lady Isadora, a radiant young noblewoman, smiled at Lucas, her teeth gleaming like polished ivory. Beside her stood her ancient governess, weathered and worn, her sunburned lips cracked and peeling, a stark contrast to Isadora's ethereal beauty.

I could only nod, envy gnawing at my insides.

As Lucas reveled in his victory, advancing to the next round, I watched him. Manhood had sculpted him over the past year, sharpening his features and draping muscle where I had none despite my efforts. My reflection haunted me—smooth, blond, slim, and always feeling less. Less than Lucas. Less than what others expected of a knight.

"Did you see Lady Isadora watching?" Lucas grinned, stepping closer, his voice low. "She's taken a shine to me. We're to meet tonight in the East wing of the castle. With death surrounding us, I'll at least die a man."

I shrugged.

"Don't be so glum," Lucas said. "You can always have her governess if you need release, though you might have to lift her teats to find her quim."

I forced a laugh. Lady Isadora was graceful and charming. Still, I resented the ease with which he slipped into her favor. I resented many things. I didn't want the mantle of knight. I didn't want to be a page or a squire, or any of what my life had become, but my parents had died of plague, and I had nowhere else to turn.

Lucas must have sensed my gloom, because as we finished our practice, he pulled me into a brotherly embrace. "I'm glad you're here with me."

"Me too," I murmured, my mood lifting.

"See you tomorrow," he said, releasing me.

"Tomorrow," I echoed.

***

I shed the sweat-soaked garb of the day, trading it for a simple tunic and red hose that clung to my slim form. In the solitude of my quarters—a spartan chamber of cold stone and sparse comforts—I collapsed onto a straw mattress that offered little warmth against the chill seeping from the castle walls.

The flickering torchlight cast shadows that flitted across the room. I lay staring at the ceiling, where cobwebs clung to darkened corners. My mind replayed the day's humiliation. The wooden sword in my hand had felt like a toy, Lucas's prowess reducing my efforts to mere child's play. Was I ever good enough?

I couldn't shake thoughts of Lady Isadora. Her name stung. I despised how she watched Lucas during training, though I couldn't quite explain why. What might Lucas be doing now? Surely his talk about meeting with Lady Isadora for a tryst was nothing more than bravado. He was probably taking a cold bath and pleasuring himself. Still, I couldn't rest. Why did I have to know?

I left my shoes in my chambers and slipped into the East Wing of the castle without candle. The corridor remained silent and still. Feeling relieved that nothing had come of Lucas's plans, I turned to return to my room when I heard a faint giggle coming from a locked anteroom nearby. Intrigued, I approached and peered through the keyhole of the heavy door.

Lady Isadora closed her eyes in the dim torchlight, her back pressed against the wall as she arched to meet Lucas. Their bodies tangled, her undergarments scattered on the floor as he plunged deep inside her. His muscular buttocks clenched with each powerful thrust, his thighs pumping with reckless abandon as Lady Isadora's whimpers filled the chamber.

Lucas looked to her for guidance. "Like this?" he panted into her ear. "You like that?"

I tore myself away and returned to my quarters, unsure if my discovery had made me feel better or worse or given me any further insight into my feelings.

I peeled off my tunic and threw myself onto the mattress. Perhaps a new day would bring clarity.

Lucas's image invaded my thoughts unbidden—the tightness of his thighs and calves as he lifted himself forward to meet Lady Isadora; the way a hand on her buttocks pulled her closer. I would have nothing like that, because I would never be Lucas.

A shiver ran through me, though not from the cold. My dismal reality had cast a shadow for weeks, growing darker with each passing day. I closed my eyes. In my mind's theater, Isadora bit her bottom lip in bliss as Lucas plunged into her warmth. My hands, traitors to my will, moved of their own accord, tracing the lines of my body through the thin fabric of my hose. I hardened, the front stretching taut. Through the cloth, I touched myself, rubbing the length of my arousal with a desperate need that bordered on pain.

I imagined being with Lady Isadora as he was, but unable to perform; unable to satisfy. Then came the dark shift.

What would it be like to be entwined with Lucas, not in combat but in forbidden embrace? The heat of his skin against mine, the press of muscle to muscle, the friction. Shame gripped my gut as tendrils of desire wrapped around my senses.

I could almost feel his touch instead of my own, the ghostly sensation of rough hands exploring my smooth flesh. I squeezed, imagining it was Lucas. The thought of bringing him to a similar state, of tasting him, drawing out moans that would erase Lady

Isadora from his lips—it was madness.

"Lucas," I whispered into the emptiness, the name a sacrament and a sin. My movements grew fervent, chasing the specter of pleasure that haunted the edges of my reality. With each stroke, I fought against the tide of longing, even as it pulled me under.

In the room's silence, save for the crackling of the torch and the ragged cadence of my breath, I played out the clandestine fantasy. A world where dragons and wars faded into insignificance.

My fingers trembled as I reached for the hem of my leggings, the damp fabric clinging to my skin. With deliberate slowness, I peeled them down, exposing myself to the chill of the room. The cold bit, but it was nothing compared to my burning need.

"Lucas," I breathed again, a prayer to a god who would never listen. The fantasy cascaded over me, relentless and intoxicating. In my mind's eye, I was entwined with Lucas, our naked bodies pressed together in the struggle for dominance and desire. Our hard dicks rubbed against each other, an urgent friction that promised sweet release.

I imagined his muscular arms around me, a bulwark against the dark threats of war and mythical beasts. In his embrace, I found safety, a place where my doubts and fears dissolved into nothingness. Only pleasure remained—raw and unyielding.

My hand moved faster, chasing the edge of ecstasy. Skin slick with sweat, I clutched at the blanket beneath me, imagining it was the rough texture of his hair under my fingers.

The pressure built, an impending storm ready to break. With each stroke, I pushed closer to oblivion, to that singular moment where nothing else mattered. In the throes of passion, there was no Aiden of Aranthia, no squire with burdensome secrets—only sensation, only want, only Lucas. Then, with a shudder that wracked my frame, warmth erupted from me, coating my hand, my blanket, and the straw mattress beneath. It was over too quickly, leaving me hollow, the ephemeral bliss replaced by a familiar tide of shame.

I lay still, breaths coming in shallow gasps. With a heavy heart, I reached out and snuffed the candle at my bedside.

2.

I had been asleep barely an hour when the stones of my world shuddered—a deep growl that vibrated through the marrow of the castle and my bones alike. Screams—high, terror-stricken—and a thunderous collapse that followed jerked me from the tangled depths of sleep.

"Armory, now! To arms!" Voices careened down the corridor, urgent, frantic. I leapt from the sweat-drenched sheets. Fumbling, I yanked the coarse fabric of my tunic over my head, covering the shame of dried stains on my hose, evidence of the desires I dared not speak aloud.

I stumbled into my boots, the clank of armor in the hallway a siren call to duty. Lucas burst into the room, his presence a force that cut through the fog of my fear. He was already half encased in steel.

"Dragon," he spat out, the word laden with dread and excitement. A beast from legend, from nightmares, alive and thirsting for destruction. "Let's go." His hand clasped my arm, a lifeline anchoring me to the present. We donned our armor in hurried silence, the metal cold and unyielding against my skin. Each strap, each buckle, a reminder of what we faced.

We emerged into a hellscape. An eerie glow bathed the courtyard, flames painting macabre shadows across the ground. The eastern wall lay in ruins, a gaping wound in Aranthia's defenses. I could taste the acrid bite of smoke, feel it clawing at my throat.

Men lay still upon the cobblestones, their blood seeping into the earth, their valor rendered mute by death's embrace. The dragon, an inferno incarnate, soared above us, its wings blotting out the stars. It screamed—a raw sound that scraped across the sky, a herald of doom.

"Stay close," I murmured to Lucas, but it was me who kept pace with him, his steps sure and unflinching. Together, we darted between showers of sparks and debris, our bodies dripping with sweat beneath the unforgiving weight of our armor.

"Watch out!" Lucas pulled me back as a jet of flame scorched the path where I had stood moments before. The heat was a living thing, hungry and indiscriminate. I nodded my thanks, my gaze fixed on the monstrosity that sought to reduce our world to ashes.

"Stay alive," Lucas commanded, his voice a low growl that promised retribution. His eyes gleamed with the reflection of fire, a warrior forged in the crucible of battle.

"The underbelly," I called out to him, voice strained but urgent. "We must strike the dragon's underbelly!"

Lucas nodded, the cords of his neck taut. We sprinted toward a catapult standing against the burning sky, a behemoth of wood and iron. Embers danced around us like malevolent sprites, and the heat from the dragon's breath singed the edges of our senses.

"Here, help me with this!" Together we heaved a massive stone onto the launch cradle.

"Ready?" Lucas asked, his gaze locking onto mine, fierce and unyielding.

"Now!" I shouted back.

With a grunt of effort, we released the mechanism. The catapult groaned, a sound of ancient fury unleashed, as the stone hurled through the air. It struck true—underneath the beast's shimmering scales—and the dragon let out an ear-piercing shriek. Its massive form wavered, then retreated into the dark sky with a flap of its mighty wings, chased by the echoes of our defiance.

We watched it disappear, the threat lifted for now, but the night still writhed with terror. The taste of ash lingered on my tongue.

"Damnation," Sir Tristan growled, emerging from the smoke. His face was a mask of frustration beneath the flickering light of the torches. "It lives to bring havoc upon us another day." He turned away, his cloak billowing like a dark cloud.

In the quiet that followed, my eyes found Lucas once more. The firelight danced over his body, casting him in a play of light and shadow that twisted my insides with a yearning I could not quell.

"Good thinking, Aiden," he said, the corners of his mouth lifting in a weary smile. His praise washed over me, a tide of warmth that both soothed and seared.

Our gazes held, and in his eyes, I saw the reflection of a bond forged in the crucible of peril—a connection that transcended the flesh. My pulse thrummed with a need for closeness, a desperate hunger to bridge the chasm between us.

The moment passed, and only the wreckage of battle remained. Ash from the dragon's fire still warmed the air as I picked my way through the shattered stones. The scorched scent of ruin filled my nostrils, a grim reminder of the narrow escape from death's fiery jaws.

"Lucas!" The cry cut through the tumult, a siren call that drew his gaze away from me.

Lady Isadora stood beneath the archway, her emerald eyes wide with terror and relief. Her chestnut tresses fell in disarray, framing a face that mirrored the night's turmoil—a visage of beauty untouched by soot or blood. Lucas's body tensed, every muscle ready to respond to her silent plea.

"Isadora," he breathed.

With barely a glance back, Lucas crossed the courtyard, the cobblestones a blur beneath his boots. They disappeared inside, the heavy door closing behind them with a finality that punched the breath from my lungs.

I stood alone, the smoldering remnants of the castle mirroring the desolation spreading like poison through my veins. Jealousy gnawed at my insides, ravenous and relentless. My jaw clenched, the pain in my teeth anchoring me to the present, staving off the images of Lucas and Isadora entwined again. The raw vocabulary of my body screamed betrayal, even as my mind waged war against the truth of what I wanted—what I craved.

"Control yourself, Aiden," I muttered, the words a bitter incantation.

Lucas would never look upon me with the same intensity he reserved for her. I would never command his attention, his protection, or his love.

"Damn it," I hissed, turning my back on the door that sealed away my heart's foolish hopes. The shadows clung to me, whispering seductive lies of fulfillment through forbidden passions. But no shadow could ease the ache that throbbed within, the ache that Lucas unknowingly nurtured. The dragon might have fled, but the beast within me remained. I would endure, as I always had, in silence and solitude. For now, the dawn approached, indifferent to the battles fought and the desires left unfulfilled.

3.

The following day, we returned to training. The sun dipped low, its final golden rays glinting off our taut bowstrings as we stood in silence. I watched Lucas notch an arrow, his broad shoulders flexing beneath his tunic. The target loomed ahead. Lady Isadora's silhouette graced the edge of the training grounds, her emerald gaze once more landing on Lucas. He caught her smile, a secret shared in the open, and released his arrow. It flew true, striking the bullseye with a satisfying thud.

"Good shot," I murmured, my words lost in the gathering dusk.

"No thanks to a fair distraction," he replied, his lips curving up at the edges.

Evening crept upon us like a shroud, and Lucas and I retreated to the armory. Our bodies glistened with the day's exertion, perspiration tracing the lines of our labor. We were alone, surrounded by the lingering scent of oiled leather and cold steel.

"Damn armor feels like it weighs a ton," Lucas grumbled, peeling off his gloves and boots. His movements were deliberate, each layer discarded a minor act of liberation.

"Where did you go with her last night? After the dragon flew away?" The question slipped past my guard, fear knotted tight in my chest.

"Isadora?" he asked, fingers deftly undoing the buckles of his heavy leather jerkin. "We wandered the gardens. Hours spent... exploring." His voice dropped to a husky whisper, and I could almost feel the softness of her skin beneath my own hands.

"Exploring," I echoed, the image unwilling to leave my mind.

"She's intoxicating, Aiden," he confessed, tossing aside his tunic. "Last night I... we... coupled. She was warm and wet as an April morning." His gaze became distant. "She fit like a sleeve, Aiden. I slid up and down inside her, each thrust claiming her. But we didn't finish. Interrupted by the dragon, and later by her governess."

The fabric of his smallclothes strained against him beneath the waist. I couldn't look away. My eyes betrayed me, drawn to the evidence of his arousal. The air grew thick, charged with an energy that spoke of raw, unspoken needs. Silence stretched between us, a void filled with unuttered confessions.

"Does it haunt you? Her touch?" My voice barely rose above a whisper, each word a tremor that threatened to bring down the walls

I had built around myself.

"Every second," he admitted. Something akin to pain flickered in his gaze—a yearning for something just out of reach. "We'll do it again. Once I finish inside her, I'll be a man fully made."

"Looks like she's got you good and ready," I said, jesting weakly and pointing to his hardness.

He flushed. "Seems she's got us both," he laughed, eyes flickering down to where my body echoed his arousal. I hadn't even noticed my heat until he pointed it out. A strange thrill raced through my veins, a mix of dread and desire. A challenge flickered between us, unspoken until Lucas voiced it with a cocky tilt of his head. "Let's see who can hold back the longest."

"What do you mean?"

He shed his clothing and gripped himself. I had never seen him so exposed—the closest until now was last night when he buried himself inside Isadora. Now he tugged and twisted his fist up and down his shaft. "The first one to spill, loses."

The suggestion struck like flint to tinder, and our competition began in earnest. I shed my undergarments, the last barrier to our naked ambition.

My fingers closed around my delicate yet firm length. A gentle tuft of hair above my dick seemed almost shy in Lucas's presence. His grip encased a bold, thick shaft, tan skin stretched tight over pulsing veins. His testicles hung heavy with a virility that stirred a primal envy.

"Ready?" His voice was rough, eyes dark with desire.

We started tentatively, exploratory brushes of fingertips that slowly morphed into firmer strokes. Pleasure wound within me, each pull a step closer to the precipice I dared not cross.

Lucas matched my rhythm, his movements brazen and unashamed. The sound of our hands moving over heated flesh filled the room, an intimate symphony for an audience of two. Our breaths were ragged and uneven as if our need charged the air itself. I edged closer, then retreated, the cycle repeating, a dance of flesh that left my body quivering.

Lucas was relentless, his strokes sure and strong. I glimpsed the vein pulsing at his neck, his jaw clenched in concentration. The sight sent a jolt through me; I wanted to touch him there, feel the life beneath his skin.

His rhythm faltered, a low groan escaping him. "Gods, Aiden... Her warmth. Her tightness."

I didn't dare respond, my focus narrowing to the sensation building within me. I could scarce hold on, watching him. Then, without warning, Lucas tensed, a guttural sound tearing from his lips as his release erupted, streaking across the space between us.

Hot wetness splashed onto my foot, startling me. I looked down, the white against my skin stark and shocking. Lucas panted, his chest heaving, his expression a mix of triumph and frustration.

"Damn it," he cursed, trying to regain his composure.

My heart hammered against my ribs, the primal part of me responding to the sight, the warmth on my skin. Desire warred with confusion, a tangle of emotions I couldn't unravel.

Lucas nodded my way as I raced toward the finish. "Don't feel bad if you can't," he said. "Your young body has not yet caught up to mine."

My balls churned as they had never before. I climaxed, and my essence streaked across the room in magnificent bursts from a well deep within me, defying him.

His eyes widened, and when I finished, he laughed. "Who knew you had it in you?" He examined my spillage. It was more than his by half. "How on earth?" he asked.

I shuddered, coming down from my high.

"Can I see it?" asked Lucas. I released myself, and he stood beside me, comparing our yardage. He met my gaze, something unspoken passing between us. The contest had ended, but the air remained heavy, laden with questions neither of us dared voice.

Our bodies still thrummed with energy, the flush of arousal not yet faded. In the dim light, our eyes locked, and for a moment, I imagined closing the distance between us, replacing competition with something deeper, something forbidden.

"Next time," Lucas said, a challenge lingering in his tone, his breathing still unsteady. But next time what? The words hung between us, an invitation to a future where lines might blur and rules could break. We dressed in silence, but every glance, every accidental brush of skin, spoke volumes.

As I left the armory, the night air cool against my flushed skin, I couldn't shake the image of Lucas undone, nor the thrill that coursed through me at the thought. What lay ahead, I couldn't say, but the possibilities stretched out, vast and uncharted as the starry sky above.

4.

The next morning, I faltered again, my blade clashing awkwardly against a training dummy. Sweat dripped into my eyes, blurring my vision, but it wasn't fatigue that weakened my stance; it was the tempest that had raged within me since yesterday. After recovering from our contest, Lucas consumed my mind. He stood at the edge of the courtyard, his laughter a distant thunder amidst the clanging steel. I needed him to see me—not as a squire but as something more.

"Focus, Aiden!" Sir Tristan's voice cut through the noise, sharp as the sword I could barely wield. "Focus, damn you!"

Lucas wasn't even watching. He was looking for Isadora.

"Focus, damn you!" shouted Sir Tristan. I met his gaze, defiance rising like bile in my throat, and threw down my sword. "How much focus do I need to best a straw dummy?" Around us, the clatter ceased, heavy silence falling like a cloak. Lucas turned, his eyes finally on me, and I felt a perverse thrill.

Sir Tristan became still. "See me after," he intoned, the cords in his neck taut with restrained anger. His presence loomed large as he turned on his heel and strode away, each step an assertion of power.

My mouth went dry as I approached Sir Tristan's quarters later, the door looming like the gate to some forbidden realm. I hesitated only a moment before pushing it open. He sat with his back toward me, not bothering to turn.

"Explain yourself," he commanded without preamble, his frame silhouetted against the window's waning light. "That was unlike you today."

"I'm sorry, Sir," I said. "I'm preoccupied lately."

"Lady Isadora?" he asked. "Are you having difficulty because she has eyes for your friend? I see it happening."

I bristled, his words reigniting an inferno in me. I bit my lip. "Sir Tristan," I said at last, "I must resign as your squire and remove myself as a candidate for knighthood."

"Because of Lady Isadora?" he chortled.

"Because I have feelings—unnatural feelings—not for Lady Isadora, but for Lucas. They're tearing at my flesh. Please, let me exile myself."

"Denied." Sir Tristan's eyes softened, the stormy blue becoming the calm at the center of my hurricane.

"Squires horseplay all the time. Most go on to take wives and have families," he continued.

I opened my mouth to reply, but he silenced me with a finger. "Yet, some don't," he continued. "I know their desires not as flaws, but as much a part of them as their skills with a blade."

"I don't even have skills with a blade," I muttered, staring down at my hands as if they were traitors.

"Even the mightiest oak was once just a seedling," he mumbled, stepping closer. "Perhaps you simply need space to grow, to explore who you are without fear."

Sir Tristan's arms, corded with the strength of countless battles and brandished with scars, were a testament to his prowess. I could not tear my eyes away. He was what Lucas—what we both—aspired to become.

He noticed my gaze and smirked. "Have you ever been with another?"

Last night, with Lucas in the armory, was the closest, but I dared not recount that tale.

"Would you like to touch?" he asked, voice low, as if reading my thoughts.

My mouth hung agape, and I tore my eyes from him. "I shouldn't."

"But will you? Touch my arms."

I couldn't believe what Sir Tristan offered. Sir Tristan! Not some squire or a dirty stable boy. My pulse became an erratic drumbeat of nervousness and need. I reached out tentatively, the heat from his skin beckoning. My fingers traced the valley of muscle, igniting a current that jolted through me.

"Let me guide you," Sir Tristan murmured, his voice a velvet command. He took my hands in his, our skin contrasting—his rough, mine trembling and smooth. A shiver raced up my spine.

"Close your eyes," he instructed.

"Yes, sir," I complied, the darkness behind my lids amplifying every sensation. His hands guided mine downwards, over the landscape of his body, each ridge and plane a territory to be explored. And then we were there, at the hard bulge straining against his breeches.

I gasped and looked into his eyes. He smiled.

He pushed me away with gentle force, his hands lingering on my skin before he shed his clothing and stood before me, naked and confident. His body was a work of art, every muscle, perfection. The lines of his abdominals were like ridges carved into marble, and his powerful limbs spoke of strength and agility. As my gaze traveled lower, I couldn't help but admire the sight of his manhood standing at attention, ready for whatever lay ahead.

He nodded, beckoning me to advance. "Explore it, if you'd like."

I wrapped my fingers around him, the girthy length pulsing with life. It was for me—this powerful knight stirred to hardness by someone as insignificant as me. Disbelief warred with the undeniable truth beneath my hesitant grip.

"You're more worthy than you see yourself, Aiden," he said. "Move your hand," he breathed, his voice now a husky whisper, guiding my motions until a rhythm took hold.

Each stroke was a discovery, each groan from Sir Tristan a reward. Power surged within me, a heady mix of control and submission, knowing I held his pleasure in my grasp just as he directed my every move. In this intimate dance, I found a measure of solace, my doubts momentarily quelled by the raw force of our shared desire.

Beneath my tunic, the calloused pads of Sir Tristan's fingers traced every curve and line of my body, each touch sparking a fire that consumed me. His hands seemed to worship the softness of my skin with utmost devotion, leaving me breathless and wanting more. With delicate care, he removed my shirt.

His lips found the tender expanse of my stomach. His kisses seared paths of desire across my flesh. I was unmoored, adrift in the sensation. My muscles tensed, then melted under the heat of his mouth, my sighs punctuating the still air of his quarters. His arms enveloped me, a fortress of sinew and strength, and I felt safe yet exposed—laid bare before this paragon of masculinity.

"Please, Sir Tristan," escaped my lips, though I hardly recognized the voice as my own—strained, desperate for more of the ecstasy he drew forth so effortlessly.

"Surrender to it," he whispered, guiding me down onto the bed, the coarse fabric scratching against my back. "Let go, squire."

I obeyed, my body a vessel for the pleasure he bestowed upon me, a whimpering mess of need on the knight's bed. He pulled my leggings down to my ankles, exposing me fully before him.

My thoughts scattered like leaves in a storm, unable to take shape or form. There was only sensation—the weight of his body pressing down, the power in his hands as they explored, claimed, owned. The room spun, and I spiraled with it into the dark abyss of pleasure, every nerve alight, every part of me craving his touch, his control, his fulfillment.

He sat upright and guided me to his lap. I felt his erect manhood pressing insistently against me, teasing the place where aching need blossomed with every brush. His hands held me with an intimacy that left no room for doubt or fear.

I closed my eyes, head thrown back as he took hold of my arousal, his hand moving with practiced ease. The world narrowed down to the touch of his calloused skin against mine, rough yet so perfect, fanning the flames within me higher and higher. Faltering moans escaped my lips as he stroked me toward oblivion.

"Look at you," Sir Tristan murmured, his hot breath on my neck sending shivers down my spine. "So ready, so responsive." He cradled my hanging balls. "Heavy," he said. "Let it out, Aiden. Let everything out."

With each pull, the ecstasy built, spiraling out of control. I squirted once—only once—into the air. A cry tore from my throat. Sir

Tristan's low chuckle vibrated against me, his surprise evident in the pause before his movements resumed, now more intense, relentless.

"Your body speaks truth where your words falter," he said, stoking the fire anew.

My legs kicked in the air. Sensation overwhelmed me, and again I came apart—dripping, shivering, squirting again. My body thrashed, instinctively trying to escape the intensity, seeking respite from the pleasure that bordered on pain. But Sir Tristan's arms were iron bands, unyielding as they held me firmly in place, guiding me through the storm he conjured.

"Stay with me," he ordered, his tone brooking no argument.

My climax approached like a wave cresting, ready to crash down upon me. A cramp seized my lance, and I arched into him, every muscle taut. Then, release surged through me, a force so powerful it left me gasping, quaking as I throbbed in his grasp and spilled myself into his fist.

"Good, squire," Sir Tristan praised, milking me, his voice a lifeline anchoring me to the here and now as I floated in the aftermath, adrift in the dark seas of fulfillment.

Reeling from the torrent of pleasure, Sir Tristan released me and slapped his hardened cod against his calloused palm—a sharp, commanding sound. He looked down at me, his blue eyes piercing through the haze of my lust.

"Will you take me into your mouth, Aiden?" His voice was a low rumble, a challenge wrapped in an invitation.

I nodded, my eagerness clear as I leaned forward, my lips parting to welcome him. I was struck by the power I held to please this formidable knight. Sir Tristan groaned above me, his hands threading through my hair, guiding me with an assured touch.

Each of his thrusts pushed me further into a world where only sensation mattered. The taste of him flooded my senses, and I lost myself in the act, driven by the deep sounds he made.

"Swallow it," he commanded when the time came, his voice thick with impending release.

I steeled myself, feeling his body tense. Then, a rush of warmth flooded my mouth. With a reverence bordering on desperation, I swallowed, savoring each drop of my mentor's potent release. With each bob of my Adam's apple, I imbibed his essence—his strength, his virility, his confidence—hoping it transformed me into a man. Sir Tristan trembled, his grasp on me easing as he surrendered to the throes of his release.

Catching my breath, I wiped my mouth with the back of my hand, the pungent tang of him lingering on my tongue.

"Look at you," Sir Tristan said after a moment, his tone proud yet tender. "A squire no more in spirit. You've taken to this with a natural grace few possess."

Lying there, spent and bare, I felt something shift within me. My boyish body still hummed with the echoes of ecstasy, but it was his words that wrapped around me now—comforting, empowering.

"Your body is beauty in its purest form, Aiden," he continued, gesturing to the lean lines of my form. "Never hide from it. You're still growing, in strength and in confidence, but until you do, be proud. Trust in that, and trust in me."

I nodded, a soft smile curving my lips as I basked in the glow of newfound acceptance. Sir Tristan was right. I was more than just a squire; I was a vessel of desire and pleasure, reforged under his careful guidance. In the quiet of his quarters, I found solace, and in his commanding presence, fulfillment.

5.

I left Sir Tristan's quarters at dawn. The sky was a brooding canvas, heavy with dark clouds that promised fury. Lucas, joining me on my patrol, jabbed me in the side, his voice ripe with a boyish boast. "Lady Isadora's lips were like the sweetest ale last night," he said, grinning like a fool.

I nodded absently, my mind drifting to the secret heat of Sir Tristan's touch, the way his strength had enveloped me, leaving traces of power and longing etched into my very soul.

"Storm's coming," I murmured, eyes fixed on the bruised horizon. My heart thudded, not from Lucas's tales but from the memory of whispers in the dark, of the dominant knight's firm hands guiding me through shadows of desire.

"Look there." Lucas pointed to the bridge into town, swaying ominously in a wind that grew fierce. The bridge was already overdue for replacement—wars and dragons took precedence—but was indispensable to the castle. It carried all manner of food and medical supplies over an unforgiving river and was the only way in and out of the fortress.

Isadora's governess, old and half-crippled, could not stand on the swinging bridge and clutched the rope for dear life.

"We have to help her," I said, urgency lacing my voice, "and fortify the bridge." The first drops of rain splattered against my skin, cold and sharp as steel.

The skies opened. We ran. Mud sucked at our boots, but we pushed on, racing time and elements. Rain lashed at us, a whiplash of nature, stinging and relentless.

"Take that side!" I yelled over the roar of the rising river, my words almost lost in the tumult. Lucas nodded, muscles flexing as he leapt into action.

I grabbed the old lady and rushed her to safety, then worked together with Lucas, our movements synchronized in desperate rhythm. Rope burned my palms, rough and biting as we tied knots, reinforcing what little hope remained for the bridge. Water surged beneath us, clawing at the stone and wood, hungering to drag us into its depths.

The deluge mocked our every move, a relentless opponent. Water thrashed against stone, churning with wild abandon as if the heavens had unleashed their fury upon our small kingdom of Aranthia. Lucas and I traded a glance, both sets of eyes wide, mirroring the same unspoken dread. Could we hold back nature's wrath with mere hands and hearts?

"Stay with me," I urged, my voice barely piercing the roar of the storm. We were but squires, yet in that moment, the weight of the world seemed thrust upon our shoulders.

A sudden surge of water grabbed at Lucas, hungry to claim him as its own. My heart lurched.

"Lucas!" Instinctively, I lunged, seizing his arm with a strength I didn't know I possessed. Our fingers locked, slippery and desperate. Pulling him back, I felt the rush of victory—not over him, but the cruel grasp of death.

"Thanks," he gasped, his usual bravado washed away, leaving raw sincerity.

"Stay alive," I replied, my tone fierce, betraying my fear of losing more than just a comrade.

Time lost meaning as we battled, pushed to the brink. Every second was survival, every heartbeat a prayer that the bridge—and we—would endure. And then, as abruptly as it had begun, the tempest relented. The rain softened, the winds sighed their last, and a hush fell over the land.

We stood panting, soaked through, and victorious. The bridge, stubborn and proud, remained intact, a testament to the fortitude of Aranthia and the determination of two young men who refused to yield.

"Look at us," Lucas said, a grin breaking across his weary face. "We did it, Aiden."

I nodded, unable to summon words, emotions tangled like the ropes we'd used to tether the bridge. Relief flooded through me, mingled with an unfamiliar sense of pride. I had not only saved the bridge—I had saved Lucas and Isadora's governess.

Where was the old nag? Gone. Gone without a word of thanks.

The journey back to Aranthia was a silent pilgrimage, the sun emerging to bathe the world in a gentle glow. The scent of pine fresh in the air, the storm's rage a mere memory. Side by side, Lucas and I walked in the warmth, our clothes clinging to our skin, an uncomfortable reminder of the ordeal. Within that discomfort, however, lay a new closeness. We had been tested, thrown into the maw of chaos, and emerged not just unscathed, but stronger. Bonded by the fight, by fear, by conquest.

"Good work today, squire," Lucas said, clapping a heavy, reassuring hand on my shoulder.

"Yours as well." I managed a smile, feeling the tension ease from my muscles.

We passed a secluded cove beyond the rush of the river—a small pool often used as a bath, but empty today.

"Let's wash off," said Lucas, looking at the mud covering him. "Don't fancy Lady Isadora seeing us like this."

I nodded. We stole away to the inlet—a hidden gem, cradled by willows that swept their fingers over a surface remarkably clear despite the recent rains. Tranquility cloaked the space, a stark contrast to the earlier cacophony.

Lucas approached the water's edge, a smirk playing on his lips. With swift, sure movements, he shed his muddy garments, revealing his rugged body beneath. Sunlight flashed along his sinewy back, muscles rippling with each movement. His skin was a tapestry of tan lines. Stripping his boots and dropping his breeches, he stood naked and unabashed, virility incarnate, before diving into the crystalline embrace of the river.

"Come on, Aiden," he called out, his voice echoing against the stillness. "What are you waiting for?"

My heart hammered against my ribcage, an erratic drumbeat spurred by memories of the night prior—Sir Tristan's lessons more intimate than any combat. Emboldened by the experience, I cast away my own soiled clothes, exposing my smooth, less battle-worn form to the elements.

Lucas watched me, surprise etched onto his features, as I followed suit and plunged into the cool depths. Water enveloped me, cleansing and raw. When I surfaced, gasping for air, he whistled lowly.

"What's gotten into you?" Lucas remarked, his brows raised in a challenge.

"What do you mean?" I asked.

"Saving the bridge must have emboldened you. You're never one to dive in without calculus or forethought. It isn't the Aiden I know."

"Perhaps you know less than you think."

"Are you calling me dense?" Lucas smiled.

"No," I grinned. "I'm calling you stupid."

Water lapped at my waist as I squared off with Lucas, the playful glint in his piercing eyes a taunt that needed no words. We traded jabs of wit, each verbal thrust parried with a chuckle or a smirk. Then, with a surge of boldness that surprised even me, I lunged forward, initiating a tussle that sent droplets flying through the air like miniature crystalline projectiles.

"Is that all you've got, Aiden?" Lucas taunted, his voice thick with feigned disappointment. His hands gripped my arms, strong and sure, but his laughter betrayed the lightness in our struggle.

I retaliated with a splash aimed for his face, and he splashed back.

I collided with Lucas, our eyes dripping with water, and my fingers brushed against flesh not meant to be touched in jest. The hardness of him was unmistakable, an undeniable truth beneath the cool water. Lucas recoiled as if stung, his eyes wide with something akin to horror.

"Damn it, Aiden," he spat out, backing away and covering himself with a hand. The fun had ended. "It's not what you think. Isadora won't release me from her grip, is all."

"Of course," I murmured.

Lucas shifted gears, his expression morphing from mortified to mischievous in the span of a heartbeat.

"Ever abused yourself underwater?" he asked with a grin that held too many secrets.

"Once or twice," I admitted, my voice barely above the sound of the river's gentle flow.

"Let's see who lasts longer, this time." Lucas's stance was casual, but his eyes were alight with competitive fire. "We tell stories, get ourselves off. Loser has to... I don't know, clean the other's armor for a week."

"Fine," I agreed, the word escaping like a challenge thrown down.

Our gazes locked, two warriors on a different kind of battlefield, where victory was measured in breaths and heartbeats.

"Begin," he commanded, and our hands moved beneath the surface, the only evidence of our duel the ripples that danced across the inlet.

"Imagine her," Lucas started, his voice low and throaty, "Lady Isadora, her skin pale against the dark silk of her gown..."

I listened, my own strokes gaining rhythm, even as my mind wandered to places and pleasures far removed from the lady in his tale. Each pull beneath the water was a silent admission, a confession of the flesh that bound us together in this secluded world of our own making.

"Keep going," I urged when his voice faltered, driven by a need to hear more—to hear him—over the rush of blood in my ears and the slow burn building within.

Lucas, his back to a gnarled tree branch, was a study in primitive beauty as he worked himself. His broad shoulders, the only part of him above the murky depths, flexed with each pull. The water distorted his submerged form, but I could imagine the firmness of his muscles, the coarse hair trailing down his stomach. His voice, when it broke the silence, dragged me back to our shared reality.

"Her breasts... like two perfect orbs, untouched by the sun," he murmured, and I couldn't help but inch closer, drawn to the raw edge in his tone.

My thoughts strayed, unbidden, to Sir Tristan's chambers. To the weight of his hands on me, heavier than any armor I'd borne. Nothing Lucas and I did here could touch that memory, the pure bliss of submission and the clarity it brought. Yet there was something within this quiet rebellion that called to me, something untamed and urgent.

As if compelled by the ghost of those hands, my own reached out towards Lucas. The ridges of his abs were stark under my touch, and for a moment, everything stilled—the water, the air, my breath. Lucas's eyes flew open, wide with a shock that mirrored the rapid drumming of my heart.

"Sorry," I whispered, the word dissolving into the space between us.

But then, something shifted. He exhaled, a sound that seemed to carry all his trepidation away on the breeze. His body relaxed, and he leaned into my hand, a low moan vibrating through the water and into my palm. It was permission and surrender all at once, and I found myself anchored by the weight of it.

I clutched his hardened masculinity. His skin under my fingers was slick with river water. With each deliberate caress, I felt Lucas shudder, and something wild unfurled within me. My grasp tightened, emboldened by the way he yielded, the tremor in his breath matching the rhythm of the ripples in the pond.

"Yeah," he groaned, his hand finding me beneath the cool surface. His touch was unexpected, a jolt of heat racing through my veins. His fingers wrapped around me, firm and insistent, echoing the hunger in his eyes.

Our breathing grew labored, the sound filling the secluded inlet as we pleasured each other in an unspoken dance. The world narrowed to the space where water met flesh, where power and desire were one and the same. I lost myself in the cadence of our strokes, the sensation amplified by the weightlessness of the pond.

Lucas's moans punctuated the stillness of the forest, raw and uninhibited.

"It's wrong," he whimpered. "What we're doing is wrong."

"Do you want me to stop?" I asked.

He didn't answer, and groaned in need as I continued.

"The other night," he asked in a low whisper, "How did you pump so much sperm? Twice my amount." His voice caught. He arched into my grasp, his body a testament to unbridled yearning.

"It came from a place deep in my balls," I said.

"Show me?" he asked, his voice barely audible.

I quickened my pace and squeezed his length hard, my own need clawing its way through me, desperate for release. He stammered, "L-Lady Isadora's touch was so soft, but yours... it's so... it's so... Gods, the way you grip me!!"

His grasp on me tightened, likewise. Lucas's muscles locked, his breath seizing, the sound reverberating through the trees that bordered our secluded inlet. The world melted away, and all I could feel was the intense connection between us.

"My stones," Lucas whimpered, "They've never been so tight... Oh God, Aiden... Oh, God! What are you doing to me? I'm losing my mind! I'm... I'm..."

With a shuddering moan torn from the depths of his being, he surrendered to the height of ecstasy. His body curled. Beneath the water's surface, I could feel the powerful throbbing of his release. It was a potent rhythm that resonated in my fist. My hand moved to his balls, drawn tight against him, and gave them a gentle squeeze as they pulsed. The uncharted depth from which he released his seed had been dormant, a place he himself hadn't known existed until this very moment.

As his pleasure surged through him, it ignited a fierce explosion within me, a cramping sensation seizing my body as I put my cheek to his and spilled into his hand. My seed, too, dispersed into the welcoming embrace of the lake.

The aftershocks of bliss were fleeting, chased away by the stark chill of the water as Lucas recoiled, his touch vanishing like smoke. His eyes—once warm and inviting—now blazed with an inferno of shame and confusion. He scrambled back, his nakedness suddenly vulnerable beneath the dappled sunlight filtering through the leaves.

"Damn you, Aiden." The words were a raw wound, each syllable laced with betrayal. "What have you made me do?"

I stood paralyzed as he hauled himself onto the shore, muscles tense and movements erratic. The air was thick with unspoken questions, the silence punctuated only by the slap of wet skin against stone as he dressed in haste.

"Lucas, wait—" My plea fell on deaf ears. With one last tortured glance, he vanished into the woods, leaving me alone with the ghost of our shared touch.

A heavy sigh escaped me as I rose slowly to my feet, the water cascading down my body in rivulets of regret. I was adrift, caught between the power I had wielded and the control I had lost. Sir Tristan's lessons seemed distant now, overshadowed by a cavernous void where connection once flourished.

"Fix this," I murmured to myself, a vow etched in the forest's stillness. I would find Lucas. I would confront the storm raging within him and within me. We were bound by more than just the secrets we shared in these hidden depths; I would not let our bond shatter so easily.

6.

I had no time to reconcile with Lucas. At night, the dragon came again. The castle walls trembled under its wrath, its fiery breath a relentless storm against stone. I stood alongside Lucas on the battlements, our armor hot to the touch as the beast circled above us, the air thick with the scent of brimstone and fear. The beast's roar shook my bones.

"Lucas!" I screamed, approaching him. My voice barely cut through the chaos, my words lost in the inferno's howl. He didn't turn. His gaze locked onto the courtyard below where Lady Isadora fled, her emerald eyes wide with terror.

"Stay away from me," he commanded.

"Damn it, Lucas," I muttered, my heart like a caged bird seeking escape. I reached out, grasping at his arm, the muscles beneath the steel cuirass flexing as he pulled away.

He looked at me, but his eyes were distant and cold. "She needs me."

And just like that, I was alone. Abandoned on the edge of hell. I watched Lucas descend, his broad form slipping through the smoke and panic, every step taking him further from me.

"Fuck," I cursed, my hands clenching into fists. Betrayed by a friend. By desire. By some twisted fate that left me hollow.

Yet the dragon loomed, demanding my attention, promising destruction. My blood roared in my ears, a symphony of dread and defiance. I couldn't let Aranthia fall. Not to fire. Not to fear.

"Come at me, you winged bastard," I snarled, stepping forward, the heat scorching my cheeks, singeing the edges of my resolve. The cobblestones beneath my boots vibrated with the promise of ruin.

I charged, alone, toward the beast that threatened everything I knew. Maybe I sought death. Maybe glory. Or maybe I yearned to prove that I could stand without Lucas. That even without his touch—his acceptance—I could still be strong.

"Here I am!" I screamed, my voice tearing through the smoke, a challenge flung into the face of the dragon's fury.

Above, the dragon turned, its baleful eyes fixing on me. In that moment, there was only the two of us. Predator and prey. Hunter and hunted. It dove, jaws gaping, claws extended like the spears of fate itself.

And I ran headlong into the fire.

The searing heat clawed at my back, a relentless beast all its own. Ash swirled around me, the world tinted in an apocalyptic hue. Every breath scorched my lungs, each step a defiance against the ravenous flames that pursued me. The stone beneath my feet cracked, blackened by the dragon's wrath.

Then, like a vision amidst the chaos, Sir Tristan emerged. His broad silhouette cut through the smoke, sword in hand, gleaming with a light that seemed to defy the darkness itself.

"Aiden!" He threw me a nod that steadied my spiraling thoughts. "Stay behind me!"

I fell into step with him, grateful not to be alone. We faced the beast together, our shadows entwined on the trembling walls of Aranthia.

Tristan advanced, the embodiment of strength, his armor glinting with the promise of protection. With each swing of his blade, he carved a path of resistance, a testament to his prowess and unyielding resolve. Yet, as the dragon reared, spewing forth a torrent of flame hotter than the depths of any hell I'd imagined, I saw it—the flicker of uncertainty in Tristan's gaze.

The dragon was overpowering us, its might an overwhelming force that no single knight, however valiant, could quell.

"Damn it," Tristan grunted, parrying a swipe of the dragon's lethal claws. His muscles tensed, the strain evident even through the layers of his battle-hardened exterior.

"Sir Tristan!" I shouted, fear lacing my words.

It was then that she appeared. Isadora's governess, cloaked in mystery, her very essence seeming to still the air around us. Power thrummed from her, a silent storm that held the dragon's fury at bay.

"Who—" I began, but my words died in my throat.

"Watch and learn, young squire," she said, her voice a soothing balm amidst the roar of fire and steel.

The air crackled with the Old Lady's power, a force that seemed to emerge from the very stones beneath our feet. Her lips moved, ancient words weaving through the tumult of battle, a chant that reverberated against my skull, burrowing deep within.

"*Esse mortalis...*" she intoned, her voice rising above the chaos.

The dragon reared, its monstrous head swinging. Flames sputtered from its maw, a desperate attempt to quell the threat. But her spell was relentless, an invisible tide washing over the beast.

"*Conteram te,*" she finished, her hands outstretched, palms facing the inferno.

A blinding light erupted, and for a moment, it was as if the sun had descended upon us. The heat was unbearable, singeing the hairs on the back of my neck, searing my lungs with each labored breath.

Then, silence. A hush fell over the battlefield, punctuated only by the sound of settling dust. I blinked against the brightness, and when my vision cleared, the dragon was gone. No bones, no flesh—nothing but a fine gray powder that swirled in the gentle breeze like some grim mockery of snow.

I stood frozen, the taste of ash in my mouth, the weight of what had transpired pressing down on me. How could such power exist? And in the frail form of the old lady?

She turned to Sir Tristan, who stood as if carved from stone, his sword still raised in a now pointless defense. She stepped closer to him, her movements deliberate, unhurried. She murmured into his ear, her voice a low hum that seemed to vibrate through the air between them.

He leaned down, his helmeted head bowing to receive her words. I strained to hear, to catch some fragment of the secret that passed from her lips to his ear. But it was not meant for me.

Their exchange was brief, a whisper lost to the wind, and yet it shifted something within him. Tristan straightened, his posture altering subtly, a new understanding dawning in his eyes.

"Aiden," he said at last. "Find Lucas. Meet me in my chambers in twenty minutes."

7.

I found Lucas with Isadora. He was pulling up his trousers and said nothing to me as we walked to Sir Tristan's quarters, the air still thick with the scent of char. The dragon's roar still echoed in my memory—a cacophony that drowned out the throb of my pulse. We had survived, but this encounter, summoned by Sir Tristan himself, promised a different kind of trial.

His door loomed ahead, a portal to some infernal reckoning, and the weight of our actions pressed down on me, more burdensome than any armor. I could feel Lucas's warmth beside me, that fierce energy of his, yet neither of us dared to speak or even meet each other's gaze. Our secret entwined us, binding us together while simultaneously tearing us apart.

Inside, the chamber was a crypt of shadows and flickering light, with Sir Tristan standing as its formidable guardian, a statue hewn from stone. He regarded us with eyes that peeled away every layer of defense, every excuse we might have conjured.

"Your performance tonight was disgraceful." Sir Tristan's gaze pierced us, his disappointment a palpable force in the room. "You fight like squires at odds, not allies. Explain."

I swallowed hard, my throat dry. Words lodged there like boulders, heavy with the truth we feared to voice. I dared a glance at Lucas, whose jaw tightened, muscles twitching with unspoken confessions.

"Speak, Aiden," Sir Tristan's command jolted me back, and I felt trapped. My voice, when it emerged, was barely a whisper.

"We... we let you down, Sir."

"Indeed." He stepped closer, the firelight casting shadows over his scars—each a testament to battles fought. "But why? What is this rift between you?"

Lucas shifted beside me, a silent giant grappling with secrets. Neither of us could articulate the intimacy we shared, the forbidden connection that bound us in ecstasy and now, in shame.

"Lady Isadora's governess witnessed you two bathing," Sir Tristan revealed, his gaze locking onto mine. The truth struck me like a cold slap. "The old crone not only saved us from a dragon but provided me with all the information I need. I want to hear you say it."

Desperation clawed at my insides, a beast with no escape. The revelation hung between us, an unbreakable chain tethering us to our actions. Lucas stood resolute, the façade of bravery cracking under the weight of our reality.

"Sir, we—" I began, but my words faltered, the confession too raw to articulate. "It was a moment of passion," I murmured, my voice barely audible. The words tasted like ash, hollow and bitter. "We were alone, and the world outside... it vanished."

Lucas's voice broke through, desperate and pleading. "Lady Isadora, she haunts my thoughts, Sir. Her image drives me beyond reason." His confession was raw, stripped of his usual bravado.

"Unchecked desire can bring kingdoms to ruin," Sir Tristan warned.

My own promises felt fragile as I spoke. "I will master myself," I asserted, but doubt gnawed at my insides. Could I truly contain what had been unleashed?

"Knighthood demands discipline," Sir Tristan stated, his voice unwavering. "And you both lack it." He paused, allowing the weight of his disappointment to settle over us. "Remove your armor. Stand before me."

The clinking of metal filled the room as we fumbled with buckles and straps, our movements awkward with anxiety. My hands trembled as I let my breastplate fall with a heavy thud, followed by the rest of my armor. The cool air of the chamber brushed against my skin, raising goosebumps.

Beside me, Lucas's armor hit the stone floor piece by piece, revealing the coarse hair and sinewy muscles that covered his large frame. I forced my gaze away, focusing on the flickering torch on the wall.

"Undergarments too," Sir Tristan commanded.

With trembling fingers, I loosened the string of my breeches, letting them and my smallclothes fall away until I stood bare, exposed before my mentor. A shiver coursed through me, not from chill but from the weight of scrutiny. Lucas paused for a moment before he too shed his final garments, standing tall and resolute.

"How do you feel?" Sir Tristan inquired.

"I feel nothing," Lucas asserted, his voice unwavering. "I could remain here all night, and desire would not reach me."

I envied his certainty, the ease with which he clung to his facade. I stayed silent, the truth of my longings a silent presence between us, refusing to succumb to his denial.

Sir Tristan's gaze roamed over me, a quiet evaluation that left my skin tingling with discomfort. "Your bodies have grown strong and capable," he noted, his voice echoing in the stillness of the room.

His hand descended upon me, and I stiffened at his touch. The roughness of his fingers explored the sensitive skin of my groin, a firm grip igniting an unwilling arousal within me. As he continued to caress, my breaths quickened, and my body betrayed me, responding with undeniable eagerness.

Lucas observed, his jaw set tight, the muscles in his neck taut. His eyes met mine for a fleeting moment, a spark of unspoken understanding passing between us before he looked away.

"Will your body react similarly?" Sir Tristan directed his question at Lucas.

Lucas flinched. Without releasing me, Sir Tristan's opposite hand encircled Lucas, drawing a gasp from his lips. He stuttered out excuses, his facade crumbling as his body yielded to our knight's skilled touch. He stiffened.

"The desires of the flesh can overwhelm," Sir Tristan murmured, almost to himself.

I could barely nod, caught in a whirlwind of pleasure and shame, the latter etched into my very being.

With deliberate slowness, Sir Tristan removed his own garments. His physique was a testament to strength, muscles shifting with each precise movement. My mouth went dry at the sight of his impressive arousal standing proudly against his powerful legs.

"Lucas?" Sir Tristan asked, his tone direct. "Do you wish to touch?"

"No," Lucas replied, his voice a sharp break in the heavy atmosphere. "It's one thing to be aroused, but I won't initiate anything with another man."

The refusal lingered between them, both a challenge and a declaration. Sir Tristan simply nodded, a knowing glimmer in his eye that suggested he understood far more than he revealed.

Sir Tristan led us to a short upholstered bench at the foot of his bed.

"Side by side," Sir Tristan commanded. "Heels up on the padding."

Lucas and I sat, our legs raised in vulnerability at Sir Tristan's command. His hands roamed over us, warm and commanding, his fingers cradling our balls with an intimacy that sent shivers through our bodies. The touch was almost reverent, exploring the sensitive skin behind and applying gentle pressure I could feel in my back teeth.

He traced the edges of our openings, and we gasped in unison—a duet of surprise and awakening pleasure. As he entered us with his fingers, sensations blossomed within me, heat spiraling from where his digits moved. Lucas and I locked eyes, reflections of each other's torment and bliss. Our hands fumbled, reaching for one another, wrapping around each other's eager lengths. The slickness of pre-cum coated our palms, and our strokes became rhythmic, desperate. Sir Tristan's fingers delved deeper inside us, each thrust urging us closer to a precipice I wasn't sure I wanted to scale—or could resist climbing.

Sir Tristan's mouth found mine, his kiss deep, as if trying to consume the moans that escaped me. Then he turned to Lucas, claiming him with the same intensity, leaving us both breathless and marked by his lips.

"Lucas," he asked, voice low and penetrating, "have you ever taken another?"

Lucas hesitated before revealing his encounter with Isadora—how he had taken her but found no release. Sir Tristan nodded, as if fitting a piece into a larger puzzle.

He turned to me. "Roll onto the rug," he commanded, and I complied, the fabric rough against my heated skin. I lay on my side, observing as Sir Tristan assessed us, two squires exposed before our knight.

The rug felt abrasive beneath me, a stark contrast to the intimacy of the moment. My gaze was fixed on Lucas, his broad form hovering over me with a hesitance that seemed unusual for someone so assured in battle. Sir Tristan's voice broke the silence, low and commanding.

"Lucas, prepare him—open him for your entry. Think of this as... practice for Lady Isadora for now, if you must."

I noticed Lucas's hands quiver slightly—a flicker of uncertainty in the torchlight—before he reached for a vial of oil Sir Tristan offered from a shelf behind him. I shivered as Lucas's calloused fingers, now slick with the viscous liquid, traced the sensitive skin where Sir Tristan had been moments ago. His touch was cautious at first, but under Sir Tristan's watchful eye, he grew more confident.

"Now, position yourself behind him. Align yourself, and press in slowly," Sir Tristan instructed, his tone a guiding force in the dimly lit room.

Lucas entered me, and I gasped, the sensation unfamiliar yet somehow right, filling me in ways I hadn't realized were empty.

"Gods, Aiden..." Lucas's voice was a gravelly whisper, filled with awe. "You're so warm... so smooth."

"Good, very good," Sir Tristan praised from somewhere beyond my line of sight. "You both are discovering the balance between strength and tenderness."

Time stretched, each of Lucas's thrusts measured and deliberate, until a rhythm emerged—a dance of bodies finding harmony in their movements. Surrounded by the scent of sweat and oil, I melted into the plush rug, feeling whole with Lucas moving within me until he shuddered.

"Enough," Sir Tristan commanded, his voice halting Lucas. "Lucas, stand up. Face the wall."

I watched, my chest tight, as Lucas complied, his muscular form illuminated by the flickering light. His length was tight with desire and dripped from the tip. He turned away.

Sir Tristan kneeled, and with deliberate hands parted Lucas's cheeks, exposing him. "Wh...what?" muttered Lucas.

Sir Tristan's tongue found its target, and the room filled with Lucas's moans. He shifted, one leg lifting, granting better access—a silent plea for more.

Sir Tristan worked for a time, lapping at Lucas's most forbidden part, Lucas's head rolling in circles, his eyes closed.

Our knight then stood as Lucas panted, catching his breath.

Sir Tristan positioned himself behind Lucas. They locked eyes and Lucas nodded. "Relax," said Sir Tristan. "Breathe."

The air was thick with anticipation. Lucas winced when Sir Tristan entered him, his frame trembling against the wall. His breaths came in short gasps, each exhale punctuated by a soft grunt. Pleasure and pain intertwined on his face, a look I recognized all too well.

"Trust in the sensation, Lucas," Sir Tristan said, his words steady as he moved within him. "Let it guide you to pleasure."

An insatiable hunger gnawed at my core as I watched Sir Tristan, a living embodiment of raw masculinity, assert his dominance over

Lucas. His rigid form disappeared into Lucas with an authority that left me breathless. The sight of Lucas's face contorting in a wince etched into my mind, yet Sir Tristan remained unyielding, his confident thrusts taming the young squire beneath him. As I watched Lucas succumb to the intoxicating rhythm, I felt an overwhelming longing clawing at my insides. The sight was a sharp lance to my chest—desire and envy warring within me. Every clench of Lucas's muscles, every thrust from Sir Tristan, sent a surge of heat through my veins. It was an agony no training could have prepared me for.

Sir Tristan's pace intensified, his powerful hips driving into Lucas with a force that resonated through the stone walls of his quarters. Each thrust elicited a primal groan from Lucas, the sound raw and visceral as it filled the dimly lit space. His hands gripped a tapestry before him, knuckles turning white as he surrendered to the overwhelming pleasure coursing through him.

Sir Tristan's breaths grew uneven, matching the rhythm of his movements. The shared sounds were instinctual, perfectly synchronized with each pulse of Sir Tristan's desire. With a final deep thrust and a low growl that rumbled in his chest, Sir Tristan released himself deep within Lucas. The moment hung heavy in the air, their bodies entwined and slick with sweat.

From my vantage point on the bench, my own arousal pressed painfully against my thigh. Yet a pang of sorrow gnawed at my heart—an ache born from witnessing an intimacy I feared would forever elude me. My gaze lingered on Lucas's muscular back glistening under the torchlight, my mind filled with fantasies of tracing every line and contour with eager fingers.

As if sensing my thoughts, Sir Tristan turned to me, his piercing blue eyes meeting mine in silent invitation. "Aiden," he said softly yet firmly. "It is your turn."

My heart raced as I hesitated on the threshold of desire and fear.

But when Lucas glanced back at me over his shoulder, hunger burning bright in his eyes as he beckoned for more—all doubts melted away.

"Aiden..." Lucas urged breathlessly; it was all the encouragement I needed to step into their world of unrestrained pleasure.

My heart thudded in my chest as I positioned myself behind Lucas. My hands trembled slightly, the unfamiliar power coursing through me igniting my nerves. Sir Tristan's guiding hand rested on my shoulder, a reassuring weight that grounded me amidst the intoxicating scent of sweat and desire. The slick warmth of Lucas's entrance was an invitation, the remnants of Sir Tristan's release coating me with an intimate testament of our shared pleasure.

"Take him," Sir Tristan commanded, his voice low and resonant in the dimly lit chamber. "Claim what is yours."

With a shaky breath, I pushed forward, my cock sliding into Lucas's tight channel with an ease that made me gasp. I felt the heat enveloping me, the residual essence of Sir Tristan inside Lucas serving as a potent reminder of what I yearned for—to be desired by Lucas as much as I desired him.

As I thrust into Lucas, something shifted within me. My movements grew less tentative and more assertive; each stroke was firm and deliberate, driving deeper into my friend's body. My muscles strained under the effort, but it only fueled my growing confidence. I could feel it all—my balls tightening in anticipation, my body ripening from boyhood to manhood under this fervent display of raw masculinity.

Lucas groaned beneath me, pushing back against every powerful thrust. "Damn... I never thought you'd be so good at this," he panted between labored breaths. There was admiration in his voice—an awe that bolstered my confidence further. My muscles flexed with each movement; thighs tightened as I drove myself relentlessly into Lucas.

"Come inside me," Lucas pleaded raggedly after what felt like an eternity of pleasure-pain throbbing between us. My heart swelled at the request, my climax building like a tidal wave within me. With a final powerful thrust and a guttural howl, I released myself inside Lucas.

As I collapsed onto Lucas's glowing back, panting heavily, I sensed Sir Tristan's approving gaze upon me. The knight's smile radiated satisfaction—pleasure in witnessing his squires discover intimacy and strength in one another under his watchful eye.

With newfound confidence, I turned my focus to Lucas's throbbing length.

"Touch me like yesterday?" he asked,

With a coy smile, I enveloped him with my lips as the essence of his desire filled my senses.

"Shit!" he shouted, twitching. "With your mouth? Like the French? Isadora never... Isadora wouldn't.... Unnnngh!" his head rolled.

I could feel his heat and firmness swell against my tongue, a clear indication of his imminent release. His protests grew more urgent, his voice strained as he fought against the rising tide of pleasure. His body tightened, a clear indication that he was on the brink.

"I can't!" he whimpered. "I can't!"

"Surrender to him, squire... embrace everything you truly desire."

The words ignited something within Lucas—a yielding not just to us, but also to his own desires. Then it happened: the final cramp of ecstasy, warm and slick against the roof of my mouth. He shouted to the almighty. His manhood pulsed within me—warm and briny—each throb sending ripples of pleasure through him. I knew it came from deep within him—the place he had been curious to discover. Swallowing every drop was a sweet triumph—a testament to the ecstasy we had drawn from Lucas, a taste of his submission.

I wiped my lips with the back of my hand. Sir Tristan summoned his servants to prepare a bath, and Lucas trembled.

8.

Side by side, in separate tubs, ladies-in-waiting attended to me and Lucas. For twenty minutes, we remained silent. Finally, I broke the stillness.

"Will you return to her?" I asked, the thought of Lady Isadora now distant and insignificant.

Lucas met my gaze, and in his eyes, I saw my own reflection—a mirror of longing and newfound devotion. "Why?" he breathed. "I've found what I seek right here."

I stifled a giggle.

Power, control, fulfillment—they swirled around us, intangible yet as real as the soap that clung to our skin. In this chamber of shadows and whispers, we had unearthed ourselves. And in each other, we had discovered everything we needed.

A few weeks later, the king knighted me and Lucas. Sir Tristan stood by our side. Lady Isadora and her governess were present, but Isadora was already dreaming of another squire. Her governess—the old witch—smirked. A feast was planned soon after, but the king received word of an invading army on the horizon. I made my way to the armory with Lucas.

"Stay close to Sir Tristan," I advised. "Fortune favors him."

"I'll stay near Sir Aiden," Lucas replied. "No one is to touch him."

I smiled. "I have plans for you when this is over."

Lucas wove his fingers through my hair and kissed me deeply. "Good," he said. "Let's claim victory."

WILDWOOD HEAT

I wanted to feel Mike Sullivan's arms. I wasn't supposed to be thinking it, I know, or looking at him that way – he was my best friend – but I wanted him to myself and I couldn't help it and it was making me miserable.

It was August, 1984. The wide, endless expanse of sand at Wildwood Crest stretched toward the Atlantic Ocean from the boardwalk, almost too vast to comprehend. Seagulls lazily picked at forgotten pizza crumbs in the late afternoon sun. A breeze rolled in from the ocean, carrying the faint scents of coconut oil and salt, as if the beach exhaled summer. I curled my toes into the warm sand, feeling the heat slip beneath my feet, grounding me. My friends lounged nearby, sprawled on faded towels, discussing plans that reached far beyond today. I focused on the waves, entranced by their rhythmic rise and fall, each one smoothing over the traces of the last, trying not to get hard.

Brian and Mike sprawled out on their towels like gods surveying their domain. Brian leaned up on one elbow, sunglasses crooked on his nose, nodding toward a group of girls walking past. "Yo, the one in the red bikini? Absolute ten."

Mike didn't even look up. "Sure, if you're into girls who'd rather fuck the lifeguard."

Brian flipped him off. "At least I'm aiming high. You're still hung up on Emily, like she's not out here banging half of North Wildwood."

Mike rolled onto his back, grinning. "She's loyal, man. To me and the other five guys she's dating."

They cracked up. I tried to laugh, too, but it got caught in my throat, so I coughed instead.

"What's wrong, Jorge? Not enough scenery for you?" asked Mike. His smile was razor-sharp, daring me to say something.

"Just zoning out," I muttered, kicking at the sand. My legs were too skinny for swimshorts this short despite my running every morning, and I hated the way my chest looked—flat and smooth, nothing like Mike's.

Mike snorted. "Dude, you gotta stop with that loner shit. You look like you're auditioning for a music video. Girls aren't into the whole brooding thing unless you've got abs to back it up."

Brian laughed. "Or chest hair."

"Or a chest," Mike added, laughing again.

I flushed, glancing down at my body. My skin was dark from the summer sun, my limbs wiry and awkward next to their tanned, muscled ease. I hated how I looked next to them—how I felt next to them.

Mike threw a hand over his eyes like a bad actor. "Ah, yes, the existential angst of Jorge Guillen. Always so *deep*. Let me guess: you were contemplating the meaning of life again?"

"Maybe," I said, feeling the tips of my ears burn.

Brian shook his head. "You gotta stop with that. No girl's gonna fuck a guy who stares at the ocean like he's about to recite a poem."

"At least he's got a tan going for him," said Mike

Brian laughed. "Yeah, not in the way girls like. More like in the 'I just crossed the border' way."

The two cracked up again.

I forced a laugh that felt like sandpaper. "You guys are hilarious."

Brian smirked, satisfied. "I know."

They turned their attention back to the girls, already forgetting me. I let them, digging my toes into the sand, wishing I could sink straight through it and disappear.

Brian's attention snapped to a girl further down the beach. "Holy shit, check her out," he whistled.

A volleyball smacked into the sand nearby, and two guys jogged over to grab it, all tan skin and ropey muscle. One had fiery red hair, while the other sported chestnut brown locks. They laughed, playfully shoving each other, and the redhead's hand lingered on the other guy's arm for a beat too long. The guy with the brown hair caught my eye and smirked. I looked away fast, pretending to brush sand off my chest, like I hadn't been staring.

Like I wasn't always staring. What was wrong with me?

"I dare you to go talk to her," Mike's voice cut through my spiraling thoughts.

"Huh?" I replied, realizing he was addressing Brian.

Brian puffed out his chest. "Watch and learn, boys."

With a confident stride, Brian swaggered off. Mike's attention shifted, his eyes narrowing as he spotted the two guys I had been watching. "Well, well. Looks like we've got ourselves a couple of fags at one o'clock."

"What?" I croaked, struggling to keep my voice steady.

Mike jerked his chin toward the two guys. "Those two over there. Absolutely disgusting."

Brian returned, a triumphant grin plastered on his face. "Got her number!"

Mike high-fived him. "Nice! But seriously, Jorge, maybe you'd be better off with one of those guys, huh?"

I rolled my eyes, trying to dismiss the sting of the words.

"Yo, faggots!" Brian suddenly yelled. "This is a family beach. Take your shit somewhere else!"

The two guys tensed, exchanging pained glances before hastily gathering their things.

"Yeah, that's right. Get lost!" Mike added.

As they hurried away, a familiar laugh rang out. Emily Parker approached, her blonde hair shimmering in the sunlight. Mike's face lit up at the sight of her.

"Em! Over here!" he called, waving enthusiastically.

She jogged over, her tanned legs moving with effortless grace. "Hey, boys!"

Mike pulled her close, kissing her lips. I forced myself to look away, focusing on the grains of sand between my toes.

"Jorge, you remember Emily, right?" Mike asked.

I nodded, managing a weak "Hey." They started dating in July, and I hated every moment.

Emily smiled warmly. "How's your summer going?"

Before I could respond, Mike wrapped his arm around her waist. "Babe, you should've seen it earlier. These two fa—"

"Mike," I interrupted, surprising myself, "let it go. They're gone."

"Whatever, man," he replied dismissively.

"What?" Emily asked, confusion clouding her expression.

"We chased off two fags," Brian chimed in.

She had a laugh, then shrugged it off. "Want to go for a swim?"

They dashed toward the water, laughing and splashing. I watched them, a dull ache spreading through my chest. They looked so right together, so normal.

Surrounded by familiar faces, I felt more alone than ever.

As the sun set, painting the sky in vibrant hues, I sat there, wondering how long I could keep pretending. Would I ever find someone who could make me feel whole? And if I did, what price would I pay?

***

I trudged through the door of my house, the creak of its hinges echoing in my ears. A *For Rent* sign hung in the window, advertising our back bedroom. It had been there all summer. People came to look, but no one had taken it.

The smell of chicken and rice enveloped me like an embrace I couldn't return. My mom, Marisol, stood by the table, her eyes weary but a smile playing on her lips.

"Jorge, come eat before it gets cold," she said, already halfway out the door, keys jingling with the urgency of her double shift at the warehouse.

"Thanks, Ma." I pecked her cheek. "Any takers on the room?"

"Not today. Maybe tomorrow."

"Are we going to make the mortgage next week?"

"I'll borrow from my sister."

"You did that last month."

She offered her worn-out smile. "Don't worry about it, *hijo*. It's my concern," she said, leaving as the car's engine faded into the night like a tired heartbeat.

I shoveled the food into my mouth, barely tasting it. My stomach was full, but everything else felt hollow. I cleaned up with robotic precision and headed to my room—the corner one with its enormous picture windows. The space was mine, tidy and ordered. Model airplanes suspended in eternal flight above me, untouched books lined up like soldiers on a shelf.

I sat on my bed, the springs creaking under my weight. "Is this it?" I muttered, tracing the lines of an airplane with my finger.

Here I was, eighteen with a face too young and a life too old. Most of my classmates were a year younger, ready to start their senior year, but I was a year behind. When I was five, dad got caught up in some legal mess that kept us on the move for a year. Mom never talked about it, but I paid the price by not starting kindergarten on time. Class of 1985, and I should have my diploma, already.

A photo of my dad sat on my dresser, stuck in a cheap plastic frame Mom picked it up at the dollar store. He had a crooked grin and eyes that crinkled at the corners. I hadn't seen him since I was eight—the night he slammed the door and didn't come back. Mom said it was important to keep his picture, even though I didn't understand why. He was a brutal man.

I looked around. Everything was in its place, everything but me. My friends didn't worry about being too old or rent or food; they worried about dates and cars. Girls came naturally to them. I clenched my fists, feeling the anger rise—a burning tide against the dam of my chest.

"Useless," I muttered, flipping onto my side to face the wall.

The memory of Mike earlier on the beach floated into my mind. The way he'd chased off the volleyball guys with a string of insults, then slung his arm around Emily. She leaned into him like it was the most natural thing in the world.

Mike hadn't always been like that. Back when we were kids, he was the kind of friend who'd share his Lunchables even if it meant he went hungry. He'd make dumb, goofy faces that had me crying with laughter, and he never cared when I couldn't keep up with him on the playground.

Something shifted between sixth and seventh grade. When summer began, Mike and I high-fived, promising to hang out as much as we could. Then his dad sent him off to Colorado for some athletic camp, and summer stretched long and hollow without him.

When we got back to school in the fall, I barely recognized him. His legs had become hairy and thick and tan, his shoulders broader, his voice deeper. He walked differently—chin up, like he owned the hallways. When he saw me, he grinned, but there was something in his eyes, like he was sizing me up.

"Hey, Jorge," he said, his voice low and smooth, while mine squeaked like an unoiled hinge.

He'd point out the girls who'd blossomed over the summer. "Check out Megan," he'd whisper, nudging me with his elbow. "Who knew she'd grow tits that *huge*?"

I didn't know what to say to that. I felt like I was in some holding pattern while Mike had already taken off, flying miles ahead. Even when my voice finally cracked and the hair came in, it wasn't enough. I was never going to be him. I would never be good enough.

I flung myself onto the bed, face buried in the pillow. My hands clenched into the sheets, seeking something to hold. A deeper connection, a goddamn sign that there was more to life than this never-ending cycle of longing and loneliness and being a step behind.

Then, it happened. I knew it would. My body betrayed me with its rising heat, a swelling tension I tried to quell by pressing into the mattress.

This had also been happening since about seventh grade—sometimes thinking about Mike, sometimes thinking about Brian, but never outside the confines of my bedroom. "You're pathetic, Jorge," I muttered, words muffled against cotton.

My fingers fumbled over the blinds until the room sank into shadows, evening light cut off from my private tempest. My clothes became confining, suffocating. I shed them desperately. My shorts hit the floor, ankles entwined for a split second before I kicked free, heart pounding a wild rhythm against my ribcage.

My dick had become a tight, rebellious curve against my

briefs—the one part of me that refused to bend to my will, smooth and demanding attention. I dropped my underwear. A scant patch of hair framed my cock—a teasing promise of manhood that mocked me. I snatched my beach towel from where it lay slumped over a chair, spreading it across the mattress like an altar for my frustrations. The fabric scratched against my heated flesh as I belly-flopped onto it, every fiber igniting my senses. Eyes closed, I let myself sink into the fantasy—the beach, the sun, the sound of waves.

The rough terrycloth was a poor substitute for the touch I longed for. My skin burned where I ground into it, each coarse fiber dragging sensation from me. I moved my hips in slow circles, feeling the tug and release of my foreskin. I pictured a world different from the one I knew - a world where I held a secret power over Mike, my fantasies painting vivid scenes of stolen moments and hushed confessions.

In my mind, we slipped away from Emily and Brian, seeking the intimacy of a hidden corner under the boardwalk, away from prying eyes. My fingers tightened around the towel, knuckles paling as I gulped in air, my imagination running wild. I'd kiss him. He'd recoil and push me away and call me a faggot, then relent. Confused, like me. Not knowing why it felt so good, like me. Wanting more, like me. I'd feel his heavy cock through the leg of his shorts.

Mike's voice, a rich baritone, echoed in my head. "Suck me, queer," he demanded, his words laced with a dangerous thrill that sent shivers down my spine. "Don't you dare say a word to Emily. Understand?" My pulse quickened at the thought, adrenaline mingling with arousal as I imagined myself obeying him willingly.

"Suck that dick" Mike's voice rumbled again, approval dripping from each word as I envisioned taking him into my mouth. The image of his muscular legs flexing and tensing in rhythm was almost too much to bear. I could practically feel the hard planes of his glutes under my grasp as they pumped against me—each thrust pushing deeper into the heat of my mouth. The rawness of it all was intoxicating; the taste of him, the primal rhythm of our bodies moving together—it was a dance unlike any other.

My ass tightened and my hips bucked against the towel as I envisioned his moans, echoing in my ears, telling me how good I was, "Em can't do it this way," Mike said, leaning back on his elbows in the sand. "God!" he growled "Why's it feel so good?"

I'd milk him for every sound, every ragged breath, every whispered praise.

The clench in my gut tightened as I pictured Mike losing himself, coming undone in my mouth, his pleasure caused by me, and only me. My torso moved in time with my imagined rhythm, the speed increasing, chasing the high that was waiting just out of reach.

I recalled the first time I did this—the first time ever—how my hardness broke and gave way to the rhythmic throbbing of release; how I didn't understand what my body was doing; how I felt ashamed and shocked by the mess and the smell, yet somehow more relaxed.

I was no longer naive. I knew what was to come. I drove harder against the mattress. Imagined Mike unable to hold himself together and spilling into my mouth. Then it happened—a moment suspended in time. My muscles locked, straining as a surge of ecstasy cascaded through me. Sticky warmth burst forth, filling the space between me and the towel. My breath released in a ragged moan, the sound swallowed by the walls that enshrined my solitude.

The aftermath hit me like a rogue wave, cold and relentless. Shame crept over me, a shadowy specter reveling in my vulnerability. A bitter laugh escaped my lips, hollow and mocking. "What's wrong with you?" I whispered to the empty room. It didn't matter. None of it did. Mike was nothing more than a dream fading with the harsh light of reality. My dad's picture stared at me, a reminder that I had to confront the truth about life. It didn't suffer feelings like mine gladly.

"Never again," I vowed, pulling the soiled towel from beneath me and using it to wipe off. The world would never understand the hunger tearing at my soul—a hunger for a fulfillment that seemed as distant as the stars peering through the blinds of my window.

***

The last week of summer break dragged like a bad hangover. Every day felt heavy, stretched thin by the looming return to school, made worse when mom called one morning from the laundry room, her voice muffled by the hum of the dryer.

"Jorge, we found a renter for the spare room," she said.

"Who?" I asked, trying to sound indifferent.

"Friend of a friend. He's a college student. Very polite."

"Is he gonna stay out of our business?"

Mom poked her head around the corner, folding a towel. "We've talked about this. We need the money. He's renting a room, not adopting us."

"I just don't want some weirdo hanging around," I muttered.

"Then lock your door," she said, half-joking. "But be nice, okay?"

I didn't say anything, but a knot tightened in my stomach. I imagined someone older, boring, maybe balding. A nobody I could ignore. That would've been fine.

Nothing prepared me for the knock at the door that afternoon—or the face I saw when Mom opened it.

It was the volleyball guy from the beach. The one Mike called a fag. Brown hair, easy grin, a posture so relaxed it was practically a dare. He looked like a postcard of summer, brought to life and standing in my doorway.

"Hey," he said, his voice low and steady. "Kevin Sebathia."

My throat dried up. "Uh... hi."

Mom ushered him in, chatting about rent and rules, but her words dissolved into static. Kevin stepped over the threshold like he'd done it a thousand times, like he belonged here. Like he belonged everywhere. His eyes flicked toward me briefly—casually—but my pulse hammered as if he'd looked straight through me.

I bolted to my room before I could embarrass myself.

Inside, I paced, cursing silently. My room was a mess. It probably reeked of dirty laundry and—God, I didn't even want to think about it. I sat on the edge of my bed, gripping the comforter, trying to steady my breathing. My thoughts wouldn't stop: *He's hot. Too hot. Stop thinking that. What if Mike or Brian saw you looking at him? What if he saw?*

After twenty minutes of spiraling, I told myself to grow up. It was just a guy. A guy who happened to be renting a room. That was all. No big deal.

I knocked lightly on the open door to what used to be the empty guest room. Now, it was *his*.

Kevin was mid-change, tugging a shirt over his head. His back muscles rippled under skin bronzed from the sun, and for a second, I forgot how to breathe.

"Shit—sorry," I stammered, my face burning as I froze in the doorway.

Kevin glanced over his shoulder, entirely unfazed. "It's cool, Jorge." He pulled the shirt down, flashing me a quick smile that felt like a jab straight to my chest. "What's up?"

"N-nothing," I managed, trying to sound casual but failing miserably. "Uh... welcome, I guess."

"Thanks." He turned, leaning against his desk, perfectly at ease. "Nice place. Better than my last one, at least."

I shifted awkwardly, wishing the floor would swallow me. "Why'd you move?"

"Bad breakup," he said with a shrug. "Needed a fresh start. My ex cheated, so... here I am."

I blinked. "Oh. That sucks."

Kevin's eyes narrowed slightly, just enough to make my stomach churn. "You were at the beach last week, right? I thought I recognized you."

My heart stopped. "Uh... maybe?"

His smile tilted, amused. "Yeah, you were there. Your friends called me a fag. Didn't bother me, though."

Heat crept up my neck. "I—I didn't—"

"It's fine," he said, cutting me off. "I was more curious about how it made *you* feel."

His words hung in the air like a challenge. I wanted to deny everything, to push him away before he saw too much, but my voice caught in my throat.

"It's... Whatever, man," I muttered finally, leaning against the doorframe and trying to look indifferent. "Just do me a favor and don't be around when my friends come over."

"Got it," he said with a nod, his expression unreadable. "Wouldn't want to cramp your style."

There was something in his tone—light, teasing—but it made my chest tighten. As I left, I felt his eyes lingering, like he could see every storm raging inside me.

***

Golden hour bathed Wildwood Crest in a honeyed glow, the sand and sea shimmering like something out of a dream. The boardwalk buzzed with energy—laughter, carnival rides, the distant crackle of fryers. I tried to focus on the horizon as I trudged along the beach, hoping the ocean could drown out the heaviness in my chest.

"Yo, Jorge!" Brian's voice snapped me out of my thoughts. He and Mike were camped out near the dunes, surrounded by a trio of girls whose laughter cut through the evening air. Brian gestured me over.

"Get over here, man!" Mike called, leaning back on his elbows with Emily perched on his lap. His hand rested on her knee, casual and possessive. "We were just talking about you."

I hesitated, but I didn't want to look weak. I walked over, forcing a grin. "What's up?"

Brian gestured toward one of the girls. "Jorge, meet Mia. She thinks you're cute."

Mia smiled shyly, her cheeks pink, and for a second, I wanted to believe this moment was real. But Mike snickered, and Brian smirked, and the whole thing felt like a setup.

"Go on, man," Mike said, his voice dripping with mock encouragement. "Say something. Don't be rude."

Heat rose in my face. "Whatever," I muttered, turning away.

"What's your problem?" Brian called after me. "Can't even talk to a girl without running off?"

"Leave him alone," Emily said, but her laughter was soft, like she was in on a joke, too.

I walked faster, the sand dragging at my feet. Their laughter followed me, biting at my back, and my chest tightened with anger and shame. I didn't fit in with them. I never had.

The beach stretched ahead, quiet and nearly empty, as the sun dipped lower into the horizon, casting long shadows over the sand. The neon hum of the boardwalk buzzed faintly behind me, a distant, electric pulse against the crash of the waves. Somewhere in the distance, the faint thrum of music floated on the breeze—a dance beat, unmistakable and insistent. *Duran Duran.* The kind of song that could pull you out of yourself if you let it.

I stepped to the edge of the water, where the waves curled gently over the shore, cool against my feet. The music grew louder in my head, syncing with the rhythm of the ocean, and I couldn't help myself. My body moved, tentatively at first—a sway of my hips, a roll of my shoulders. Then the beat took over, like it used to when I was a kid and didn't care.

I danced. Alone, on the beach, with only the encroaching night as my audience. My arms stretched out, fluid and free, the song coursing through me like it was part of the tide. Each movement pushed back against the heat that had been curling in my gut. Here, I could forget—about Brian, about Mike, about the gnawing confusion inside me.

The music crescendoed, and I spun, the wind catching my shirt as I stretched toward the darkening sky. For a moment, it felt like I was flying.

As the final beat faded into the evening air, I stilled, breathless and flushed. Applause broke the silence, slow and deliberate. My stomach dropped.

"Bravo," a voice called out, smooth and teasing. Kevin stood a few yards away on the sand. His oversized T-shirt hung loose on his lean frame, and his short swimsuit revealed legs that seemed carved by the gods. His arms were crossed, but the grin on his face was playful, almost smug.

"You've got moves," he said, stepping closer.

I froze, heat rushing to my cheeks. "Didn't think anyone was watching," I muttered, brushing sand off my palms as if I could shake off the embarrassment.

"Would've been a shame to miss that." Kevin's grin widened, his eyes catching the last glint of the sun.

I let out a hollow laugh, more out of nerves than humor. I shifted my weight, trying to look anywhere but at his thighs. "Just killing time," I said, my voice rough.

"More like owning it," he replied, his tone light but edged with something I couldn't quite place. He walked toward me, his bare feet silent on the sand. The oversized shirt swayed in the breeze, but his presence felt anything but soft. It filled the space between us, tangible and electric.

I let out a hollow laugh, more out of nerves than humor. "Guess I got carried away."

"Nothing wrong with that," Kevin said. "Passion's good. Makes life worth living."

"What are you doing out here? Are you following me?" I asked.

"No," he said, stepping beside me. "Getting away from everything. Seems we had the same idea, but I can't dance."

His voice was calm and steady. The wind tugged at his shirt, revealing a sliver of sun-kissed skin. I found my voice getting caught as I tried to speak. "What's there to get away from? You seem like you've got it all figured out."

Kevin chuckled, low and easy. "You'd be surprised."

"Your ex..." I started. I didn't even know where to go. Maybe she dumped him because he got too close to the redhead. Maybe it was none of my business.

"What about him?" said Kevin.

"Wait," I said. "So that guy you were with the other day..."

"I don't want to get you into shit with your friends, but yeah. My ex."

"They aren't my friends," I said. "Maybe they used to be. I don't know, anymore. Friends do fun stuff. They don't pressure you, and they do stupid shit, like get funnel cake and race you to the end of a pier."

"So that's the problem? Not enough stupid stuff in your life?"

I shrugged.

Kevin gestured toward the distant pier, silhouetted against the purpling sky. "Race you to the end?"

I laughed nervously. "I was only saying. I hate running."

"Then you'll have to swim," he said, pulling his shirt over his head. His torso gleamed in the fading light, lean muscle rippling as he tossed the shirt onto the sand.

I hesitated, caught between wanting to look and wanting to bolt. But then he darted toward the water, and the challenge sparked something inside me. I stripped off my shirt and ran after him, the humid air clinging to my skin. No time to debate whether my chest was good enough.

We hit the water at the same time, the cold biting against the lingering warmth of the day. My arms cut through the waves, my legs kicking hard as the pier loomed closer, its barnacled pillars like ancient sentinels against the darkening sky.

"Come on, Jorge!" Kevin called, his voice carrying over the rhythm of the sea. I pushed harder, the burn in my muscles fierce and alive. The race wasn't just about the pier—it was about proving something, to him and to myself.

When we reached the pier, our hands slapped the rough wood at almost the same time. We surfaced, gasping and laughing, the water lapping at our shoulders.

"I won," I panted, grinning despite myself.

"No way," Kevin said, splashing water at me.

"Call it a tie," he suggested, his grin wide and disarming.

"Never!" I splashed water at him, droplets catching the remains of the light and transforming into liquid fire. He retaliated, and soon we were both half-blinded, sputtering and laughing as the saltwater invaded our eyes and mouths. We shook off the sting, the cold droplets mingling with the warmth of our skin in a tantalizing contradiction.

"Okay, okay!" I surrendered between coughs, holding up my hands in mock defeat. But Kevin was relentless, sending another wave crashing into me, and I couldn't help but laugh at the absurdity of it all—slapping the ocean like kids under the watchful eye of dusk.

With reckless abandon, I launched myself at Kevin, wrapping my arms around his broad shoulders. Laughter bubbled up from deep within us as we tumbled through the gentle waves, the water swirling around us. He was strong, but I matched his strength with determination.

Then something shifted.

Our laughter faded, our movements slowing until they were no longer about winning or losing. Kevin's hands, still holding my arms, lingered. His grip loosened, his touch softening as if testing the boundaries of what was allowed.

I didn't pull away. Should I have? If I were really a guy like my friends, I should have punched him in the face.

Instead, his fingers slid down, brushing against my shoulders, tracing the curve of my spine in a way that made my teeth chatter. It wasn't aggressive or even intentional—it was careful, almost curious. My hands found their way to his chest, hesitant at first, resting lightly on the planes of muscle. Beneath my palm, his heartbeat was steady and strong, grounding me in a way I hadn't expected.

"Sorry..." I said in a near-whisper.

I didn't know what I was sorry for.

I exhaled as his touch grew bolder, trailing down my sides with a deliberate gentleness that made my skin hum. The water lapped around us, cool and quiet, but every place his hands touched felt warm, like the last rays of sunlight still clinging to my body. If I was sorry, he offered absolution.

I let my fingers move, tracing the contours of his chest and shoulders, feeling the rise and fall of his breath beneath my hand. It wasn't just about desire—though that burned low and insistent in the background—it was about something deeper, something I couldn't name but didn't want to let go of.

His leg brushed against mine, tentative at first, then more intentional. The contact sent a jolt through me, not of fear but of something unfamiliar, something almost comforting. I gasped softly, and he stilled, his eyes searching mine in the fading light.

"Is this okay?" he asked, his voice barely above a whisper, carried on the rhythm of the waves.

I nodded, unable to find words. My hand moved instinctively, settling on the curve of his shoulder, holding him there, anchoring us both in this fragile, weightless moment.

The world around us blurred—the pier, the horizon, the distant hum of the boardwalk. All that remained was the quiet press of our bodies, the warmth of his touch, and the way my chest felt lighter, like I'd been carrying something for years and had finally set it down.

My fingers found Kevin's chest again, tracing the lines of his muscles as they moved with each breath. A pang of envy twisted in my gut as I felt the brush of hair against my palm.

"I wish I had more chest hair," I admitted, my voice barely louder than the lapping waves. It felt trivial to say, with our bodies so close, but the words slipped out, wrapped in layers of insecurity that clung to me like seaweed.

Kevin chuckled softly, a sound that wrapped around my heart like a warm embrace. "You're adorable the way you are." His eyes held mine, brimming with sincerity. "Can I feel your legs?"

"Why? They're like toothpicks."

"You think so?" he argued.

"Compared to Mike..."

"Stop comparing. You have great muscles."

I wanted to call him a liar; to remind him I was a pathetic, skinny, sicko who jerked off to thoughts of guys instead of girls like normal people, but before I could, his hands began their journey downward.

The ocean enveloped us, a blanket of secrecy, as we submerged deeper into the fading light. Kevin's fingers traced the length of my calves with intention, every stroke deliberate and full of promise. The touch of his hand on my thigh ignited a blaze of sensation that rushed through my veins.

His hand ventured under the leg of my swim shorts. His fingers grew bold, daring, grazing my flesh where it ached for contact the most. I gasped at the intimacy, a thrill of fear mingling with burgeoning desire, as the coolness of the sea contrasted with the heat of his touch.

"Good boy," he whispered.

"Kev..." My voice faltered, all bravado washed away by the tide. I wanted him to continue, to dismantle the barriers I had built around myself, brick by brick.

"Shh," he murmured, silencing my uncertainties with a single word, his fingers exploring, promising power, control, and the fulfillment that had eluded me until now.

The sounds of Wildwood's nightlife were now muffled by the water lapping at my skin, the shouts of children a distant echo. I turned, facing away from Kevin, his body an anchor in the fluid world that swirled around us. I backed into him, my head finding comfort in the curve of his neck. His solid form pressed against me from behind, our shorts offering little resistance to the connection. The unmistakable hardness I felt against my backside was a revelation - startling, affirming, confirming. It sent a jolt through me. Could a hot college guy have feelings similar to mine... or even for me? How was it possible? My mind spun with this new reality, thoughts tumbling over each other in a dizzying rush.

His arms encircled me, a vice of muscle and warmth, keeping me afloat, keeping me close. I shivered. His hand again slipped up the inside of my thigh, this time all the way, his fingers finding their way to my hardness. His touch was deft, strokes calculated to stoke the fire building within me. It was too much and not enough all at once, pleasure bordering on pain, the kind of agony you never wanted to end.

"Sorry," I found myself whispering over and over, an echo of insecurities that clung like the salt on my skin. "For being so... I wish I was, bigger, you know? And cut..."

"I like it this way. It's working just the way it should," he said, his words both steel and velvet. There was no room for argument in his tone, just an undeniable assertion that left my heart hammering. His fingers didn't falter, didn't pity. They took a break to squeeze my balls, then worked with a purpose, coaxing shivers and twitches from my body, each pulse a step closer to the edge he was guiding me towards.

I clenched my teeth, fighting the urge to succumb too quickly to the cresting wave. In the depths of the water, in the depths of the moment, my desire peaked—a mountain climbed, a precipice reached. Kevin was my sherpa, leading me to heights I'd never known, his hand the only thing tethering me to the earth as I teetered on the brink of release.

A swell of laughter bubbled up from my chest as I felt the pressure build, an involuntary reaction to the overwhelming sensations Kevin wrung from my body. I squirmed under his touch, a dance of flesh in the water that refused to be still.

"Never done this before, have you?" Kevin's voice was a low hum against the twilight sky. I shook my head in the negative. His hand moved with a rhythm that had me unraveling thread by thread. "A squirmer, huh?" he chuckled, the sound mingling with the lap of waves around us.

"I can't help it," I laughed through the haze, my voice betraying the pleasure that seized me. "It feels so amazing."

He gripped harder. Stroked faster. My legs kicked out, thrashing beneath the surface like a marionette's, strings pulled by the puppeteer's skilled hands. Kevin's arm tightened around me again. Then, with a sudden jerk that sent my heart into my throat, he yanked my swimsuit down so that it hung from my ankle, baring me to the ocean's embrace.

"Shit!" I wept. "Terrified" didn't cover it. "Thrilled" didn't come close. Exposed and on the edge, I could only gasp out, "Keep going!"

He did. His fist clenched around me, pumping ever faster under the surface of the water. My heels found his knees. I spread my bent legs wide like a butterfly, letting him access me. Giving him everything. Thrusting into his fist. I didn't want it to stop, but I was tightening, like I would into the terrycloth towel.

"Kevin!" I said. "I can't hold it! I'm sorry! I'm gonna... I'm gonna..."

The climax crashed over me like a rogue wave, washing away thought, washing away time, leaving nothing but the raw pulse of existence. In Kevin's fingers, I throbbed—a desperate, clinging rhythm in the midst of the sea's vastness. My release spilled into the water, warmth diffusing into the cold depths.

The afterglow pulsed between us, a vibrant entity born of salt and skin. Our bodies, still entwined beneath the water's surface, clung together with the desperation of those who have shared something sacred. Each breath I took came slow and heavy, a confession of the pleasure I had just experienced.

I raised my gaze to meet Kevin's, our eyes locking in a silent conversation as the light dimmed around us. The taste of seawater lingered on my lips, mingling with the sweetness of release, and I found it impossible to look away from him, even if the tides themselves commanded it.

"Wow," I whispered, the word barely escaping before the ocean's song swallowed it whole.

Kevin's smile was soft, his expression tender, yet an intensity simmered beneath the surface, holding me captive.

"Yeah," he replied, his voice a low hum that vibrated through the water and into my bones.

"What about you?" I asked, curiosity edging my tone.

"I can take care of myself later. This moment was about you," he said.

We floated there, suspended by the sea, caught in the gravity of each other's presence. His fingertips traced idle paths along my arm, stirring the waters around us as if he could map the contours of my soul.

"Kevin," I began, my voice cracking under the weight of emotions I struggled to name. It wasn't just longing in his eyes; it was a promise, a vow that transcended the physical.

"Shhh," he soothed, pressing his forehead against mine. "We're here. That's all that matters."

In that moment, I grasped the essence of true power—not the kind derived from force or fear, but the strength found in vulnerability, in the give-and-take of bodies and hearts. Control became a mere shadow on the sand, shifting with the whims of the moon.

The lapping water was a quiet reminder that the world would continue its relentless march. But for now, we lingered in the stillness, two souls adrift in the vastness of the night.

***

The next morning, I woke up hard, a pulsing reminder of yesterday's heat with Kevin. Underwater, where no one could see us, his hands had traced my secrets. Now, in the morning light, shame gnawed at me, but the craving still burned fiercely.

I dragged myself out of bed and clutched my erection, willing it away. It throbbed through my fingers, betraying my resolve. I turned from the photograph of my dad and stumbled toward the bathroom, desperate for relief.

"Morning," Kevin's voice cut through the hallway like a lifeline—or a noose.

"Hey," I mumbled, avoiding his gaze. His chuckle resonated low, a sound that vibrated straight to my groin.

"Your mom still at work?" he asked, casual as ever.

"She'll get home when I'm at school," I replied, my voice tight.

His eyes flickered down, lingering on the bulge straining against my briefs.

"Did I not do my job well enough yesterday?" The tease in his words felt like a velvet touch.

"Shut up." I couldn't help but laugh, the sound edged with nerves. "It's the first day of my senior year," I reminded myself more than him. "I can't be late."

"Of course, you can't," he agreed, his tone dripping with molten promise.

I bolted into the bathroom, my heart racing, and slammed the door behind me.

The shower water cascaded down my back, but I kept my hands firmly on the tiled walls. No matter how much my body ached for release, I wouldn't give in. Not today. The cold droplets felt like a baptism, a futile attempt to wash away desires that clung tighter than my own skin. I dressed quickly, the fabric of my navy blue tee shirt clinging to my still-damp body. I wriggled into my cotton briefs—carefully chosen for discretion—and then stepped into my khaki shorts.

I glanced down at the short leg openings, acutely aware of how close they came to revealing too much. I pulled a pair of tall white tube socks over my calves, to my knees, and searched for a blue pair of Converse shoes.

In the kitchen, Kevin sipped coffee, the early light casting a halo around him. His presence soothed the frayed edges of my mind, a balm I hadn't realized I needed. It had been years since a man's voice filled these rooms, and the timbre of his offered an unexpected comfort.

"Jorge," Kevin began, his brown eyes locking onto mine. "I know what happened yesterday was intense and happened quickly." His voice flowed gently, pulling at my resolve. "If you did not like it or don't want to do it again, I understand. I just don't want you to feel uncomfortable with us living together."

His words should have granted me relief, a chance to retreat into normalcy. Instead, something inside me cracked, a fissure spreading through the brittle facade I'd constructed overnight. I wanted to scream, to beg him to never stop what we'd started, yet fear gripped my throat.

I swallowed hard, nodding once, betraying nothing. "Okay," I managed, my voice barely above a whisper. I turned away, grabbing an apple from the bowl on the counter, feeling the weight of Kevin's gaze as I left the safety of his presence behind.

I was supposed to nod, agree, and be grateful for the out. But it felt as if he had flipped a switch inside me, and all the circuits fired wrong.

I turned back. "I don't know what I want," I sputtered. My hands fidgeted with the hem of my T-shirt. "Everything with you—it was..." Words failed me, so I let them hang, unfinished.

Kevin chuckled, low and warm, standing to approach me. His laughter wasn't mocking; it was understanding. "You're really tense," he observed, his hand finding my shoulder, grounding me. "Did you not jerk off in the shower? Do you need some relief before school?"

"You're too much," I replied, blushing. "Besides, I'll be late."

"Have it your way," he said, a hint of amusement in his tone.

I dashed to my room to grab my book bag. I had to leave. On my way out, however, I slowed. "What would you do to me if I stayed?" I asked.

He tilted his head toward the living room, and I followed him as if tethered by an invisible string.

Sunlight leaked through the blinds, casting lines across the sofa where Kevin gestured for me to sit. I complied, feeling the cushion yield beneath me.

"Be quick," I said.

He knelt before me, his presence a fortress as he spread my legs apart with firm, assured movements. His hands began at my knees, a gentle pressure climbing up my thighs, teasing the edges of my shorts. I was hard, already, and he knew it.

"I don't know why I'm like this," I confessed into the charged silence, my voice barely a whisper amidst the ticking of the wall clock. "I'm 18. I've always had urges, but I've never felt this needy."

He looked up at me, his eyes dark pools of empathy. "You're still developing," Kevin said, his voice a caress. His hands swept down to massage the backs of my legs through my socks, thumbs pressing into the muscle with a careful strength that made my whole body hum.

"You're so damn cute," he murmured, and I flushed at the compliment, unfamiliar warmth blooming within me. "It's sad none of your other friends see it."

I leaned back, draping my arm over my eyes, shielding myself from the intensity of his gaze. "Are you going to do what you did to me yesterday?" Anticipation coiled tight in my stomach, a mix of fear and desire.

"Your body needs more than that," he answered, his voice low and inviting.

His fingers crept higher, a bold trespasser scaling the border of my shorts. I felt his touch, deliberate and knowing, as it found the tender warmth beneath the fabric—a gentle pressure that elicited a gasp from my lips. My world narrowed to the sensation of his fingers tracing the outline of my hardness, a sculptor shaping molten desire.

"I never saw it last night," Kevin's voice was low, a velvet darkness. "Can I see it now?"

"Can I see yours first?" The words tumbled out, a plea wrapped in curiosity.

Rising to his feet, Kevin stood before me, the embodiment of masculine allure. His hands hooked into the waistband of his shorts, and with a fluid motion they cascaded down his hairy thighs. Exposed, he revealed his proud erection—it stood as if saluting the morning sun that filtered through the blinds.

"You did this to me. It's for you," he declared, a simple truth hanging in the air between us.

My fingers trembled as they reached out, brushing against the rough terrain of his legs, a stark contrast to my smooth skin. Touching him felt like unlocking a forbidden tome—each page filled with secrets I yearned to read aloud. I caressed the heat of his dick, the weight of his balls, the wildness of his pubic hair; textures alien yet beckoning.

"I can't believe I'm doing this," I confessed, my hand now moving with intent along his length. Each stroke was a silent question, each moan his whispered answer.

And then, with a resolve that surprised even me, I leaned forward. His taste invaded my senses, a heady mix of salt and musk. For those few seconds, as I took him into my mouth, the world ceased its relentless spinning, and in that stillness, I surrendered to the moment's raw command.

"You like sucking cock?" he asked. I wiped my lips with the back of my hand.

Kevin returned to me with a wink that carved through the morning air, charged with unspoken promises. He knelt between my thighs, and his fingers curled around the hem of my shorts and my briefs, pulling everything down past my tall socks in one swift motion.

My erection stood, defiant and eager, a single bead of precum glistening at the tip. With a deliberate touch, Kevin spread the moisture around, his thumb pressing into my foreskin.

His breath was warm against me as he leaned in close, and then his mouth—oh god, his mouth—found me.

I gasped as he took me in, his lips soft yet insistent, his tongue tracing patterns that spelled ecstasy across my senses. As he sucked, each pull drew out threads of pleasure that wove a tapestry of heat throughout my entire being. I was teetering on the edge, the world narrowing to the feel of him, the slick warmth of his skilled mouth enveloping me.

Beneath the onslaught of sensation, my legs kicked out and beat an erratic rhythm in the air. My heels at last dug into the sofa, finding purchase as I thrust into the cradle of his lips, seeking more, always more.

I threaded my fingers through his hair as he sucked me gently and played with my tip with his tongue.

"Oh no!" The words tumbled from my lips, tinged with laughter and edged with desperation. I squirmed again, as I had last night under the intensity. My toes curled in my socks.

"You're such a squirmer," Kevin murmured, amusement lacing his voice. His arm wrapped around me, holding me tight to the sofa, anchoring me to reality. Yet reality had no place here, not in this moment of surrender, of giving myself over to the tempest brewing at my core.

He sucked harder and faster, his lips gliding over my foreskin. I tried to pull away, tried to push him off, the sensation too powerful. His grip was too tight. His lips too soft.

I cramped—harder, tighter, fiercer than ever before. I bent forward, and came with a force that shook me to my core, my laughter transforming into a crescendo of guttural sounds that echoed in the stillness of the room. My calves tightened, my back arched—every muscle contracted as pleasure surged through me in pulsating waves.

Kevin didn't pull away. Instead, he swallowed every drop, his throat working in silent testimony to his determination and the care he took in receiving all of me.

In the aftermath, my breaths came in ragged gasps, my heart raced wildly within my chest, and my thoughts scattered like stars across the night sky. He wanted me. He wanted everything about me and wanted me to feel good, like nobody had, ever before.

I at last stumbled out of his embrace, my legs weak and unsteady as he steadied me with a firm hand. His fingers brushed against my skin with the same tenderness he had shown moments before, wiping away the remnants of our encounter with a tissue. I flinched at the touch, not from discomfort but from the struggle to reconcile the gentleness with the intensity that had just coursed through me.

"My turn," Kevin's command echoed in the stillness of the room. He stood, and I again took in the sight of his erection. He was beautiful like this, exposed and wanting under my gaze.

His hand found its way to the back of my head, guiding me closer until I could feel his heat against my lips. Tentatively, I brushed my tongue against him, tasting salt and skin and something uniquely Kevin.

I loved this. Loved having him in my mouth, feeling him harden even more under the attention. There was power here too - a different kind than before - but it was intoxicating.

Kevin's grip tightened in my hair as he guided me deeper onto him with each thrust. His glutes clenched rhythmically. His thighs tensed as my hands explored them.

His balls tightened, and he tried to pull away, but this time I held *him* steady. His fingers dug into my scalp.

He let out a magnificent grunt. I felt the tightness and the release; the rhythmic throbbing against my tongue. Then, there it was: his essence, hot and bitter-sweet filling my mouth, raw and unfiltered as he surrendered himself completely to me.

I swallowed him down with determination etched into every line of my body. I wanted him inside me. This was us now – raw and honest – baring ourselves completely for one another without fear or hesitation.

He pulled away, at last.

"Put these on," Kevin said, handing me my shorts, his voice a low hum that vibrated in the stillness of the room. I dressed in silence, each piece of clothing feeling like a layer of armor being clumsily fastened around me—a feeble attempt to shield myself from the emotions I had begun to confront.

"Off you go," he said with a slight smile.

"But..."

"I'll see you after school."

I nodded, unable to find words that could bridge the chasm yawning between us. Stepping outside, the crisp morning air slapped against my flushed face. I was as light as a feather, totally at ease.

***

The halls of Wildwood High echoed with the sounds of lockers slamming and hurried footsteps. Everything appeared as it always had, yet it all felt different. I didn't want to be there, nor did I want to endure another year of monotony. I would—I had to—but while everyone else carried on, I knew other, better things awaited. I couldn't shake thoughts of Kevin from my mind. What we had shared that morning. How he had made me feel.

"Hey, Jorge," Mike called from down the hall. A smirk twisted his lips as I approached the trio by the lockers. "Where'd you go yesterday?"

"I saw you swimming," Brian chimed in. "Was that the guy from the other day? What's going on? Something you want to tell us?"

My mouth went dry, the taste of the morning lingering bitter on my tongue. "He's renting a room from my mom," I muttered, desperate to deflect their scrutiny. "Nothing more to it."

But there was so much more. My mind churned with images of Kevin's hands, his mouth, the heat that had enveloped us both. I pushed those thoughts down, burying them under layers of fear and self-loathing. It wasn't right; it couldn't be.

"Oh, shit!" Mike exclaimed. "He doesn't come into your room at night or anything, right?"

"I lock the door," I lied.

"Drink this," Brian said, shoving a flask into my hands. The smell of liquor cut through the fog in my head. "I'm sure you need it."

I took a swig, the alcohol burning a path down my throat, igniting a rebellion in my stomach. But I welcomed the pain, a distraction from the chaos swirling inside me.

"Jorge's no queer," Emily chimed in, her gaze flickering with something like concern or perhaps judgment—I couldn't tell. "My cousin is gay. Jorge's not like that."

Their laughter filled the space around us, a cacophony that seemed to mock the silent plea struggling within me. I craved their acceptance, longed for the simplicity of being part of them, untouched by the complexities that now threatened to pull me under.

"What if I was queer?" I wanted to ask. "Would you ever talk to me again?" Instead I said, "I have to get to class," and handed back the flask, my resolve hardening.

I had to end things with Kevin. There was no place for what we shared in the world I inhabited, a world where labels like "normal" were wielded like weapons.

As I sat through the lectures, the teachers' words washed over me, meaningless against the turmoil roiling in my chest. The need for touch battled against the chains of expectation, leaving me adrift in a sea of uncertainty.

The bell rang, its shrill tone echoing my discordant thoughts. As I walked out, I felt the tug of two worlds—one filled with dark corners and secret touches, the other bathed in the harsh light of judgment. I found myself caught in the middle, an exile of my own making.

The first chill of autumn clawed its way through Wildwood. Tourists enjoyed the last days of Indian summer, arriving later and leaving earlier.

When I got home, Kevin chatted with my mom, helping her cook and laughing. She left for work a short time later, and I approached him.

"Look, I know we live in the same house, but I can't do things with you. Okay?" My words fell flat, a barrier I built with every syllable.

"Sure, man," he replied, his smile not reaching his eyes. "Whatever you want."

I wanted him to beg or plead, but he didn't. His inaction nagged at me.

A week dragged by. Each day, another leaf fell, another layer of pretense added.

At home, I feigned indifference with Kevin. With Mike and Brian, I played a part that grated against my skin.

"Did you see the legs on that new girl from New York?" Mike nudged me in gym class.

"Uh, yeah. Legs for days," I muttered, the lie tasting like rust on my tongue.

"Damn straight," Brian chimed in, clapping me on the back with a force that made me stumble forward. "Gotta love a girl who knows how to fill out a pair of jeans."

"Definitely," I echoed, the word hollow. They laughed, oblivious to the tremor in my voice. I hated the mask I wore. But they believed it, and for a moment, I let myself bask in the false warmth of being taken seriously.

***

That night, darkness gripped me, thick and suffocating. My father's voice sliced through the silence of my sleep. I was no longer in my mother's house but back in Hackensack—in the apartment where my parents fought, where I watched my dad throw dinner against the wall because there wasn't enough spice.

"You can provide for your child," he screamed when she finally kicked him out. "Don't count on anything from me."

Your child.

Now his venomous words echoed in the void. "You're nothing, Jorge. Just a fraud." I could not see his face, but I almost felt his breath, hot and heavy with disappointment. "Everyone knows. They all see it. There are no faggots in this family."

Did he know? Had he known? Was that why he left?

I thrashed in the sheets, limbs entangled as if bound. The alarm clock crashed to the floor, its digital numbers blinking out of existence. A gasp tore from me, and my eyes snapped open to a darkened room. I snatched his photograph and threw it into the garbage, my mother's feelings be damned.

"Jorge?" Kevin's voice cut through the remnants of my nightmare, the door creaking open. "You okay?"

Tears betrayed me before I could lock them away, carving wet trails down my cheeks. His arms found me, and I crumbled into the embrace, letting go of a façade that had become my skin. "I can't do this anymore, Kev," I choked out, the confession raw against my throat.

"Hey, come on," he coaxed, his tone soft but steady. "Let's walk. It's nice out."

Under the silver glow of the moonlight, we walked toward the marina nearby, where boats bobbed gently on the water.

"I have to fight just to... be. It's a beast, you know?" I said, sniffling.

"I know." His words soothed me, easing the weight of my own

doubts.

"Is life ever going to be fun? Will it ever be real?" I blurted out, desperation creeping into my voice. "Or do I just keep pretending forever? I can't shake the feeling that I've been doing it wrong all this time, but I don't know what else to do."

My voice stumbled over the uncertainty that enveloped me. I probably wasn't even making sense.

Before I could spiral further into my thoughts, Kevin took my hand, warmth radiating through me. He led me toward one of the boats, a mischievous glint lighting up his eyes.

"I didn't know you owned a boat," I said, my heart racing.

"I don't," he replied, a grin spreading across his face. "But it will help you to be a little bad."

The boat rocked gently as we stepped onto it. We stepped below deck, the world above fading into an afterthought. Inside, everything was neatly tucked away. The bed was just a bare mattress.

"Why do you even care about me?" I asked. "I'm too old for high school, but stuck there. I have nothing to offer. Are you into Hispanic guys or something?"

Kevin did not answer. Instead, his gaze locked onto mine and he leaned in, our lips meeting in a kiss that was both a lesson and a revelation.

"I've never kissed..." I admitted.

He kissed me again, this time teaching me how. "I hate how you think about yourself," he murmured against my mouth, his breath warm and intimate. "I think you're incredible. Kind. Honest. I want you to have everything good."

His words resonated within me, mingling with the erratic beat of my heart. He saw something in me that I had yet to recognize.

We continued to kiss, a slow fire igniting between us. Kevin's fingers found the bottom of my shirt, coaxing it upward and away, exposing my skin to the air and his burning gaze.

His lips traced the path of my pulse down my neck, each kiss a promise of more. Then, his mouth closed over my nipple, a wet heat that drew a gasp from deep within me. He bit gently, and I arched into him, silently pleading for more.

My nipples—sensitive and neglected until now—tightened under his attention. When his tongue swirled around one, then the other, a shiver coursed through my body, a current of desire I couldn't name but desperately craved. His hands roamed, exploring the hard lines of my abs.

My hands ventured across his skin, once more feeling the contrast between his hairy chest and my smoothness. The texture thrilled me, stirring a wildness within. The ruggedness of him, the solid reality of another person wanting me just as fiercely, turned me on.

"Jorge," Kevin breathed, "I want you to suck on me like you did before. Suck on me until I'm good and hard. Will you do that?" He dropped his shorts to the floor, revealing himself.

I didn't hesitate, descending upon him, my mouth embracing his pulsing length. The taste of him flooded my senses. His subtle moans fed my eagerness, each sound a confirmation of my ability to give pleasure. I worked him, taking him deeper, feeling him grow rigid against my tongue.

"God, yes," he groaned as I brought him to the brink of ecstasy and back again. His hands cradled my head gently, guiding the rhythm, never forcing.

He withdrew and laid me back on the bunk, and lifted my knees over my head.

"Are you going to fuck me?" I asked, my voice shaking.

"I have work to do, first," he said. He lowered his head between my thighs and licked – not my hard-on, but the space between my thigh and my balls. I jolted, but he held firm, licking then sucking—one nut, than the other—with a pressure neither too delicate nor too painful.

"Kevin!" I moaned. He gripped the back of my legs and forced them further above me. His tongue found my entrance and lapped back and forth.

"Oh God!" my head thrashed. "W-what are you doing?"

He redoubled his efforts, licking my ass harder and faster. I was losing my mind against the sensation – kicking again into the air, my dick pulsing.

He drew back. "It's time, Jorge," Kevin rasped, his words raw with desire. "Will you let me?"

"Will it hurt?" My voice sounded young, uncertain.

"A little," he admitted softly, "but in a good way. Is that okay?"

I nodded, laying myself bare on the bunk, flesh against coarse fabric. "Go slow?"

His fingers traced my thigh, a silent reassurance before making their way to my crack and pressing inside, preparing me. There was pain—a pressure that bordered on too much—but his eyes held mine, steady and reassuring.

"Ready?" His voice was a low promise.

"Ready," I whispered back.

Kevin slickened himself with spit and entered me, slow and deliberate. Each increment felt like an invasion, something foreign testing the boundaries of my body. My teeth clenched against the initial sting, my breath breaking in my throat as I braced for each new intrusion. Yet, amidst this discomfort was a strange sense of progress, of crossing a threshold I had long feared.

His hips pressed against mine, joining us in a union that was as intimate as it was unfamiliar. The pain, once sharp and unwelcome, morphed into something else—something complex and profound. It was an intermingling of sensations that transcended the physical realm; we were merging on a deeper level than just our bodies.

Kevin moved within me with gentle precision, his rhythmic thrusts gradually persuading my body to surrender its resistance—to yield to this new experience. His movements were patient yet persistent, guiding me through this uncharted terrain with an understanding that eased my apprehension.

And then he found it—that elusive spot hidden deep within me. The sudden burst of pleasure caught me off guard; it was as if fireworks had ignited behind my closed eyelids. A yelp tore from me as I clung onto him desperately, arms and legs ensnaring him like a lifeline pulling me out from an ocean of uncertainty.

I drew him closer still, inviting him to delve deeper into the recesses of my vulnerability.

"Jorge," he murmured, his strokes gaining confidence, "you're incredible."

"My body needs this," I said in rugged gasps. "I need this. Please don't stop!"

He pinned me beneath him, every thrust a stroke of lightning across my nerves. He drew out every last shiver of pleasure from my body with his relentless rhythm, taking me harder, driving deeper.

The sensation built, a mounting pressure as he jerked me off in time with his thrusts. My belly slickened with precum, and the heat grew tighter. I tried to hold on, but couldn't.

"Kevin!" I warned. "I... I..."

It was too late. The dam burst, and my release came as a flood, hot and uncontrollable. It painted his chest, marking him with my pleasure.

He caught my gaze, his eyes dark, and whispered through gritted teeth, "I'm so close."

"Inside me," I urged, voice laced with a need I didn't fully understand until that moment. "I need it in me."

His pace quickened, a crescendo of movements that echoed in the cramped space below deck. The sound of flesh against flesh, his balls smacking against my skin—it was the only thing I could focus on. Then, his body tensed like a bowstring pulled taut. He released and warmth flooded my core, the scent mingling with the remnants of my own climax.

We were laughter and sweat-dampened skin as he withdrew. Our mouths met in a kiss that spoke of things deeper than words ever could.

The moon hung like a silent witness over the marina, its silver light spilling through the porthole. The atmosphere felt heavy, the only sounds our synchronized breaths and the distant hum of Wildwood nightlife, muffled by the boat's walls. My skin still buzzed from Kevin's touch as we lay entangled, limbs heavy and hearts light. I traced the lines of his forearm, feeling the steady thrum of his pulse beneath my fingertips. Outside this boat, this stolen moment, the world seemed distant—a storm held at bay.

"Jorge," he said softly, breaking the silence. His voice rumbled through the darkness, vibrating in the air between us. He shifted beside me, an arm reaching across my chest as if to anchor me to this moment. "I have something to tell you."

"Okay." My voice barely rose above a whisper, almost lost in the cabin's close confines. "What is it?"

"I accepted a job... in New York City." He paused, letting the words linger like the thick humidity outside. "It starts next month."

New York City. The words echoed in my mind, each syllable a dull thud against my consciousness. A chasm opened within me, a sense of loss so immediate it felt as if the sea had risen to claim the ground beneath us.

"Wow, that's—" I began, but my throat constricted, choking off the rest of my thoughts.

"Big?" he offered, gently squeezing my shoulder.

"Big," I agreed, feeling small in comparison.

We lay there, our naked bodies a tangle of limbs, silently acknowledging the finite nature of what we shared. The connection we had built, formed from skin and vulnerability, now bore an expiration date. Yet instead of despair, a twisted gratitude took root within me.

"Guess we should make the most of the time we have, right?" Kevin's voice remained calm, but I sensed the undercurrent of emotion.

"Yeah." The word emerged stronger than I expected. "We will."

He muttered something about a subleaser for my mom, but I didn't listen. The conversation drifted off, leaving us in a comfortable silence. I let myself get lost in the feel of his body against mine, memorizing every detail—the firmness of his muscles, the rise and fall of his chest, the heat radiating from his skin.

Hours slipped away as the night deepened around us. While Kevin's breaths grew deep and steady in sleep, I lay awake, staring into the shadows.

This was power—the stark, raw kind that comes from facing truths. In the dark belly of that borrowed boat, I realized control wasn't about holding on; it was about letting go and choosing which currents to ride.

Then there was fulfillment. Not just the physical rush that had pulsed through my veins earlier, but something deeper. A fulfillment that came from being seen—truly seen—and not turning away from the reflection.

By the time I closed my eyes, the first light of dawn crept into the sky, painting the world in shades of possibility. When I stepped back onto land, I would be different. Ready to face my senior year with a confidence born not of pretense, but of truth. Walking the halls of my high school again, I would be someone unburdened. Someone real.

With that thought, a smile tugged at the corners of my mouth as I surrendered to sleep, prepared for whatever came next.

Still Hard?

Buy Filthy Gay Stories Today!

Author C.D. Truncheon brings you six of his best short stories in one convenient volume at one low price! Get a rise out of this spicy, gay MM collection that features enemies-to-lovers, friends-to-lovers, age gap, first-time, straight-to-gay, coach/player, daddy/younger, and hurt/comfort tales.

Coach's Assistant
Brian Hwang, a college dropout, returns home to assist his old soccer team. Can he handle his feelings for the alluring coach, or will their dynamic heat up in unexpected ways?

All-State Champ
Former wrestling champ Aaron Strickland struggles with self-acceptance after graduation. Torn between his dad's expectations and

his love for neighbor Gabriel, Aaron must confront his identity before he loses everything.

Swimmer's Build
High diver Carson Ryan transfers to a New England college, facing initiation rituals and forbidden feelings for his tough coach. Can he balance desire and self-discovery to achieve perfection?

Senior Trip
On a trip to London, Alex wrestles with his feelings for ex-girlfriend Alyssa and best friend Shawn. As Shawn moves on, Alex must sort out his heart before it's too late.

Greatest of All Time
At 19, speed skater Jason Jenson is unstoppable—until forbidden desires shake his world. Can an irritating nurse's assistant thaw JJ's icy facade and show him what really matters?

Teenage Runaway
Adam Evans befriends Brady, a troubled runaway tangled with a dangerous man. As Adam's feelings deepen, he must find a way to protect Brady before it's too late.

From Mayonnaise Press. *We won't tell.* ™

Also Available

Russian Ballet Reform School

"Shameful... A series that sensationalizes boarding school hardships and perverts the hard work and athleticism of young male ballet artists, reducing them to objects of desire in tights."

Banished to a Reform School at the Edge of Siberia!

Forrest Nikolev is certain he's asexual. A senior in a Detroit high school, he thinks little of guys, and past experiences with girls have left him cold.

When his abusive, alcoholic father sends him to the Siberian Ballet Reform School for Boys in remote Russia, however, everything changes.

Inexperienced in dance and stripped of dignity in the brutal institution—a place where the handsome, authoritarian dance instructor trains students to do more than tendu and doles physical punishment in his office at night—Forrest's desire awakens.

For the first time in print, this six-book series is a spicy, erotic, gay coming-of-age series for adult readers only. It will satisfy those who like multiracial characters and enjoy teacher/student tales, first-time discoveries, watching and yearning, guys in tights, and dirty mm fantasy.

From Mayonnaise Press. *We won't tell.*™

Content Advisory: This series contains explicit portrayals of power dynamics in an academic setting intended for titillation, exploring themes some may consider offensive or tabu. Reader discretion is strongly advised, particularly for those who may be sensitive to exploitative depictions of authority. 18+ Only.

Review Us!

Word-of-mouth is crucial for any author to succeed. Talk us up on social and, if you enjoyed this story, please leave a review. It makes a world of difference. Thanks!

Our catalog: https://books2read.com/CDTruncheon

Our newsletter: https://mayonnaisepress.substack.com

Printed in Dunstable, United Kingdom

68099097R00137